I ONLY CRY WITH EMOTICONS

Zalkow, Yuvi,author.
I only cry with emoticons :novel

2022
33305254830213
sa   06/08/22

I ONLY CRY WITH EMOTICONS

:´(

a novel

Yuvi Zalkow

Red Hen Press | *Pasadena, CA*

I Only Cry with Emoticons
Copyright © 2022 by Yuvi Zalkow
All Rights Reserved

No part of this book may be used or reproduced in any manner whatsoever without the prior written permission of both the publisher and the
copyright owner.

Book design by Mark E. Cull

Library of Congress Cataloging-in-Publication Data

Names: Zalkow, Yuvi, author.
Title: I only cry with emoticons: novel / Yuvi Zalkow.
Description: Pasadena, CA: Red Hen Press, [2022]
Identifiers: LCCN 2021041434 (print) | LCCN 2021041435 (ebook) | ISBN
    9781636280370 (hardcover) | ISBN 9781636280387 (epub)
Subjects: LCGFT: Humorous fiction.
Classification: LCC PS3626.A6273 I16 2022 (print) | LCC PS3626.A6273
    (ebook) | DDC 813/.6—dc23
LC record available at https://lccn.loc.gov/2021041434
LC ebook record available at https://lccn.loc.gov/2021041435

The National Endowment for the Arts, the Los Angeles County Arts Commission, the Ahmanson Foundation, the Dwight Stuart Youth Fund, the
Max Factor Family Foundation, the Pasadena Tournament of Roses Foundation, the Pasadena Arts & Culture Commission and the City of Pasadena Cultural Affairs Division, the City of Los Angeles Department of
Cultural Affairs, the Audrey & Sydney Irmas Charitable Foundation, the
Meta & George Rosenberg Foundation, the Albert and Elaine Borchard
Foundation, the Adams Family Foundation, Amazon Literary Partner-
ship, the Sam Francis Foundation, and the Mara W. Breech Foundation
partially support Red Hen Press.

First Edition
Published by Red Hen Press
www.redhen.org
Printed in Canada

for anyone out there stumbling towards an IRL connection

Contents

I ONLY CRY WITH EMOTICONS

PART ONE

"the only thing to #fear is fear itself. and maybe
also your day job. and parenting. and sex. and
most of all, fear honesty. that shit is fucking
terrifying." —@F_D_Arrr

Chapter One: HelloWorld.java

My boss tells me it's embarrassing that I've been here for six years and I'm
still at Goldfish status. Ever since we installed the gamification plug-in, he
knows exactly how many Likes I've gotten from coworkers, exactly how
many Comments I've made, exactly how many Best Answers and Virtual
Pints of Beer I've received, exactly how many Blog Posts I've posted. He
even knows how many animated cat GIFs I've giffed, which is zero. We
get points assigned to these various activities and are assigned a status level
based on our points. I'm a Goldfish even though some six-monthers have
already leveled up to Penguin. My boss is a Blue Whale. People think Blue
Whale is the highest level, but there's an even higher level that no one has
ever achieved.

He tells me this morning that I need to @ mention more people in my
Posts. The Chief Technical Officer needs to know what I'm up to. Especially after the layoffs last year. And I can't overlook the Algorithm group.
They were the ones who wrote the algorithm for the Trending Topics plug-
in in the first place. People need more visibility into what I'm doing.

But what I'm doing a lot of the time is hiding in the bathroom and
writing stories about my dead grandfather and failing to @ mention the
people I especially don't want to @ mention because I'm all @ mentioned
out.

Look. CollaborationHub is not a bad place to work. They're good
people. The online collaboration software they make is a good product.
They give my family—or at least me and my boy—good health insurance.

And they actually Help People Collaborate Effectively in This Modern World™. It's really true that they Take Collaboration to the Next Level™.

But I don't happen to like collaborating in this modern world. I don't like this level or the next one. I also don't think I know how to get a proper job any longer. I've coded my way out of employability. I'm no longer a catch for an employer, if I ever was one.

When I get back to my desk, I see that I have some private CollabHub messages waiting for me at my laptop. They're from Anne, my coworker who has dedicated too many office hours trying to save my floundering life. She says she'd be happy to set up a personal profile for me either on OkCupid or just on our internal dating group. At CollaborationHub, we use our own software to collaborate with each other, and we have over four thousand social groups, which is pretty impressive (and pretty horrifying) for a company of 321 employees.

Anne sits at the desk next to me. She looks so focused at her two 25" monitors, like she is doing nothing but serious work. There's a small desert rose cactus between us, sitting on her desk, that she overwaters. She claims it has a beautiful flower, but I've never seen one.

We've moved beyond cubicles around here. Cubicles are so twenty years ago. Even half-height walls are old school. Here we just have these big ugly slabs of pressed wood pushed up against each other—making little islands of desks, about four together at a time. Anne is on my desert island.

I lean over and talk to Anne old school—with my actual mouth. *Just what I need*, I say to her. *To date an effective collaborator at the next level.*

She whispers to me over the cactus, *I can @ mention you in the Singles group or the Just For Fun group or the Divorcé group.* She has these cute chunky cheeks with dimples but also long gray strands in her black hair, and it's impossible to gauge her age, except that she somehow captures the best of both worlds, old and young. Whereas I'm the worst of age forty-five: too old to have fun, too young for wisdom.

I remind Anne, again, that I'm not officially divorced.

She says she's even willing to @ mention me in the SSFW ("Semi-Safe For Work") Kinky group. And Pet Lovers. And Lonely Guys.

I hate pets, I tell her.

She gets up and walks right next to me. I can smell her perfume. Some kind of flower that my wife—and probably my son—could identify instantly.

Saul, it's been two years since she left you. Divorced or not, y'all are done for. Anne's Southern accent comes out when she's frustrated with me. It's comforting, her accent. Even though I know it came along with some history of abuse. And collard greens.

I also grew up in the South. But living in the suburbs of Atlanta with Jewish parents threw off the accent.

Anne makes it seem like two years is a long time. But it doesn't feel so long to me. Some days I still unthinkingly drive home to what is now my ex's house.

I'm trying to finish my novel, I tell her.

She takes a deep breath and then sighs.

I love my friend. She never lies to me. When she's exasperated, she exasperates.

Anne thinks I'm wasting my time with my book. She likes to remind me that I've been working on the stupid book longer than my boy has been alive. I regret confessing that detail to her. My debut novel was published to a lukewarm audience ten years ago, and the audience is not even lukecold at this point.

This book is toxic to you, she says. *I see it on your face.*

I take a selfie with my iPhone and look at it. And delete it before it syncs with the cloud. She's right.

I need to finish it before my father dies, I say. *He's the only one still alive. I need to finish telling our story.*

So whose story is it exactly?

I don't watch regular TV, if such a thing still exists. I particularly don't watch courtroom dramas. But I understand enough about entrapment to know what she is doing.

I fall for it anyway.

It's my grandfather's story. But also my dad's story. But maybe also my story. I tell her all this even though she knows all this. I know she is about to point out that since it is my story, I can tell it anytime. There's no ticking clock even if my dad is eighty-eight years old and going blind and deaf.

I mean, she says, *did the Klan even try to destroy your grandfather's store?*
Anne looks at me like she won the game.

My friend takes things too literally. She doesn't understand that fiction is more true than what really happened. In the novel, my Polish, Jewish grandparents open up a dry goods store in 1938 in a place called Stella, Georgia. In real life, it happened in 1931 in Waynesboro, Georgia. In real life, a drunk man stumbles into the store and warns my grandfather about the Klan and then vomits on the floor, and that's that. In the novel, this man is *in* the Klan. And he nearly destroys my family.

It's a brilliant book. It's a disaster.

What about your boy?

He's not in the book, I say.

But he's already seven years old.

You're a hell of a counter, I tell her. *I'll @ mention you in the Math Is 4 Fun group.*

Go take him somewhere fun. Get to the beach before the summer is over. Take the attention you give to the book and give it to your son. Worry about the book when your son is off to college or culinary school or the Marines or Mexico. Let the book go. Imagine what you could do if you let that turd go.

It hurts when she calls it a turd. A burden, yes. A thing that is killing me, yes. Something that destroyed my marriage and has stunted my growth emotionally, maybe. But a turd! That's going too far.

I say, *My boy isn't the Marine Corps type. And the beaches here are cold and rocky and windy.*

When I was a kid, we would visit my grandparents in Savannah and swim at Tybee Island. The beaches there were warm and beautiful. And there was that rickety dock that I loved to sneak onto when my parents weren't watching. I would look out at the ocean and pretend that the Germans were attacking because my dad once told me he did the same thing back in 1941. Except I didn't know much about Germans—I had seen those pointy helmets from WWI movies—and so that's what they wore when I imagined them capturing me on the beach.

And how come, Anne says with that tone she uses when she's discovered another of my flaws, *you always call Auggie "my boy" and Julia "my ex"? You know they exist separately from you, right?*

Shush, I say to Anne in a whisper, like she's my boy and it's late and it's time for him to stop talking and fall asleep.

My grandmother died in 1983, when I was twelve. My grandfather— Papa as we called him—died five years later. Those five years were the years I got stuck listening to his stories. I hated being around him in those years. I did it because you have to do those things. But he scared me. His beard smelled like a rotting log, and he would weep into his ice cream cone. At the time, I focused on the wasted ice cream.

Now that I'm forty-five years old and failing to write a novel about him, and that failure has taken me nine years and seven drafts and counting, I know that I should have been paying more attention. The poor old man.

It's easy, when you sense dying, to run away. But now I know that dying means it is time to come in even closer and listen to the whisper of it.

Papa, I want to say to him, *I'm sorry I only paid attention to the ice cream.*

Snap out of it! Anne says. *Why don't you do one Post about your dead granddad and then move on?*

My boss overhears us talking about me doing a Post, and so he walks up and says, *If you don't @ mention the Algorithm group, then I don't want to hear a story about your dead grandfather.* He makes it sound like a joke, but there is no joke here. What sucks is that I feel every bit of his frustration inside of me.

The failure to @ mention the Algorithm group was an innocent mistake. They were helpful, and it was stupid on my part to overlook them. My @ mention brain was out to lunch. It isn't necessarily one of my Top 10 Regrets—which is a type of Post we're required to write once a quarter—but it is maybe Top 500.

My boss also tells me he needs a write-up about the Bang Blog functionality. He says they are now spelling it as five letters: !-b-l-o-g. I try to tell him that the first character isn't a letter, it's a symbol. And that "Bang Blog" is a horrible name. It's like a feature for a porn site. He says that if I have a problem with it, I should @ mention the product marketing group before the task is shifted from "In Progress" to "Done Done."

I tell him that it is 5:00 p.m. and I have to pick up my boy from school. He shrugs like that's my problem, which it is.

#

I get in my car and drive over to my boy's school. As a writer type, I should be able to describe things well. But I struggle with real-world descriptions. When I describe an object, like my car, I forget to say what color it is. I won't say whether it is a sedan or a hatchback or sports car or one of those old station wagons that has somehow survived all these years, which I inherited from my mother when she died ten years ago and I keep repairing even though I should just get a new car. I don't describe whether the car is clean or if it has stains. Like a big vomit stain on the seat from when my mother broke into the liquor cabinet that one last time and then went for a drive. None of that comes out. Just, "car."

#

My boy is excited to see me when I get to his school. With his arms around me, I can totally forget about Blog Posts and Blue Whales. But he hugs me tight enough that I immediately worry if he has had one of those days when other kids teased him for one reason or another. The boy got the most-sensitive-kid-in-the-class genes from me. He's not such a small kid, but he always struggles with the more boyish boys. They don't like that he prefers dance to basketball. That he'd rather paint a picture of a butterfly coming out of a cocoon than of Spiderman punching a bad guy.

After the hug, we get in the car, and I say, *How was your day?*

My ex never liked how I ask these open-ended questions. She said they were too hard to answer. She tended to ask more specific questions like, *Do you think you can stop obsessing over your novel in the next thirty days or should we just get separated now?*

My boy doesn't bother to answer my question. He says, *Can we watch The Octonauts when we get home?*

I tell him we can. It'll give me a few minutes to work on my novel. I keep hoping to find the secret to this story to make it all come together, to stop it from feeling like a bunch of disparate, desperate anecdotes without a clear throughline.

As we're driving home, I get a text from Anne: *sometimes letting go is the only way to move forward.* I don't know if she is talking about my marriage or my novel or just quoting some dead guy for fun. She is very involved in the Famous Dead Guys group at work.

My wife and I are not officially divorced. But unofficially, we're divorced. Big time. Our joint custody situation is good, though. We even share a Google Calendar. Things are so clean and clear that I suggested to my wife—my ex-wife or semi-ex or quasi-ex or whatever she is—that we're so good at being separated that we should get back together again. She didn't like my suggestion. Or even worse—she liked it enough to laugh at me.

The boy splits his week between us. It was a hard few months for him when we first separated, he kept asking why it had to be that way, but he seems fine with it now. At least he is more at ease with it than I am.

#

When *The Octonauts* are over, he says, *Can we get gelato?*

Who wouldn't want to get gelato? I'm no idiot.

He grabs his scooter, the purple one that he loves with the bell in the shape of a sunflower. I grab my iPad, just in case I get an idea for the book.

He says, *Dada, can I play with your iPad at the place?*

Why? I ask.

If I check in from a dessert place, I'll be able to serve zombies ice cream.

I say, *We'll see*, as if what he said makes perfect sense.

My favorite Octonaut is Tweak Bunny. Who's your favorite?

I can't remember their names. *My favorite is also Tweak Bunny*, I say.

I knew it, he says. *Tweak Bunny talks just like your dad.*

My boy's whole life has been here in Portland. He doesn't know much about accents, other than the Japanese girl and the Nigerian boy who are in his classroom. And that his grandfather talks differently because he's from the South.

I worry often about my father. He survived cancer, heart disease, three marriages, a depression, the Depression, twelve Bush years, Trump, but now it is his failing vision that is killing him. You can only increase the font size so much before it becomes impossible to read a digital book about quantum physics.

My son asks me if rabbits can swim. I tell him I don't think so, and I think about Glenn Close in *Fatal Attraction* boiling the pet rabbit. I shake my head to make the image go away.

I remind him to stop at each intersection so many times that he finally says, *Dada! I know! I do it right every time.* He stomps his foot and his scooter on the sidewalk. He has a clip to keep his long hair out of his eyes, and it falls to the ground as he stomps.

I choose not to use a clichéd parenting speech here about safety, save it for another day. There are so many confusing and scary things about being alive. Sometimes I want to hug my son and never let him go.

I pick up the clip, and he grudgingly accepts it.

Before getting the gig at CollaborationHub, there was a six-month period when I was unemployed. My boy was just a baby and my ex—nearly ex, almost ex, virtually ex, viciously ex—was my happily-ish-married wife back then, just getting her social work degree. She made it seem like it was good timing because I could take care of the baby while she wrote her papers. *And you can work on your book while he naps*, she said with a smile. I knew it scared her. At best, I was a reluctant parent. At worst, I resented her and the baby for what they took away from my once quiet life. Plus, we had nothing in savings. Of course, I didn't write a damn thing. I worried. I stared at my sleeping, snoring, pooping boy, and I thought about how I would manage to take care of this creature until he became an adult. My so-called skills are very particular, and I worried that I'd never get a job again. It didn't help our life that, at night, I'd drink, and instead of writing, I'd order crap online that we didn't need and couldn't afford.

An R2-D2 robot that (supposedly) responded to voice commands. A six-(but-really-three)-in-one step stool. A two-(but-really-one)-year supply of razors and wet wipes. A zucchini spiralizer.

My boy happily scoots ahead. He occasionally looks back at me, but acts like he is just checking out the scenery around him. He's in that place between being a little kid and being a big kid. I'm not sure how much distance he wants.

I get another text. It vibrates on my iPhone, but also beeps on my iPad at the same time, which means we must be around a Wi-Fi hotspot. One of the houses around us naively left their router with the factory settings, unaware of what a malicious hacker could do to them.

Anne says: *marriage = false. novel = false. boy = true. date = true. beach = true. #salvation*

It drives me crazy when people use hashtags. #The #hashtag #is #a #distracting #symbol.

Anne thinks the beach can solve all of life's problems. But the only solution to life's problems is being dead.

Anne is married, BTW. Happily. I even like the dude. But she is taking me on as a project. I am a thing she is trying to fix.

We park the scooter outside the gelato store, don't bother with a lock since it's a pretty safe neighborhood, and as we walk into the shop, I rub my hand over my boy's head. He says, *Stop that, Dad.*

My dad used to do that to me, and I hated it too. I thought he was just being mean. I wonder if Papa used to do that to my dad. Even though I know my boy doesn't like it, sometimes I don't know what to do with this feeling for him. I try to avoid these selfish gestures of affection, but occasionally they just burst out.

He gets vanilla gelato no matter how many times I try to convince him to pick something more interesting.

I get vanilla too.

He wants to use the iPad. *Can I can I can I can I?*

I say he can't until after he finishes his gelato and washes his hands.

You're a party pooper, he says. *I'll get extra points if I serve zombies ice cream from here.*

Why not eat your real-life ice cream?

It's gelato.

I'm not sure whether or not to let him play these games. He is so into this alternate world that seems so empty to me. He'll spend hours watching YouTube videos of people playing this game. It's so weird. These young guys who make these videos are probably just around twenty years old and have ten million subscribers and make a living off recording themselves playing games.

We focus on our gelato. Quietly. Nobody @ mentions anybody. But still we are connected. Silent collaboration.

Then my boy asks if I think he's getting too old for *The Octonauts.*

I say if he enjoys it, then he isn't too old.

But they make fun of me at school.

Who?

He pokes his spoon into his gelato and doesn't look up at me. I burn with the pain of knowing that kids tease him.

I say, *You don't have to tell others about it if you don't want, but if you enjoy it, you can watch it. To hell with them.*

He takes a bite of his gelato and then looks at me, smiles, and says, *How long ago were you my age?*

In my novel, my father is my son's age. This makes things confusing because sometimes I write the character as my dad, and sometimes as my son. But they are two very different creatures. My dad was the scientist. My son is the storyteller. My dad was into insects. My son is into cartoons about insects. My dad had a buzz cut and was in the Boy Scouts. My son is into scooters with flowers and has a clip to hold back his long hair. In the novel, the character has both qualities. Which means he is a mess. It got so messy that in the latest draft, he is reduced to a character who just digs a hole in the backyard in search of China. All novel long. Poor kid. I want to apologize to my son. And to my dad. And to the character in my book. So I rub my hand over my boy's head. *Stop that, Dad.*

Anne sends another text: *we found someone for you.*

#

I call in sick the next day. In my sick post, I make sure to @ mention my boss and Anne.

Within seconds of that post, Anne sends a message that makes it clear she downloaded the stupid haiku-ify app:

```
blue whale in water
knows who pretends to be sick
future uncertain
```

I ignore her attempt at seventeenth-century poetic Japanese sassiness. Instead, I lazily loiter on Twitter, mute a few trolls saying nasty things, and search for something meaningless that I can retweet.

Chapter Two: The Blind Date

The first thing I ever wrote that wasn't homework was a *Choose Your Own Adventure* book, except unlike the *real* book series, mine had no plot or consequences: *If you want to stay in your room and sleep another few minutes, turn to page twelve. If you want to pee and brush your teeth, turn to page thirty-two.* I was in fourth grade, and I was embarrassed about it, so I wrote it while pretending to nap.

Of course my mom knew I was bullshitting. She always knew. When I told her I was napping, she came in my room with that Mom suspicion, she sniffed the air, and then quickly lifted my sheets.

She reached for the pages before I could stop her and she stepped back and read some of my story. Closely enough that she had to flip back and forth a few times until she got to an ending.

Her laugh was a familiar kind of laugh. The kind of laugh adults make when their kids are doing something cute.

I said to her, *It's just a stupid story.*

She stopped laughing. She looked straight at me. She threw the pages onto my chest and said, *Don't let anyone tell you that your story is stupid. You keep writing your story and you don't stop for anybody or anything.*

She walked out of my room like she was furious with me.

But I still quit writing for a long time after that. It wasn't until after she drank herself to death that her words came back to me, and the writing picked up again.

#

After enjoying my fake sick day, I grab my boy from school and take him to my wife's house. He runs inside the house and before my wife closes the door on me, I tell her that Anne has set me up on a blind date.

She says, *Why are you telling me this?*

She always looks so good when I drop the boy off. Never with dirty sweatpants and an exhausted look, but fresh out of the shower, that long wet hair smelling of honey, a nice tight blouse. Surely she should be messy from a messy day working with messy clients in her messy social work gig. Maybe she likes to clean herself up as a way to welcome the boy—I know I have my own prep rituals—or maybe she does it just to make it hurt worse to see her.

I don't know why I'm telling you, I say. *I thought it might be kind of like the piña colada song, you know, where the couple mistakenly cheats on each other with each other.*

Umm, she says. *I don't think it's going to go that way.*

It's hard figuring out how humor works when you're separated.

Yeah, I say. *I guess not. Tell the boy that I love him more than Tweak Bunny loves kelp cakes.*

She reminds me that it is Tunip, a creature who is half-vegetable, half-animal, who loves kelp cakes. Even this mundane back-and-forth feels like another piece of evidence for her, proving that I'm a failure as a parent and a husband.

Of course. Turnip, I say.

No, she corrects. *T-U-N-I-P. Half tuna, half turnip.*

Of course.

I don't know why I tell my wife about the date. I miss her, I guess. Hearing stories from the boy, I know she's been on a few dates. It's hard to imagine us together again anyhow. Nothing is different from when we split up. She has no reason to think I've changed. Because I haven't.

But I still like to pretend.

#

Anne's husband gives me an exaggerated, *How are you doing?* when he lets me inside. Which is the encrypted password for: *I-know-every-detail-about-your-life-but-can't-admit-it-because-you-haven't-actually-told-me-directly-so-I'm-stuck-with-vague-phrases-like-how-are-you-doing.*

The blind date lady they set me up with is running late because she's driving in from Suburbaville.

Suburbaville? I say, and make my disgust obvious as if I used the nausea emoji. *You have a friend from Suburbaville?* Suburbaville was in the paper this week because there's a burglar running around stealing jewelry and leaving behind blurry VHS tapes of his previous robberies. They say he's not well, but he seems like he has a more clear plan than anyone else I know. And he has an affection for obsolete technology, which gives me some affection for him. At least he didn't choose Betamax.

It's just temporary, Anne assures me. *She's moving next week to the Hawthorne district.*

I ask Anne if she had fun today—completely forgetting that today was supposedly a workday—and she says, *Good, except that I've spent the whole day writing a Post about the Bang Blog feature because my selfish coworker pretended to be sick today.*

Oopsy Daisy, I say, in the same way my boy says it, which I think is the best I can do under the circumstances. *Did you remember to @ mention the Algorithm group?*

She looks at me in that angry way that makes me realize that the rules for funny are a little different when your friends have been cleaning up your mess.

I spent the day working on my novel thing. The Klan is about to send a brick through the front window of my grandfather's store. His son is digging and digging and digging all alone in the backyard, in search of the other side.

Anne's husband, who—in my head—has already been assigned the username Hubby, asks if we want gin martinis.

We both say YES in all caps.

Anne says, *I bet you worked on your dumb novel while I worked on your dumb work.*

I did, I say with fake pride. *It's almost ready for you to send off to your big shot agent friend.* I know that Anne has a powerful literary agent friend in New York. But in reality, I'd be terrified for my impossible novel to see the light of a New York day.

Not likely, she says.

Then we talk about Hubby's projects. Since they don't own a car, he is converting the garage to his own personal brewery and movie theater. He has a projector, and he plays 1970s movies on the inside of the garage door while brewing beer. He is currently working on a lager, two IPAs, and a stout with molasses and ginger and Earl Grey tea.

I enjoy hearing him talk about it. I like men who are into projects. Not little writing projects hiding inside the circuits of solid state drives, but real-world, physical projects that involve touching real-world things to produce real-world results. Anne teases him about his obsession, but she doesn't try to save him the way she tries to save me. I don't know whether to be flattered or offended or something else.

We get so far into the martinis and the brewing talk and his insistence that every self-respecting American needs to watch *The Godfather* at least once a year that when Blind Date from Suburbaville walks in the door, we look at her like she's the VHS Burglar.

#

She's probably in her forties like me, but her body is shaped like an athlete, and I start to worry. I force down my tight, always-at-the-computer shoulders and I push out my flat, always-at-the-computer chest and I imagine that my bike commute to work is more than just a few miles of meandering slowly while thinking about my dead grandfather. She has this fabulous long brown hair almost to her waist that probably takes a year to dry. For the most part, I focus on her smile, which is pixelated slightly since I'm wearing my reading glasses by mistake, but I can still tell the smile is nice. It's sad too, there's a hesitation, and it makes me want to know more.

She checks me out, just for a split second, while hugging Anne, and she doesn't leave the house immediately. Level one complete.

Suburbaville Blind Date tells me her name is Kitty, which sounds like it's straight out of the porn name generator that I created last month for Hackday. I try to roll with it.

Kitty shakes my hand and I fake a sturdy handshake. Hubby makes a first martini for Suburbaville Blind Date and a second round for everyone else. Hopefully this drink will give me the confidence to survive the night.

There are pimento olives in there. The Martini group at work would be impressed.

Hubby says that we can watch *Taxi Driver* in the garage later tonight, which is either cool or creepy.

Kitty and Anne talk about a beach trip they're planning. Girls only. I force myself not to ask if I can come along. Even though I hate beaches, I want to go with them anyway. I bet they'll talk about bad blind dates and all kinds of other juicy stuff. When I was getting my engineering degree, I always felt out of place with the other guys. I wanted to hang out with their girlfriends, talk about relationship issues instead of how to hack into the school servers. Luckily, CollaborationHub has been good about hiring women lately. Even though sometimes it feels like the women have to out-man the men to stay in their roles. Which is a big matzo ball of a topic that I don't know how to approach.

I notice that in the time we take to finish our second martinis, Kitty has caught up to us, and we all drink a third drink together.

While they talk, Kitty wiggles her hips like she is dancing in the chair. I hope she isn't a dancer type. Dancers make me realize how uncomfortable I am in my own body.

Kitty says she wants to go for a swim in the ocean before summer is over.

In the real-life, physical ocean? I ask. *Isn't the Pacific cold and dangerous and horrible and violent? And cold?*

She looks at me for too long like she doesn't understand the language I'm speaking. So I look at Anne and Hubby, hoping someone could save my sinking ship. Kitty finally says, *When you swim in the ocean, you can't think about anything else except staying afloat.* She stares at the ceiling like there is some kind of beauty to this experience.

She's a skinny woman, but her arms are all muscle. They are used for a lot more than QWERTY on a keyboard.

Another thing about swimming in the ocean. She lifts up a finger and shakes it towards me a few times. I'm expecting another profound insight. She says, *It stops me from fantasizing about cutting off my ex-husband's cock.*

She closes her eyes. She takes a deep breath and presses her hand to her chest. And then looks at me.

Oops, she says. *I wasn't supposed to say that out loud.*

It is exactly this line in the code where I like this girl.

There is something between us. My divorce trauma fantasies are not as colorful as hers, but they're there. Some days are more desperate than others, but those first few months were no fun. Drinking too early, not eating, not sleeping, dirty underwear, writing and deleting and writing and deleting and writing and deleting a thousand horrible and cruel emails, not leaving my couch for entire weekends, the kid asking why I keep getting the flu. I may not know about cock cutting, but I could get there from here with just a short TriMet bus ride.

I ask Kitty what else she's into. It doesn't come out right. I probably come off like a pervert.

I'm into novelty piggy banks, she tells me.

I start to giggle, but notice nobody else giggling.

So I ask, *What do you do for a living? Sell piggy banks on eBay and Etsy?* She tells me, *Yes.* She's serious.

I work on my martini and wait for the life rafts.

Hubby is quietly drinking his drink like he has diplomatic immunity to small talk. Anne looks up from texting someone on her phone, which somehow makes me jealous, and says, *Saul's a writer, you know,* which she says with a kind of pride I've never heard from her about my writing. *He even published a novel a few years ago.*

More than a few, but I'll take the compliment. This is when Kitty looks at me. Really looks at me. Like I've been put up for auction on eBay. I get itchy all over. She says, *So are you one of those shame-filled writers?*

I say, *Is there any other kind?* I think I smile, but it's not helping. We're no longer on the same side. It's worse than not being on the same side. I feel like I'm on her ex's side all of a sudden.

What do you write about? Kitty is all business.

I can feel Anne and Hubby watching us.

I look at my smartwatch and say, *Look at the time. I need to call in sick somewhere*, even though Anne knows that I turned off the time feature on my watch so it only shows me random lines from my broken book.

Anne talks to me like a dog, *Stay*.

I write about screwy families and screwy relationships, I say. Which is a terrible description.

She doesn't smile, I'm still up for auction, but she gets softer. *Anne says you have a cute kid*.

Anne blushes, and I try to imagine her PowerPoint bulleted list of me:

```
- OK looking
- OK writer
- OK employee
- OK communicator
- Has a cute kid
```

In my awkwardness, I tell everyone that my son is obsessed with a show called *The Octonauts* and that it's about these land animals that help sea creatures and live in an underwater space station called the Octopod and drive around in Gups.

They look at me like I'm talking from an outer-space space station.

Maybe it's the martini burning through me. I look at these people around me, and I want to cry. I say, *When the boy is with me, I'm constantly trying to work on my novel, and I get irritated with him when he interrupts me. When he's with his mom, I miss him so much that I sometimes drive by her house and park a block away, hoping to see him biking by*.

Anne and Hubby don't look me in the eyes. But Kitty does. She says, *That's messed up*. She says it with such a straight and even voice that it doesn't even seem like a criticism. And she smiles at me like she's floating along on a happy memory that I've somehow instigated.

I say to Kitty, *My boy has a beautiful cowlick.*

And then to get back into the moment, I say, *So do you have an octopus piggy bank or some other quirky ocean-themed thing?*

Her breathing gets irregular, and she squeezes her eyes shut. The lift in her cheeks turns to a droop. Whatever happy thought that was in her head is now gone. My benign question somehow stuck a blade in her.

The crying echoes in her palms like she's inside a seashell.

Anne hugs her and presses Kitty's face into her shoulder as she walks them to the bedroom.

Well, I say to Hubby. *I have an effect on women.*

Hubby smiles, barely, and then he says, *She hasn't had the easiest year.* He doesn't say more and he doesn't try to make me feel better.

I wonder if I should apologize or something.

Hubby lifts his shoulders up and down. This is the kind of moment where I don't really appreciate project-oriented men who aren't into emotions. They'd rather repair something in the garage than repair something in the heart.

My mom was always so good at saying just enough to stop me from feeling like a fool—even if everyone in my first-grade class just saw me pee my pants, she'd have some wisdom that would make me not so worried about the situation. *Don't worry about it, honey. In ten years, those assholes will be so desperate for a date that they won't remember a damn thing about who pissed on what.* I miss her.

I stand up in a state of antsiness. I don't know if I want to go towards the problem or run the hell away. Both directions seem bad.

I go down the hallway to the bedroom and knock on the door. *What is it?* Anne says, like I'm no longer her friend and coworker.

Are y'all OK? I say.

She doesn't answer.

Sorry about the octopus thing, I say, taking a wild guess at what offended her. Maybe she suffered an octopus mauling while swimming in the ocean.

Give us some time, Saul, Anne says to me.

I want to hear Kitty's voice too. Just a sign. But I get nothing, so I walk back into the living room.

Look, I tell Hubby. *I think I better go.*

You sure you don't want to watch Taxi Driver?

No thanks, I say. It's actually tempting to hang out and watch a disturbing story of disconnection and loneliness right now, but instead I say, *Tell everyone I'm sorry for . . . everything.*

As I leave, Hubby says to me, *Forget it, Saul. It's* Chinatown.

#

The document conversion code needs to be fixed, my boss tells me the next morning. Otherwise, Discussions can't be converted into Blog Posts and back again without a loss of data.

I tell him that I'll get right on it. And then I daydream about the scene in my novel that I got stuck on at 3:00 a.m. while I couldn't sleep. My grandfather is always losing money at his store. Whenever my grandmother looks away, he sells an item at their dry goods shop below cost. The one-legged man whom Papa sells one shoe to at less than half cost. The Klan member to whom he sells white cloth for free. The boy with the hole in his pants who somehow walks out of the store without a hole in his pants. He may have been a disastrous businessman, but he had plenty of people visiting his store. Papa loved talking to the goys about sports and joking to them about his failures, which were never jokes to my grandmother.

When Anne gets to work, she doesn't seem pleased to see me, and I stop brooding about my writing so I can start brooding about last night.

Five minutes after she settles into her cubicle, I start getting messages from her on an ephemeral CollabHub channel.

She says: *sorry about last night* in a meme with a picture of George W. Bush standing on an aircraft carrier.

And then she says: *i think it's a little too soon*

And then she says: *i didn't realize it was too soon*

My therapist tells me that I'm the opposite of too soon. That the only way I can work out my attachment issues is by having a real-life relationship. I told her I wasn't so attached to her theories about my attachment issues. She didn't laugh.

I say to Anne: *was it my offensive piggy bank comment or the part where I stalk my ex-wife?*

As if my wife can sense references to her, she texts right then to tell me she is ready to get the paperwork together for the divorce. I tell her if she makes me sign the papers, I will brainwash our son into thinking his mother is a sea monster from the midnight zone. But she knows it's a fake threat. She also knows it's my crooked way of dealing with the fact that I'm not ready to sign the papers.

My wife says, *So how was the date?* I tell her it was DOA. She says, *Good.* I know it's a fake sentiment. She doesn't really care about the date. Even though I like to pretend that it's her crooked way of telling me that she's not ready to sign the papers either.

Anne says: *She likes you*

My iPhone rings—I mean, it actually rings like a phone, I mean, the phone app that is buried away in a hidden folder somewhere is actually doing something—and I don't even look at the display because I know it's either a telemarketer who got through my spam call filter or it's my dad, and I need to get this code checked in by the end of the day.

My boss also asks me to fix the gamification plug-in while I'm in there because Customer Support is upset that you no longer get any points when your comment is marked as Best Answer. He throws in another request that would be the type of thing that you'd mutter under your breath as you were walking away, except you can't do that online, so he just puts it in parentheses. He says, *(and it wouldn't hurt to write a Post about your fix instead of leaving right at five on the dot).*

Here's the thing: I WROTE THE FUCKING GAMIFICATION PLUG-IN. This deserves ALL CAPS. It seemed like an amusing idea at the time. To reward collaboration in game-like ways. To create a playful level system. It seemed amusing, sure, and I stole some of the ideas from my boy's zombie game, but I also didn't think anyone would actually use it. It is our most successful plug-in ever. And even though I wrote it, I'm stuck in the same virtual hamster wheel with everyone else.

I make all the changes my boss requested. I even write a Post about it and @ mention all the right people. Though I also make one tweak to the plug-in. I set it up so that you *lose* points for collaborating after 5:00 p.m. And you mysteriously level up (rather than get a warning notification) after a certain number of hours of inactivity.

#

Once the fix is checked in and tested, I listen to my voicemail. The speech-to-text engine doesn't seem to work well with my dad's Southern accent, so I have to listen to his message the old-fashioned way. *This is your father*, he says. That's how he starts all his messages. As if I didn't already have five ways to authenticate the source. He tells me his email has been hacked because he keeps having to install something called a flash update, and he also gets emails about Viagra, and Viagra is the opposite of what he needs. He tells me that I need to get my son down to Atlanta because he'd love this new sushi joint. *What is his favorite kind of sushi again?* he asks my voicemail. Voicemail doesn't answer, but he waits for a response anyway.

I book the *Battlestar Galactica* conference room with our meeting scheduler plug-in and then go there to call my dad. I get self-conscious calling him from my desk. I'm afraid that I sound too much like a little kid when I speak with him. Plus, I have to yell so that he hears me.

I take over his system remotely while on the phone with him and verify that his email doesn't look hacked. I delete the various penis-related spam he has acquired. As I'm fumbling around on his computer, he mentions that his blood pressure is too high, and the doctor is confused because the blood pressure-lowering medication makes his blood pressure go up. When I ask him what he is going to do about it, he says, *Blood does what it does.*

And then he asks me about other emails he notices on his screen.

Is that spam? Is that a phishing attack? Is that a virus? Is that a hack?

I tell him not to worry as I scan through his inbox and notice that some of his old emails to my mom are in a separate folder.

Why did y'all email? I ask him. I have to do the math to remind myself that there was email back in 1999 when she was alive. I mean, *I* emailed. But my dad? My mom? What would they know about email?

Oh, it was nothing, he says. But I see that the folder has fifty-eight emails in there before he pushes me on to other computer problems. If he was using IMAP email instead of an archaic POP protocol, I'd be able to dig into those messages straight from the server after we hang up, but maybe it's for the best that I don't have that option.

I ask my dad if he's reading any new books on physics. He is. He begins to recite things he has underlined from the book. *The only watchmaker is the blind forces of physics.* He reads the excerpts in bits and pieces, and I don't get great cell reception from this corner of the building so I can't quite follow him. I get this low-grade annoyance that is more than the bad reception. I know he is lonely, and I know I need to check in on him, let him talk, but these impatient emotions still bubble up.

Speaking of watches, I say to him in an attempt to reroute the conversation to my book. *Do you remember what sort of pocket watch your father had?*

I have to ask him three times before he hears.

Well, let me think about that, he says. And then he tells me twenty minutes of stories about him and his parents. None relate to the watch, but they are interesting. He tells me that his father had a kind of charm that could win over a sweet young lady and a mean old son of a bitch and a nervous one-legged black man. *One time*, he says, *he even stuck up for the man who tried to burn down his store. It made Mama furious. And you know what it is like when she is furious?* My dad laughs and coughs into the phone. I ask him to tell me more. I have so many questions. But he keeps saying, *What did you say?*

TELL ME MORE ABOUT YOUR MOTHER! I say loud enough that my coworkers can probably hear it through the walls.

He is quiet for a few seconds, and I know he just realized that I'm trying to swipe material for my novel.

He says, *Why don't you write about the history of the town instead? Or the story of immigrants in the South in the 1930s? Or make use of that engineering degree of yours and write a book that matters? Nobody wants to read about what Mama worried about. And how Papa kept us poor and miserable.*

I get a message from a coworker that says, *My mother is fine. Thanks for asking.* And he sends a sticker of the I've-fallen-and-I-can't-get-up woman falling down.

I try to explain to my dad that a novel isn't a historical record. But he says, *There is history and there is science. And the rest is horseshit.*

Dad, I say. *There is value in storytelling.*

He says, *Azoy, now you sound like Papa.*

What's wrong with that? Wasn't he a good storyteller?

A good storyteller. Sure. If you want to get drunk and bullshit with some-one about the Yankees, he was great. If you want someone to take care of a family, look somewhere else. Anywhere else.

I can hear him breathing. Long, deep breaths. My dad, who worked on his research for ten hours a day, six days a week, and despised his father's lack of drive.

I have more of my father in me than I'm willing to admit. Because I'm terrified of losing my day job. Even if I act cavalier about it when the Blue Whale gives me shit, I still stay up at night worrying what I'd do if I couldn't afford the Netflix subscription that sends *The Octonauts* to the iPad. But I'm also like Papa in the way that the business of making a living is so peculiar to me. Anne sometimes says that I like to shoot myself in the foot every time I have an opportunity to make something of myself. But I'm nothing compared to Papa. He would shoot himself in both feet and still be looking for more of his feet to shoot. He just didn't care about busi-ness. Or feet. With three bankruptcies to prove it. He cared about telling stories and hearing stories. He loved stories.

I wonder how the other Southerners managed to enjoy Papa's compa-ny so much even though he was this Jew with an accent who loved the Yankees. I wonder how a man can charm even when he barely speaks the language. I wonder why I like Papa more and more the less practical he seems to be. Sure, he didn't understand a damn thing about business, but he understood something about relating to people.

I say to my dad, *I'm thinking of coming to visit you with the boy next month.*

Great, he says. *How's he doing at math?*

Good.

Ready for me to teach him calculus?

He asks me this every time. And every time, I laugh along with him and then I say, *Not quite yet.*

My boy is scared of my dad like I was scared of my dad's dad. My dad leans in to tell him stories, and my son goes to the bathroom for suspiciously long periods of time.

My dad asks me if there are any women in my life. I say, *No.* He asks if my relationship to my ex is good. I say, *No.* He asks if my job is going well. I say, *No.*

Funny, he says on the phone. *You act like your job is such a burden, but it seems to me like a decent way to make a living. Didn't you say they have a shower with towel service at your office?*

Yeah, but.

But what? You get to work on these silly writing projects on the side. That sounds like a pretty good deal to me. If it were up to me, I'd do everything in my power not to fuck it up.

He pauses for a while, and I hear these deep, lungy breaths. Lungs that have been breathing every second for more than eighty-eight years. Which is over 625 million breaths.

I say, *I just don't want to fool myself into thinking this is an OK life and then wake up thirty years later having squandered my chance of doing something more meaningful.*

Without even leaving space for a breath, he says, *There isn't anything more meaningful. You just need to make enough money so that if you start shitting your pants, you can pay someone to clean it up.*

#

Instead of going back to my desk, I spend twenty minutes in the bathroom stall staring at my novel on my iPhone.

I've misconstrued the scene with Papa. When my grandmother is yelling at him for bankrupting their business and he is yelling at her back, he still has affection for her. Papa is still crookedly proud of his son even when he doesn't understand why his son is so fascinated by insects or why his son doesn't care about the Yankees or the big Joe Louis boxing match.

I just don't fully get Papa. There's something missing in my understanding of this man.

Anne interrupts my focus with a rude text: *are you toilet writing again?*

She gives me hell when I write in the bathroom.

Get with the times, I toilet text.

It's just gross, is all she comes up with.

So I keep sending her messages from the toilet. *Anne, this is a message from beyond the bowel.* I include a ghost emoji next to a poop emoji. I normally prefer old-school, text-based emoticons from before the days of these fancy emojis, you know, like :(and :) , but it's too hard to text a pooping ghost. :_(

She asks if I'd be willing to meet with Kitty again, just as friends.

I wonder why the hell Kitty collects piggy banks. Does she keep money in them? Does she pay for everything in pennies and nickels? That would make for an embarrassing meet-up. When I think about it, meeting "just as friends" sounds just as scary as meeting for a date.

I say, *I'm too busy. I don't have time for just-as-friends. I hate all humans. I made her cry. Didn't you say it was too soon?*

She says, *She could meet you at that ice cream place you like to go to.*

It's gelato, I say.

"gelato is made with a base of milk, cream, sugar, and a healthy dose of self-loathing."
—@wrongapedia

Chapter Three: The Gelato Situation

An hour before I'm supposed to meet Kitty at the gelato spot, the babysitter cancels. Her name is Genevieve and my boy and I like to say her name a lot because it's pretty. Genevieve. Genevieve. Genevieve. She's also totally flaky about babysitting. I toy with canceling on Kitty but then I freeze up about what to do next, so I just text Kitty, *the babysitter just canceled*, without making any decision. My wife hated it when I couldn't step up and make a decision for myself. Then again, she also liked making decisions for me.

Within a minute, Kitty says, *bring him along . . . i won't bite*.

I spend ten minutes staring at that word: *won't*. It should be *don't*.

\#

When my boy and I get to the gelato place, Kitty is already waiting for us inside, staring at all the flavors. She's staring into the glass like there is something so transcendent in there. I spend a moment to stare at her pretty body from behind, the way she is about the size of me, but with her, you can see the muscles and curves. Meanwhile, I'm all edges and bones.

We walk up to her and I say, *It sure is gelato*. The line was less stupid in my head.

Oh! It's you! she says. She looks confused or sad or like she wasn't expecting us. And then she looks down at my kid and her disoriented look disappears and she smiles, *And you*.

My boy stands behind me as I introduce him, which is normal for him to do, but he steps out from behind me when he gets a look at Kitty, like he has determined that she is less dangerous than most adults. And then he tells this stranger, *Genevieve gets sick a lot. My dad worries that she is annarex-six but I think she is nice. And she knows a lot about the sea creatures in the midnight zone. And she lets me have popcorn before bed.*

I can feel the sweat from the top of my bald head. I should have canceled.

I like her already, Kitty says, squatting down so she can look him in the eyes. But then my boy squats as well to mimic her gesture.

I try to remember the advice from the article that went around Facebook last month about when you should introduce your child to a new boyfriend or girlfriend. This Kitty person isn't either of those, but I still don't feel good about this gelato situation, and I'm sure the Facebook article would disapprove of this. Then again, I don't know if it was a real article or a fake article written by some guy in Macedonia with a secret agenda to destroy our democracy.

My boy orders vanilla. I order vanilla. Kitty gets a scoop of chocolate on top of a scoop of strawberry. My boy looks at her like she just robbed a bank. One part terror, one part fascination.

As we sit down, the boy asks Kitty if she is my girlfriend.

Kitty says, *No*, faster than the speed of this store's wireless network.

He explains to Kitty that the kitten character in *The Octonauts* is named Kwazii Kitten, and he doesn't follow the rules. *Do you follow the rules?* he asks her.

She moves in extra close to him and says *NO!* and my boy jumps in his chair.

Then he giggles and says, *Mama has a boyfriend. Do you believe that?*

Kitty says, *I do.* She looks at me as if just by looking at me she could have gleaned that information.

This woman scares me. Maybe she is a spy for my ex.

Wait. My wife has a boyfriend???

My iPhone vibrates on the table from a text. *Anne?* Kitty says to me. And it is. Anne says: *don't be an asshole.* Then Kitty gets a text, and I say, *Anne?* And Kitty nods.

Kitty says, *Does Anne also give you ego-boosting mantras?*
More or less, I say.

I threaten Anne that I'll call in sick again if she keeps bugging me.

I'm scared to ask Kitty about her piggy banks because I fear that she'll either start crying again or my boy will get so riveted by it that I won't know how to regain control.

I give my boy the iPad, and he says, *Already?*

Anne texts me that if I call in sick, she'll status bomb me.

She'll do it too. She knows my password, she's able to log in to my account, and she knows exactly what kind of fake status update would shame the shit out of me.

I wait a minute in silence as my boy gets immersed enough in the game that he isn't paying attention. I could just talk about the weather. I'm sure there's some weather I could discuss. I have four weather apps on my iPhone and three on my watch.

I say to Kitty, *Anne thinks I should quit working on my novel and get over my ex. The characters in my book are just as stuck as my relationships.*

I no longer understand how real-life adults converse. They probably don't even use the verb converse.

Have you tried poking? she asks.

My boy looks up at us. *Poking what?* he says.

Poking your characters. That always helps. We like to see squirming. She tickles my boy above his hip and he wiggles and giggles.

When he goes back to his game, Kitty says to me, *Grab them by the you-know-what and twist.*

My boy looks up again. *Is the you-know-what the same thing as a penis?*

This alarms me. But Kitty says, *Actually it's just the hair on their head.* And she rubs his hair.

I'm not sure I like how affectionate she is being with the boy.

So are you a writer? I ask.

Hell no, she says. *My life is enough of a mess.*

She must have dated a writer. She knows too much about the problems of writing. Dating a writer probably makes you a better storyteller than the actual writer.

I have to piss, I say.

TMI, Dada! is what my boy says to me. And then he leans over to Kitty and says, *That means "too much information." It's an acorn-nim.*

I totally agree with that acorn-nim, she says.

Would you watch the boy? I ask her.

My boy says, *I don't need to be watched*, at the exact same time that she says, *Of course I will.* And they both seem to be judging me in equal measure.

#

While sitting on the toilet, I see that my story has made no progress without me. Too bad writing isn't like rotting, where things keep moving along whether you're paying attention or not.

My father was obsessed with rotting. When he was a young chemistry professor, he told me that his first research grant was to study decay. I can't remember any of the details except that he once photographed a rotting log every twenty minutes for six weeks. When I was too young to know what the hell he was talking about, he said to me, *Son, there is no life without decay. We're all dying as we live.* I had nightmares for months about my body falling apart like a zombie.

But the book is more about my grandfather than my father, and in the book I need to understand why my Papa keeps getting up and going to his dry goods store each day. Doesn't he know that the store won't bring in any money? Doesn't he know that his son is ashamed his father has a dry goods store? Doesn't he know his wife resents his business failures? *Why do you keep at it, Papa?*

I can see the rot, but not the growth.

The toilet is one of those auto-flushers, which flushes mysteriously before I'm ready. It's a passive-aggressive toilet. It wants me out, and I take the hint.

#

When I sit back down, my boy is explaining to Kitty how the zombie game works, how you have to go to real stores to do real things in the pretend game. He says, *It's just like real life but with zombies. And the best baby zombies hatch in ice cream shops.* He shows her where you're allowed to touch the screen. *Touch here!* he says. *And here!* he says. *And swipe here!* Every time Kitty touches or swipes, her body shakes in delight from whatever happens on the screen. *Oh my,* she says so innocently, as if this isn't the woman that spoke of cock cutting the other night. *That zombie is totally adorable.*

I want to stay in the background and keep watching them play. They both look so happy sitting there. Together. Like this is exactly what they want from this moment. They are not distracted, no interruptions, no multitasking. They're just right here next to each other. A simple moment of connection between these two people . . . by way of a zombie game on the iPad. She is good with the boy. I like adults that can be this way with kids, neither talking down to them nor pretending that they're adults, and knowing that they have the capacity for amazing things just like anyone else.

My boy says, *I wish I could draw zombies but they always come out like regular people who are grumpy.*

Kitty says, *I can TOTALLY teach you how to draw a zombie. There's a secret trick to it.*

Anne texts me to say, *whatever you do don't talk about divorce . . . too messy for ice cream!*

My boy tugs on my shirt and says, *Can she teach me zombies? Please?*

I think about my wife. I wonder how long she's had a boyfriend. Did she meet him while we were married?

Suddenly this woman and my boy bonding about zombies no longer looks sweet. I don't like it. It feels dangerous. These zombies are bringing them close together. And someone is going to get hurt. And it's my job to protect my boy from zombies. And I don't yet know what this woman is made out of, or whose brains she might devour.

I tell my boy that he can't get zombie lessons and he calls me a party pooper and goes back to his iPad in a mopey way.

I ask Kitty, *How long have you been divorced?*

She looks up at me like she forgot about me. *Oh*, she says. *Yes. Two months. But he started you-know-what-ing another you-know-what about three years ago. And I found out about it a year ago.*

Damn, I say. *I'm sorry.*

My boy says, *No potty words, Dada*, while he keeps playing his game.

I tell her that I'm not officially divorced and our ending wasn't as exciting-sounding as hers. I try to use vague terms so my boy doesn't follow the conversation.

But my boy tells Kitty that his mama got tired of me working on my book instead of spending time with her.

In a sad sort of way, Kitty says, *Looks like all of us seem to be poking the wrong characters.* I don't understand what she means, but I still agree with her.

You know what's the worst thing? she says.

I'm scared to find out. So I say, *I'm scared to find out.*

He used to call me quirky.

Ouch, I try, not sure what the problem is with quirky. Isn't fucking another woman a lot worse than an adjective?

She seems like a relatively sane woman, all adjectives aside. I wonder about the bedtime conversations Anne and Hubby have about the two of us. How high on the crazy scale did they rate each of us?

How are the piggy banks? I ask. I can see her lips move in strange ways, like the conversation could go in many different directions, like she is close to crying again, and I feel bad for asking. I know what it's like to connect real-world objects to not-real-world emotions. But I also know that it helps to talk through those piggy bank emotions anyhow.

They sell, she says in a tone like she's disappointed with her success.

Really? People still put real coins in real piggy banks?

*I didn't say that. But sentimental idiots buy this crap. You just tack on the phrase COLLECTOR'S ITEM to the description and it sells like—*I can see that her lips start to say the word *porn*, but instead, she says—*gelato.*

You're not the most sentimental type, I say.

Were you looking for a particular sentiment?

I guess I'm not so good with emotions myself.

My boy looks up at me and then puts a few fingers under one of my eyes. Right in the spot that he claims is the only not-hairy part of my body. *My dad doesn't even cry.* He lifts his fingers off my face and shows them to Kitty. *See?* he says. *Nothing there.*

Hey! I say to the boy. *Enough with the inspection.*

He gets back to the game, and Kitty says, *I'm sorry for how I behaved at Anne's place. I'm a walking bag of emotional shit right now.* She covers her mouth real quickly, and then says, *I mean, a bag of poo poo.*

My boy giggles. I giggle.

Kitty leans over towards me, and I expect her to say something nice about the boy but instead she says, *You're an adorable parent.*

I blush even though I don't like the compliment.

Oh! she says. *I nearly forgot.* And she hands my boy an octopus piggy bank that materializes from her purse, which has materialized from under the chair.

He peeks in the hole and then turns it over. *I love it!* he says to the octopus.

The Facebook article would definitely not approve of a gift for your kid the first time the kid and the woman you're not dating meet. Especially when you wonder if the gift is connected to some seafaring or marital trauma she's been through, or whatever it was that caused her to disappear in tears last time.

My boy rubs each tentacle slowly, feeling the various bumps on the ceramic. He doesn't look up at us for some time.

I'm tired of judgy Facebook articles that remind me of my failures. Fuck Facebook. I'm tempted to go online and claim that I'm against vaccinating children and I stand for smallpox, polio, and a flat Earth.

Kitty leans towards me, a little too close, so I can feel the heat of her chocolate-strawberry breath. She points to the octopus in my boy's hands and whispers, *Be careful with that thing. It's a collector's item.*

#

My boy hops into my bed at 6:00 a.m., as he often does. Except he brings the octopus piggy bank in bed with us. It jingles from the six quarters he put in there last night.

The boy puts one leg and one arm on me. He says, *You're more scratchy and bony and uncomfortable.*

Than what?

Than Mama.

Oh, I say. *Maybe I'm more like a zombie body?*

Not really a zombie, he says, but he can't figure out what I'm more like, and then he says, *I wonder if your friend can really draw zombies.*

I don't know, is all I can come up with.

I feel totally hungover. Even though I didn't drink a thing last night. I can't point to any one special thing about Kitty, but it was nice to be around her. She's familiar and surprising at once.

What did you dream about, Dada?

I dreamt that my wife and Kitty were in bed together. When I tried to walk into the house, my wife sent a bunch of geese to attack me. Kitty explained to my wife that the geese are collector's items. And then my grandfather got in bed with them and started singing about anti-Semitic geese. And then Anne got in bed and said that a good story should never contain a dream. Or geese.

I tell the boy that I dreamed about singing geese.

I say, *Come on boychick, let's make some of Tunip's kelp cakes for breakfast.*

He gets up quickly after I say this—he doesn't correct my statement—which means I actually got the *Octonauts* reference correct. Once more, we survive.

#

I drop him off at school but I'm late to work, and I haven't been paying attention to my vibrating iPhone and the haptic feedback on my watch, even though I sort of noticed all the taps and vibrations. I couldn't stop thinking about meeting up with Kitty for the gelato situation. I can't decide whether her talk about poking is worth paying attention to, and whether I should use this advice for my book or my life. I hate this feeling of liking her.

When I'm just outside the building, I finally look at my iPhone.

Since I left work yesterday, I have been @ mentioned in fourteen Questions, three Posts, eleven Messages, twenty-seven Angry GIFeroos, three Anti-trophies, five Status Updates, and fifty-one Argghss.

I also have one text message. When Anne takes the time to text in capital letters, you know you're up a creek full of shit.

DANGER! Enter the office with EXTREME caution. The place is full of pissed-off GOLDFISH. And you are one soon-to-be-fired COLOSSAL SQUID.

```
"don't forget to take a vacation. and then take
a vacation after your vacation. and then . . .
forget it. just give up. go weep under your desk.
again. #recursivevacations" —@productiveAsPhuck
```

Chapter Four: The New Deal

I could easily just roll back the changes. After all, that's why we have version control software in the first place. A simple *git revert* command would do the trick. But instead, I undo the changes manually. There is something almost therapeutic about cleaning up my mess slowly. I try to really clean up the gamification plug-in while I'm in there. Not just like how it was, but better than it was. As a bonus, I grab some machine learning code I find online on GitHub that automatically scours Twitter and Facebook and Instagram and Pinterest and Pornterest every week to see what causes successful collaboration and then gives employees extra points for possessing those qualities. Phrases such as "free prize" or "most important" or "leather brassiere" seem particularly effective in inciting engagement with others.

My boss starts sending me messages on an encrypted channel and asks what the holdup is. He tells me that the entire sales engineering team is giving him hell for the delay—*the gamification demos this morning have all been shot to hell already and they can't afford any more surprises.* That is his wording. I toy with sending something sassy back, but my survival instinct kicks in and I say, *Give me five minutes.*

Anne sends me a video of an explosion, and inside the explosion you can see Obama saying *Thanks, Obama*, while trying to get an oversized cookie into an undersized glass of milk, and inside the glass of milk, there's a picture of a Blue Whale with its mouth open. I don't bother trying to look inside the mouth. I miss Obama. And I need to get back to work.

The software I took from GitHub works really well, and it's really fast, but I should probably let the QA team know about it for testing, and also the legal team about whether we can use this open-source code that I swiped, but just then I get a message from my boss: *We need it. Now.* The text red and large. And he's switched the font to Baskerville. So I *git commit* my changes. And then my boss calls me into the Serenity conference room.

#

As I step into the room, my mind is testing out a thousand inner voices. The one voice that feels like an idiot for messing up the gamification plug-in, the one that hates him for pushing me to finish too fast, the one that loves messing with the code, the one that hates this techie world, the one that is terrified to lose this job, the one that tells me that I have no actual skills in this world, the one that knows I need to do every possible thing to provide for my boy.

We sit in the room for two minutes without a word. Two minutes. That's 120,000 milliseconds of silence. My laptop could perform more than a hundred trillion instructions in that time. But we do nothing. Except I pretend to check things on my phone and he pretends to check things on his laptop.

Finally he looks up and sighs and says, *What are we going to do about this?*

Fire me?

Is that what you want?

I don't know, I say. I have never felt more confident in my lack of knowledge.

What's going on with you these days? You once did great work for this company. But you're not all here lately. You hide in the bathroom and write that . . . book. He says the word "book" like it's one of those bad words my son would call him out for. My boss sighs again, in case I missed it the first time, and then he says, *I just hope you remember who gives you those paychecks every two weeks.*

It's actually only twice a month, I say to him.

He looks at me for a long time. Right in the eyes. And I try to look at him back. We're not texting or @ mentioning. Just looking. His eyes aren't quite blue and they aren't quite green. His lips make a slightly sad shape. No emoji could capture it. He is just sad about this situation. It's the first time I realize that he actually cares about me. He doesn't want me to die in a tornado or an undersea whirlpool or a status bomb or a reorg. The poor guy doesn't even want to fire me. I have to look away.

OK, he finally says. *I want you to take a week off. Unplug yourself. Don't post a damn thing. When you come back, we find you a role that will make you happy, where you can do good work again. I've been talking to Anne, and she has some ideas—*

Wait, I say. *Anne has ideas about MY career?*

He takes a long breath. I can feel the warm air blow past me. The space between great work and lousy work. He says, *If you can't be happy here, I don't want you to come back. Not as a Goldfish, not as a Penguin, not as a Colossal Squid, nothing. Deal?*

Even though I'm a little thrown off about Anne planning my career, I appreciate this man and his kindness right now. I say, *Thank you.* And then I lift my wrist and say to my watch, *Send a message to my boss that says thank you.* And a second later, his phone vibrates. He smiles at that.

We shake hands. Like men are supposed to do. He has a tight grip but it is not too tight. There is some give.

#

As I drive the boy to my ex's house, he says, *Do you think you and Mama will live together again someday?*

I tell him, *I don't know.*

He says, *Is that the way adults talk when they don't want to talk?*

I don't know, I say again.

I never know how much to tell my boy. I know I need to have some explanation for why I'm not with his mom, but he doesn't need to hear the real story, the story I don't even want to hear. How can he understand that

I couldn't let go of my novel because I thought I had almost found the answer to it? And how she hated me writing those stories as if it threatened our relationship? How can I say that I slept in the attic for years, no matter how hot it was, instead of sleeping with her? That I did all these things even though I loved her? And that I even resented him at first. I didn't want to have a baby, and I was angry at how he made everything so much more complicated. I was selfish and she saw every side of this selfishness. And now I miss her every day and I regret my actions every day, but I know if we were together, I'd make many of the same mistakes all over again. Instead of explaining it, I drive faster.

From the backseat, the boy says, *Dada, the sign said not to turn right on red.*

This damn attentive boy. I slow down.

He says, *Do you think it's more important to follow the rules or do the best thing?*

What do you mean? I say.

The rules at school are that you should help other people, but some people are not nice people. Do you help not nice people too?

Are people not nice to you? I say. *Is anything bad going on?*

He says, *I don't know.*

In the rearview mirror, I see him looking out the window. When I was a kid, they teased me in school too. But it wasn't too bad. At least I don't remember it much. What bothered me most were my parents, how my dad was working all the time, how he'd say, *Show me tomorrow,* except he'd never come home in time tomorrow either. My mom was home a lot but she was so spacey. She'd say, *That's nice, Saul,* in an empty way even though I spent five hours building a dragon out of Legos. I was dying for more attention from both of them, either of them. I don't know which parts of this childhood map to my son.

I say, *It's good to help everyone you can. Maybe you can help not nice people get nicer.* I raise my voice a little when I say, *But you should get an adult if you get scared and don't know what to do.*

Do you think Kitty would want me to poke at the mean kids?

What? I say.

You know, Kitty said to poke people.
I don't think that's what she meant.
Oh, he says.

When my boy is quiet, it feels so loud. Everything around the car gets uncomfortably vivid. The evergreens outside are too green. The buildings are too tall. Clouds too dark. The cars all around us are closing in. And every now and then, my boy sighs. And I fear the next question will be the hardest thing in the world to answer.

He says, *Will you take me to see a real giant Pacific octopus?*

#

When we get to my ex's house, before we get to the front door, I give the boy an extra big hug. And throw him up in the air the way I used to. While he is up in the air, he smiles that way he does, and it is totally the thing I need from him right now.

When I catch him, I feel a sharp pain in my lower back that shoots down my left leg, and my toes go numb. As I take another step, the pain goes into my hips and up my back. I hold back the groan I want to make.

I don't think he notices me limping as we make our way to his mom's front door. And just as he gets ready to knock on the door with his little fist, she opens the door, and my boy hugs her leg in a way that makes me jealous.

Mama! he says. *Dada is getting too old to throw me up in the air.*

I take some deep breaths and try to get the ache to pass, but it doesn't.

She smiles at me and says to the boy, *Or maybe you're getting too big.*

Even now, she still has this kindness in her.

In a peculiar and alarming and terrifying turn of events, she asks me to come inside. Inside her house. @Me.

#

It's weird sitting on this couch in this house again. It no longer feels like my house. Or maybe it was never my house.

How is work going? she says.

I say, *I hear you've got a boyfriend.*

How did you find out? she asks.

All the way from upstairs, our boy says, *I told him, Mama!* He yells this in a purely informative tone. No guilt at all.

I point my finger up. *He knows more than we do,* I say.

We both giggle. It is funny—this thing between us. I'm not upset, even though it hurt last night. This moment right now is intimate between us. I want nothing more than to laugh with this woman.

Is he nice? I ask.

Very nice, she says. She says it too forcefully. The hurt returns. And the moment is gone.

I say, *Is he manly and sexy? Can he throw a boy up in the air without a blistering pain in his spine?*

Umm, my wife says. *You don't get to know any of that.*

I don't think I want to know. It is cleaner in the house than when I was here. It smells flowery even though I can't tell which flower. The house feels too big.

So why am I here? I ask her. It's a familiar feeling with her, this mixture of joy to be around her, and also resentment that she can tell me where to sit and I just sit there.

She takes a big breath like they do in the movies before people have big things to say, and then she says her big thing: *I'd like to have the boy more often.*

You what? I ask.

Like maybe you get him every other weekend and I get him the rest of the time. I think he'd like more stability anyhow. It's hard on him, the way he has to switch houses so many times each week. I bet you'd like to work on your novel more anyhow, right? He likes Daniel. She looks around the house for a moment like she's deciding whether to move in. And then she looks back at me. *It's nice here for him.*

She'd often do this during our marriage. Her ability to very casually and sensibly change the situation to her advantage. And I would just let her do it. Her mentioning my novel, it's infuriating, she never supported my writing, of course, but that isn't the worst part. It's the boy. She thinks I still resent being a parent because she saw me be that way once upon a time. But I'm not resentful anymore. I love him. She can't take him away from me.

I say, *I'm glad to hear about this Daniel person. Maybe he can come to our house for a fucking slumber party. I don't mind adjusting the schedule or something else to help. But I won't take any less of him. Not unless I think I'm doing him wrong.*

What I say isn't the perfect thing, but it isn't the worst thing either. I probably didn't need to throw in the slumber party part.

She says, *I won't ask for any more money to have the boy more, just so you know.*

I don't give a shit about the money, is what I say. But she knows that I'm struggling with the money. My debts from writing and schooling and other stupid things still haunt me. I say, *I just don't want less time with him.*

My ex-wife doesn't insist or threaten or try to tell me what to do. I think she tears up a little. I want to get away from here.

She takes a long breath and then says, *I'd actually like you to come over and meet him. Maybe you can come over for dinner sometime. He's a decent man.*

I don't understand why she's asking me to do this. It's a calculation of some kind, but I don't know what exactly she's calculating.

I don't know if I can do that, I say to her, and somehow this vague response feels like the most honest thing I've ever said.

Well, she says, *think about it.*

It's what she'd say all the time when we were married. And, somehow, whenever she said this line, it meant that she would get her way, and I don't know if that reflects something about her or me.

I stand up to leave. It hurts to stand.

She stands up too. She faces me and puts her hands on my shoulders. *Wait*, she says. *He cries when I drop him off at your place.*

What? I say, and I take her arms off me.

He cries.

Why?

I don't know, she says, kind of like she is just talking to herself, like I'm not even here.

We head to the front door, each of us still us trying to make sense of things, each of us still unchanged.

We hug goodbye. I almost kiss her on the lips before I remember that we don't do that anymore. It is weird, this bond between (almost) divorced parents. So intimate and so distant.

#

I spend the next day not talking to anyone. Lying in bed and only rising to eat and go to the bathroom. I pop too much Advil so my back doesn't hurt as bad when I get up. I try to genuinely unplug, as they say. I don't even use my iPhone in the bathroom. My smartwatch remains in Power Reserve mode. I get flashes of images of my boy crying on the way to my place. Getting bullied at school. Kitty crying behind Anne and Hubby's bedroom door about an octopus. My boss's firm but not too firm handshake. Me trying to explain to the unemployment officer what my skills are. My grandfather sitting in his dry goods shop, reading about the upcoming Joe Louis fight, the only white guy in town rooting for the Brown Bomber, he doesn't have any idea that the Klan is supposed to destroy his store later that night—a scene that I haven't yet managed to write. All these images in my head, and no conclusions.

The backache gets a little better.

I spend the day after the next day cleaning my apartment. I never really got past the phase after breaking up of living out of boxes, except for my boy's room, which looks like a fully-realized room. So I begin the process of unboxing. Mostly books, some programming manuals, some novels, I find an old copy of *Herzog*, a new copy of *All Grown Up*. I find a letter from my father that says: *The difference between stupidity and genius is that genius has its limits.* He used to send me quotes by snail mail every week, especially right after my breakup. A letter sent by the United States Postal Service across the country for a single quote that could easily be texted in a microsecond. I find a package of condoms that expired two years ago. I find a gift certificate to a hotel in Newport Beach for two rooms for two nights. My ex got it for me when we weren't exes, when my boy was just a baby. She got two rooms because she knew I was already having trouble sleeping next to her, especially when our boy was sleeping in the bed.

The day after the next day after the next day is Monday. I should be at work, and it feels weird being at home. I sit on my couch and make a decisive plan. Well, a sort-of plan.

I send a text to my ex and tell her that we should try a weekly schedule with the boy. I update our shared calendar with the suggested new schedule using a new color scheme. New colors can make a calendar event feel fresh and compelling. I tell her that it might be easier for the boy if he switched houses once a week rather than our crazy every-other-day scheme. I also tell her that I'd like to take him this first week because I have some time off of work and his school has a few days off for something called in-service and so I'm planning a trip. I say that I can come over for dinner to meet the new boyfriend when we get back. I text her with the authority of a Colossal Squid. Within an hour, she says, *OK. Let's try it. Just change my weeks from that prissy pink to a powerful purple.*

I send a text to Anne. I say, *So what's the deal with you planning my next career move behind my back?* She says, *Yeah, I meant to talk to you about that. What if we talk about it when you get back? You should be taking a break.* I ask her who made her a Blue Whale all of a sudden. She tells me that they're no longer using sea creatures. *What are they using?* I ask. *Natural disasters,* she says. *You know that I care about you and I want you to come back to work. Right?* I tell her, *I know. I'll be back.* Since it is an old-school SMS text message, I can't attach a voice or sticker to it, but we both know I'm saying this like Arnold Schwarzenegger from *The Terminator.*

I send a text to Kitty and tell her, *I know it sounds like a trademarked line, but I'm not ready™.* She says, *Don't feel bad. I'm still thinking about cutting off my ex's cock™.* I say, *Good.* Then I clarify: *I mean, not good about the cock cutting. But I'm glad we're in the same Octopod.* And then I say, *Do you want to go to the beach with me and the boy this week? I have a gift certificate to the Hemingway Hotel for two rooms, two nights.* She says, *You mean the real-life, physical ocean? The cold and dangerous and horrible and violent ocean?* I say, *Yes, that's the one.* And she says, *I need to get back by Thursday for a horrible collectibles convention.* I say, *We can do that. First the horrible and violent ocean and then the horrible and violent convention.* I imagine Hemingway approving of the way I'm acting like I can handle horrible and violent things.

This couch in my apartment is the one thing I took from the house after the separation. It's an old couch from my childhood, a piece of furniture that should've been thrown away a long time ago because it was a piece of crap even back in my childhood. My ex would always say things like, *How come your nostalgia couldn't take the form of smaller, lighter, less ugly things?* In that last year, she made me put it in the attic. It's true, it's ugly. Maybe she left me because of the couch. It's a 1970s plaid-looking thing with uncomfortable fabric and it squeaks and creaks when you move around. But it reminds me of my mom. Mom loved the couch. We'd sit on the couch next to each other on the days my dad worked late and I'd hold onto her elbow and she'd read to me. First Dr. Seuss. And then *Charlie and the Chocolate Factory.* And then *Lord of the Rings.* I don't know how many years between books, but I just know they happened on this couch. When you sit on the couch, you sink into it in this not-actually-comfortable way and it feels like you'll never be able to get up again, and sometimes that is exactly what you need.

PART TWO

Chapter Five: The Beach

My boy asks me if we can roll down all the windows. He doesn't mind that we're going five miles over the speed limit. He doesn't even mind that the rain is getting in the car.

We're driving to a beach that is about three hours from Portland, and my boy won't stop talking about the big aquarium that we're going to visit.

He says, *I hope they have a giant Pacific octopus there.*

They do, Kitty says. *I checked online.*

My boy says, *Woohoo!* in a way that he doesn't do with me. Then again, we've never gone to an aquarium together.

We stop at a rest area even though it's still drizzling. My back isn't collaborating effectively with this car seat and I need to stretch. The boy sees a swing set and starts swinging while Kitty and I sit on the bench and watch. Though I don't spend much time actually sitting—I do these peculiar twists with my body. I try to readjust my hip with an Elvis-like body twist. It is incredibly relieving, though I fear I'll do it one time and never walk again. She looks at me and says, *Who says you don't dance?*

She asks me what we plan to do during this trip. *I didn't bring my piggy banks or my laptop and so I'm looking for creative ways not to brood.*

I tell her that I'm also looking for a good distraction because I'm taking a break from work and a break from my novel.

Why do you bother? she says.

I sit down next to her. It aches a little to hear how easily she can write my writing off, but it's still a question I have to answer in my head a lot, so

I try to answer it outside my head: *All these stories I hear from my family are about my grandfather's failures and his incompetence, but I keep feeling like there is some kind of—*

No, she interrupts. *I mean why do you bother with that job? It seems to be distracting you from the interesting stuff.*

Wait, I say. *Aren't you supposed to pooh-pooh my creative life instead?*

First of all, I don't say pooh-pooh. Second of all, you're obviously hanging out with the wrong people. Your family's messed up story is more important than that online whatchamadoodle crap. She covers her mouth and leans toward me and I expect her to say something that she doesn't want my boy to hear, except my boy definitely can't hear us, he's high enough on the swing that it's creaking. Kitty says, *Just don't tell our mutual friend that I suggested you quit your job at CollaboDon'tGiveAFuck.*

I love her stance. And I'm dying to buy into it. But the boy needs someone to pay for the food and the doctor visits.

I don't mention that I have a printed copy of my manuscript in my backpack. It feels like I'm carrying a first aid kit. Come to think of it, I probably should carry a first aid kit.

Kitty watches my boy swinging for a while, and then she says, *Board games!*

What?

Let's board game the shit out of this trip. When the boy is awake, we do family-friendly games, and then at night—she pauses for long enough that I get nervous, but then she says, *we play grown-up board games.*

Deal, I say, wondering how the hell we're going to acquire board games.

You thought I was going to say sex games, didn't you?

My iPhone vibrates. It's Anne saying, *Have fun!* along with a picture of *James Bond*—the Sean Connery one—toasting his martini.

Kitty gently pushes my phone away from me. She says, *Let's only check our devices twice a day. 10:00 a.m. and 10:00 p.m. What do you say? I mean, just as an experiment. Next week we can superglue ourselves back to Etsy and Twitter and Snapchat and CollaboWhatever and the other sick things you're into.*

I put my phone away and say, *Deal.* I should write a plug-in that gives you an electric shock when you touch your device while on vacation. Probably wouldn't be a big hit with the execs of an online collaboration company, though.

She looks me up and down and then she smiles and says, *Hmm.*

Hmm, what? I ask.

Hmm, you don't seem to manalogue the way most men do.

What's a manalogue? I say, sort of knowing I'm walking into a gender trap.

You know, she says, *manalogue, male answer syndrome, mansplain, just how men have that habit of explaining things to women like women just landed on this planet to listen to them.*

Well, I say. *You don't know me too well. I could be a grand manaloguer.*

She looks at me some more and shakes her head. *No,* she says. *You're not a manaloguer. But you should meet my ex-husband someday. He invented it.*

I watch her for a bit until she gets uncomfortable. *What?* she says.

She feigns annoyance, but she also has a shy smile. She has this way of being tough and fragile at the same time and I'm uncomfortably attracted to it.

I say, *What did you see in your ex anyhow?*

She looks up at the clouds. *I don't know,* she says. *If he wasn't always busy running that company and fucking other women and if you squinted your eyes and covered your ears and held your nose, the guy had some real charm.*

We watch the boy swing for a while.

Kitty says, *It's so lovely to see how he does his own thing without needing you. Look at him,* she points at my boy going higher and higher. *He is totally in his own world right now. I love it.*

When my boy was younger, he was more insistent on me watching him do these things. Today he doesn't care as much. He's smiling and looking at a spot in the sky above our heads. Maybe there's a cloud in the shape of something. I wonder where he learned to pump his legs so effectively like that. How long ago was it when he insisted that I push him on the swing? I always got scared of swinging that high. There is a point at the very top of his arc that the chains loosen, and it feels like everything is going to fall apart, and then the swing comes back down, and his weight pulls on the chain again, and it's OK again.

#

When I try to cash in on the gift certificate to the Hemingway Hotel, the man at the counter says, *Umm.*

Umm what? I say.

Three things, he says. He raises a finger. *For one, this coupon is for the Idaho room and the Lost Generation room, both of which are being remodeled.* And then another finger goes up. *Second, this thing is from five years ago.*

He drops his hand to the table, giving up on counting altogether.

Kitty looks at me and says, *You didn't call in advance?*

My boy clings to my leg.

My back aches. I'm too tired to figure out how we're going to find a room somewhere else. We're not driving back. What would Hemingway do? WWHD?

I take a deep breath, and sigh loudly.

My boy holds onto me tighter. And I know he has his sad and worried face going right now. Thataboy. The man sighs and fumbles through a folder on the counter. *Let me see what I can do.*

It isn't exactly the Hemingway touch, but it's something. I'm not above sympathy.

#

The man gives us the Africa room. Which seems particularly inappropriate for us—the lion head on the wall and the wooden hyena sculpture that is taller than my boy and the bear rug and the zebra print comforter on the one big bed. I'm not sure what parts of this room are made from real animals and what parts are fake, but I appreciate that the enormous closet is covered in wallpaper with a faded photo of Mt. Kilimanjaro.

My boy immediately sits down on the bear rug and pulls out his Gups from his suitcase—these crappy, plastic, submarine-like vehicles from *The Octonauts*.

Let's test out the room, he tells the Gups. He already has Gups A, B, C, and D. He is lobbying for me to buy the Gup-S, which is the fanciest one, but I'd have to buy it from the UK and it would cost a hundred pounds. He is saving up his allowance money for it. But I'm hoping he outgrows his excitement for it before he gets enough money. He explained to me that it is easier for him to earn an allowance at my house because there is a lot more of a mess to clean up.

It's small, is what I say, as I look around the absurd room that all three of us are staying in. I pat the zebra comforter. For comfort.

My boy stops his playing for a second and looks up at me. *Don't worry, Dada,* he says. *Zebras are social animals and they live together in a harem.*

A what? I ask.

You know, he tells me, *a group of zebras.*

You know, Kitty says to me, with a smile I don't like, *a harem of zebras! Like a murder of crows.*

Crows can murder? my boy asks.

#

Kitty offers to take my boy to the beach, and even though I almost say no, I also get this intense craving to be alone. So after my boy says *Please!* a fifth time, I say *OK*, and I help him get some layers on because it's cold and windy and drizzly. We collect some sand toys and put them in a plastic bag. I ask Kitty not to let him go far in the water.

She says, *Are you kidding? It's cold as hell out there. And the undertow. I would never.* And she is genuinely offended and I feel stupid.

I say, *Sorry. Just letting you know you can ping me if you need anything.*

Ping yourself, she tells me, as she laughs and pinches my arm.

Yeah, ping yourself, my boy says, and I move my arm away before he can get to it.

#

I feel guilty for how quickly it is great to be alone. I toy with taking out my manuscript but I take out a notebook instead. An actual physical notebook. And a pencil. A real pencil. Number 2. And I write. With my goddamn fingers using the goddamn pencil on the goddamn paper. It's been so long since I've done this.

I wonder if Hemingway would be impressed with me, writing with a real pencil like a real goddamn man.

Not likely, Hemingway says. *A man can be destroyed but not defeated.*

I don't understand, I say.

He says, *In modern war, you will die like a dog for no good reason.*

What? I say.

Bullfighting is the only art in which the artist is in danger of death and in which the degree of brilliance in the performance is left to the fighter's honor.

Please stop, I say to Hemingway.

Suit yourself, he says. *But I suggest a typewriter for dialogue.*

I expect it to feel lovely. To write with a pencil. But it's terrible. My fingers ache immediately. Nobody is auto-correcting my work. I actually have to insert the punctuation myself. How the hell do you even spell *accommodate*? What do you do if you need to move sentences around?

I don't work on my novel. Instead, I write a story about a guy who's taking his boy on a trip to the beach. With another woman. Except I creatively name the other woman Catty. That'll fool them.

In the story, the narrator is attracted to Catty, but when they try to hook up at night, he can't pull it off because he is afraid his boy will wake up.

It's sort of similar to how Jake Barnes is impotent in *The Sun Also Rises*.

Jake is impotent from war, Hemingway explains to me. *Big difference.*

But it's more than that, I tell him. *He's emotionally impotent. He just can't express it.*

Hemingway doesn't respond.

After I write for a half hour, I realize I'm attracted to Catty—and to Kitty—and I'm ashamed that my stupid story caused this pretty obvious realization.

I check my phone. A voicemail from my dad. A voicemail from my ex. A text from Anne. A status message from the gamification plug-in. I turn off the phone without listening to or reading any of the messages and I look out the window.

Kitty and my boy are chasing each other on the beach. When my boy falls down, I almost can't stop myself from running out there to see if he's OK. But then Kitty races over and tickles him, and I can see he is rolling around in a sort of giddiness that makes me miss him even while looking at him.

It could just be a false memory, but there was a time when my wife and I were happy parents, together. A time when I wasn't preoccupied and I wasn't resentful. We went to the beach. Together. My boy was about three. And he held our hands and he wanted us to swing him. And we swung him. It was so simple.

I don't know why she wants me to meet her new man. I want to find out if he's a worthy human to be around my kid, but it also seems like a mean trick of hers to show me that she found someone better. She's subtle about how she makes me feel like shit. Though her loving was also subtle.

I get some clothes on and head outside. But by the time I get there, they are cold and ready to drink some hot chocolate beside the African fireplace.

#

When it's time to go to bed, my boy says, *I don't want a book tonight. Tell me an out loud story instead.*

Tell you a what? I say.

You know. A story. Don't you write stories, Dada?

Sort of, I say. The fraud inside of me grows larger.

So tell me one.

What should it be about?

Umm, he says, and he looks around the room, this little boy tucked inside this big zebra bed. *How about zebra mermaids?*

There are no such things, I say.

Dada, he whispers. *I know that and you know that but the zebra mermaids don't know that!*

Kitty laughs from the bear rug where she's sitting and digging through her backpack in search of the card game she brought for us to play when the boy's asleep. *He's got a point*, she says.

So I tell him a story about a family of zebra mermaids. And mermen, just to keep the gender balance. They have a big problem because they are running a dry goods store at the bottom of the ocean but they can't keep the stuff dry. My boy likes this. He says, *They could put everything in Ziploc bags.* So they do. And he seems really into the story, but he still falls asleep just as the mermaids have their opening-day sale and the bad guy—a seahorse—arrives. I'm relieved that he falls asleep because out of storytelling desperation, the seahorse was wearing a white robe with a pointy white seahorse hat.

I wait for my boy's muscle twitches to let me know he's been asleep for a few minutes and then I hop off the bed and sit with Kitty on the floor while she drinks hot cocoa with vodka.

Every mug in this place has a different Hemingway quote. Kitty drinks with *Happiness in intelligent people is the rarest thing I know.* And I have *The best way to find out if you can trust somebody is to trust them.*

How's it going so far? I ask Kitty nervously. I hand her the rolled-up sleeping bag that I always carry in my car for emergencies. Emergencies like right now. When we first got to the room, she volunteered to sleep on the floor, which I immediately accepted.

It's going great, she says. *I haven't wanted to weep or murder or chop the whole time.*

That's good, I say. *I was hoping this trip wouldn't have any weeping or murdering or chopping.*

How about you? she asks. *Have you been online?*

She gives me a squinty look that I remember my mom would make. It makes it impossible for me to lie to her.

Sort of, I say

Cheater! I knew it!

I wonder how she knows this. I wasn't even feeling guilty about it. *I mean*, I say, *I saw I had messages, but I didn't read them or listen to them.*

She looks at her watch. *It's not even nine o'clock. I think that deserves a spanking.*

Maybe, I say, not knowing whether I like the sound of that.

Want to play the game? she says. She's still organizing the cards, which have roads, medieval cities, and fields on them.

Maybe, I say.

So she explains the game. You have to lay the cards out while trying to control various fields and roads and cities with these little wooden stick figure guys. I barely understand the rules and she destroys me. But it keeps my mind off of how nice it is to be around her. Or how I want to kiss her. Or how maybe I do want to take her up on that spanking offer.

Play again? she says.

She's getting drunker and happier. I'm getting happier too.

Before answering, I stand up and walk over to the bed. I put my lips to my boy's head as if I can inhale all the answers to life from this action. But it doesn't work that way. What I do learn from this gesture is that my boy is soundly asleep. And that he has a lot of sand in his hair.

I get back on the floor. *OK*, I say. *But let's play beside Mt. Kilimanjaro.*

Do what now? she says, refilling her drink.

Let's go in the closet, I tell her. I point over there. *My boy is a light sleeper.*

She looks at the closet, and then looks back at me like I've just asked her to marry me. She seems almost fragile. I want to hug her. And kiss those lips.

Instead, I grab her hand, the one without the mug. *Come on*, I say. *Get in the closet with me.*

We play again. And either because I'm getting too drunk to worry about things, or because I'm actually beginning to understand it, or because it is just fun being around Kitty, I start really loving this stupid game. I'm actually out-strategizing Kitty. I'm having fun. How long has it been? She puts down the last card. And she makes the last move. And I win. I kick her cute, drunk ass. And I'm so giddy because I have figured out this one game for this one moment, that I lean over towards Kitty and kiss her.

Her lips are hot and fleshy and vodka-soaked and I rub my tongue along her lips and I pull away, and I see that she is looking at me, not even at me, but at my lips, and I can tell she is turned on, and I am turned on, and I have this vision of us fucking right now in the Kilimanjaro closet, and I try to remember if I packed those condoms.

She kisses me some more and it all feels good. Really good. I put my hands on her arms and her body feels good. Uncomfortably good. I push her away, and I look at her body, up and down, the way her shirt is tight but loose enough that I can imagine taking it off. I see the wanting in her. And the volcano photo behind her.

I want her, this Kitty woman. This could be a night that goes just like a night like this *should* go. I might not screw it up. This wanting. I could let it take me over and not worry about anything else. This is exactly what I need. Be in the moment. Step away from myself and my worries and step towards someone else. This may be the moment where I learn how to be with someone other than my wife. I reach for the bottom of her shirt to take it off.

In my head, it seems connected, it even seems like a sane thing to say, so I say to Kitty: *Would you go to dinner with me at my wife's house?*

She squints her eyes and even tilts her head, trying to match my words with what she expected my words to say, and before I understand why, I know that it has gone wrong.

She shakes her head and says, *What?*

I grab her arms with my hands—her elbows are smaller than I expected—and I say, *I'm sorry. It's probably a dumb idea, but I need to meet her new boyfriend, and it's going to be hard to go there alone.*

And you want to use me to make her jealous?

Well, I say. I squeeze her arms. *I don't mean that exactly. It's just that . . . It would be nice to be there with . . . Well . . . As long as you don't start crying like at Anne's house.* It comes out before I realize what I've said. It was supposed to be funny. It was supposed to be the kind of thing that ends with a winking face emoji.

Kitty shakes out of my grip and puts her hands out in the you-better-stop-right-there motion. She closes her eyes, takes a breath, and says, *I have got to piss.*

As she stands up to leave the closet, I say, *Wait.* I say, *I didn't mean to say that.* I almost say, *Make it go away,* just like how my boy used to say when he'd get those toddler stomach aches that I couldn't make go away.

#

When she comes back from the bathroom, she doesn't look me in the eyes, she tells me that she wants to crash on the floor now and that I should go sleep with my baby. She calls him a baby. I try to convince her that we could all sleep in the bed, like that might somehow undo my mess, even though the real idea of us all in the bed sounds terrible and crowded and uncomfortable. I just don't want the night to end this way.

Kitty? I say. And I walk up to her.

I can feel something desperate pumping through me. Like however much I've screwed up, I might screw this up even more if I open my mouth because I want to fix it all so badly.

Without my noticing, Kitty is now wearing gray, long underwear on the top and bottom, and she's working her way into the tight sleeping bag.

What? she says once she's inside the sleeping bag. She looks tired. Emotionally tired. It's not just in the eyes and forehead, but behind the eyes and forehead. In those last years of my marriage, I remember my wife had that look whenever I asked her something. Big or small, everything coming from me was exhausting to her at the end.

I'm just confused right now, I tell her.

About what? she says.

I wave my arms around the room, pointing at the hyena and the bear and the zebra and the picture of Hemingway holding on to the antelope horns and the drawing of his double-barreled shotgun, and it all makes my head spin.

You're confused with Hemingway? she asks. She's annoyed.

I put my hands down. *I don't know,* I say. *I'm a big fucking mess. I think about my damn wife too much but I want it to be nice with you and this stupid room's got me hearing Hemingway make fun of me about being a man.* I'm whispering now—because of my boy sleeping, but also because a confession needs to be whispered. *I think about my grandfather too much, who went broke while running a dry goods store, and it drove my grandmother crazy how he was always flirting with women and obsessed with sports. He'd mutter about DiMaggio or the Brown Bomber when he came home drunk, and he drank at work all the time, and my dad, the scientist, resented my grandfather for how he was always being a spaced-out dreamer about something and couldn't provide for the family and now I'm worried about my boy, who is also a little spacey, except he doesn't care for sports, and I worry about how I should be with him and how I should be with you and I don't know what kind of man is the right kind of man and even though my grandfather was a dishonest, broke, drunk, flirtatious fool with dirty jokes about prostitutes and maybe he didn't know how to be a father, I feel for the guy, I always have. I feel like maybe he has an answer for me, because I don't know how to act or what to do or who to be and I hate my job and I'm scared to lose my job and my chest hurts just talking about it.* I hold on to my chest and say, *Does that make sense?*

I guess, she says, in a noncommittal way that is worse than a "No," and she turns away from me in her sleeping bag.

I reach my hand out and touch her over the sleeping bag, hopefully against her back though I'm not sure exactly where I'm touching her. She doesn't move but I know she is listening. I whisper again, *The more I write this book, the more scared I get about being in any kind of relationship with anyone.*

She doesn't answer or respond in any way. I don't want to continue down this path. I *can't* continue because there is nothing left to fuck up.

I have to admit, there's a little relief in that.

I take off my pants and get under the sheets next to my quietly snoring boy.

I close my eyes. I try to go to sleep. I think about my grandfather eating ice cream and how much he loved his son, in his own crooked way.

But then I feel a light shining on my face, and I open my eyes to see Kitty pointing her phone flashlight right at me.

Ouch, I tell her flashlight.

She whispers, *Do you want to know why I cried at Anne's house?*

I push her phone downward, out of my face. *Yes*, I say.

She takes a big breath, and then, *I had a baby.*

You did? I say. I don't know what to do with this information and I can't quite make out the expression on her face. My eyes follow the shaking light of her phone, the long shadows of Hemingway creatures all over the room.

I called him the octopus because of how much he squirmed around in my body.

Her flashlight flashes on her face. Her eyes are moist and red. I brace myself. This story isn't going to end well.

She says, *I gave him up for adoption fifteen years ago.*

I sit up in the bed. *I'm sorry*, I say. Though I'm also relieved to think that the octopus child is at least still alive, somewhere. And that she's had time to work through it. It is an old wound. Which is better than a new wound. I think. Even though I need to ask a lot more questions to understand the where and why and how of it.

Somehow, she says, *you blabbing about your boy that night and asking me about an octopus piggy bank made me think about that year after I gave him up. It was almost unbearable.*

Oh, I say. I touch her lit phone and push it downward, with just my fingertips touching her hand, an awkward way to connect with her when I don't know how to connect. *I'm sorry*, I say.

No, she says. She shakes out of my grip. *It's OK to think of my octopus baby. It's almost sweet.* She is quiet for a few seconds and she looks up at the ceiling. *It's lovely spending time with your boy, but it does make me think a lot about my octopus. And the regret.*

Then Kitty drops back to the floor. *Well, goodnight*, she says, as she crawls back towards the bear rug.

Goodnight, I say, still seeing bright spots in my vision from that flashlight, still wanting to ask so many more questions.

I can hear her grab a spare zebra pillow from the Kilimanjaro closet, and then I fall asleep, thinking about her octopus boy.

#

Even though I like to tell stories, the stories about my mom don't come out like normal stories. They come out like flashes. Like a blur. Like blurry flashes. Like this: I'm six years old. It's the middle of the night. I open my eyes—even as a kid I'd wake up at least once in the middle of the night. I hear some rustling next to me. And there is my mom, lying on my floor. Face up. Eyes wide open.

Mom, I say. *What are you doing down there?*

She doesn't look at me. Keeps looking up. Those bright night eyes.

Mom? I say again. Maybe I'm imagining her. I did have a habit of blending dream-life and awake-life.

Hush, she says. *I'm protecting.*

I look around the room.

Protecting what? I ask.

For a split second, she turns her head towards me, and then back up at the ceiling again. She says, *I'm protecting you, silly pants!*

From what? I say.

The elements, she says.

What elements?

Go back to bed, she says. *It's late.*

So I go back to sleep.

In the morning, she's gone.

"the octopus is the only creature that is smart
enough to be a complete fucking asshole."
—@octopussypants

Chapter Six: The Fucking Aquarium

I wake up before dawn with a headache. My boy is cuddled up next to me, with his arm around me. I don't know if he is too old for this sort of thing, but it feels nice to be near him.

I get out of bed for some Advil, and as I tiptoe to the bathroom, I see that my backpack is opened up on the floor, my manuscript pages strewn around. And there are doodles in the margins that were not there before.

And there Kitty is, still lying in my sleeping bag on the bear rug, reading a book that I had in my backpack. It's not actually my book but a book my father mailed me and insisted I read.

Without pulling away from the book, Kitty whispers, *Come here! Come here!*

I tiptoe between the pages of my manuscript like they are booby traps. *Have you been looking at my things?* I say.

Someone's got to do it, she says. *Your book is amazing, by the way.*

My manuscript? I ask.

She takes her eyes off the book and looks at me. *No, dummy*, she says, and she shakes the book in her hand. *This one. It's a hell of a book*, she tells me.

I pretend my mix-up doesn't burn inside. I haven't read the book in her hands. Instead of reading it, I carry it around with me everywhere—some book by a fancy pants physicist and atheist my dad is obsessed with.

I squat down on the floor and take the book out of her hands even though she was holding it tightly. I thumb through it, making sure to lose her place in the process. *Yeah*, I say, *that's what I hear.*

She grabs the book back like it's hers.

Why did you take out my manuscript? I say. I look around at the pages on the floor. I can pick out phrases here and there. Phrases I worked on for hours. In the morning light, and with this morning headache, I can see them for how mediocre they are.

The zipper is a boundary, I tell her like she's a child. *You shouldn't open something I have zipped.*

I realize I want her gone.

Look, she says, and she pulls me towards her. She points at the book and says, *Listen to this shit*, and then she reads a quote that my father already highlighted in the book:

```
Do you want to understand where you came
from? Do you really want to know? Well,
you don't need a biblical text to get the
answer. All you need to do is look up! Look
up at the sky, gaze at those stars, those
nuclear reactors that provided you with the
oxygen, carbon, hydrogen, nitrogen, and the
other elements that make up who you are. We
are all connected to each other, connected
to the stardust from celestial explosions.
```

Kitty says, *And whoever had this book before, wrote all these things in the margins next to all the great lines.*

That's my dad, I tell her, wondering why she didn't assume I wrote those things.

She looks up at me again. *Oh*, she says. She smiles. *That kind of makes sense.* Even though this woman doesn't know a thing about my dad.

She points out a spot on a page. *Here he writes, 'When we die, what stars do we create?' Isn't that weird?*

When my father sent me the book, I didn't take it in because I was busy with some pointless work thing. And now I still don't take it in. Because all I can think about is that I wish I could hit ⌘Z on the keyboard and undo this trip with Kitty.

I say, *So do you want to go to the aquarium with us, or what?*

Are you even listening? she says. It's in her eyes, the way she is looking right through me, like her being up all night is causing her to be more irrational, but also more penetrating.

I am listening, I say. How is it that *I'm* the one who is guilty in this moment?

But you're not paying attention, she says. She slams the book shut, a gesture that looks louder than it actually sounds. She gets back into the sleeping bag. She turns away from me. She says, *Have fun at the fucking aquarium.*

#

When we drive up to the aquarium parking lot, my boy says, *Tell me again why she didn't get out of her sleeping bag?*

It's MY sleeping bag, I say. Then, *I guess she was so excited about the book she was reading last night that she didn't get enough sleep.*

When I was a kid, my mom always looked so exhausted in the mornings, like she was only half-formed. I learned quickly that if I wanted something before school, I'd need to talk to my dad—if I could catch him before work. When I'd ask my dad about why Mom slept in the morning, he'd tell me that she stayed up reading half the night. And it's true that I did find books opened all over the bedroom floor, with no pattern whatsoever, there were romance novels and westerns and appliance manuals and science fiction and detective novels and weird books on the Kabbalah and *The Joy of Sex*. When I'd ask her about them, any of them, she'd say, *Just a bunch of bullshit to pass the time.*

I don't like that Kitty isn't doing this thing that my boy wants to do with her. It's one thing that she opened my backpack, but this is another thing. A thing to hurt my boy. I hate that we're stuck with her on this trip.

My boy giggles and says, *Kitty's kind of like Kwazii Kitten.*

Why's that? I say, trying to remember any of the qualities of Kwazii other than the fact that he is a cat who talks like a loud, dumb pirate.

Well, he gets excited about things a lot. My boy thinks about the comparison for a while longer and then says, *Except Kitty is a lot smarter than Kwazii Kitten. And prettier.*

#

My boy pulls me to every room at the aquarium and to almost every display, and he reads to me every bit of text he sees on the walls. I learn about hermit crabs and water pollution and we touch sea stars, gumboot chitons, and anemones, and we learn about the gentle wolf eel, and then there is a room that is like a pretend submarine and my boy says it looks just like the Gup-A and we play in there for a while, pushing all the buttons that simulate submarine sounds and ocean creature sounds.

Eventually, we get to the giant Pacific octopus. It is curled up in the corner of the aquarium and doesn't look much bigger than a baseball. I imagine that little guy inside Kitty's belly. I wonder why she gave him away. My boy looks at it quietly for a few minutes, and then he finally says, *Smaller than I expected.*

Yeah, it is, I say. And I'm afraid he'll be disappointed. That he will wish he hadn't seen it in real life. That this trip will be as regrettable to him as it feels to me when I think about Kitty who is back in our room sleeping in my sleeping bag next to all our stuff.

And it is lumpier, he continues. *It has more suction cups.* He looks at the tank from all different angles to the point where I can see his fingerprints and his cheek marks on the glass, and I nearly say something about how he should stop doing that—he doesn't know whose face was pressed on there before. The octopus looks at us as it wiggles its way from one hiding spot to another. *And it has bigger eyeballs,* my boy says. *And it is mushier. And it is sadder.* His voice goes to a whisper. *And it is awesomer.*

#

While my boy rummages around in the gift shop and I await the inevitable negotiation about whether or not he can buy some overpriced piece of crap, I check my voicemail and messages. Because I feel so guilty about my failure with Kitty last night, I actually don't feel any guilt about cheating on our plan to abstain from technology. It's one upside to my romantic failures.

It turns out that Anne sent a message saying: *After you've had a few to drink, remember not to talk about your ex-wife or your novel.* It's an animated pic of Joe Pesci shaking his finger at me.

I ask Anne if she'll create an Octopus Lovers group at work for me, and then @ mention me in it.

After fifteen seconds, she says *done.* And then sends me the shortened URL. She makes me an administrator of the new group so I get the extra points for "facilitating social collaboration."

I also get a message that says:

```
{ error      : "oopsy daisy",
   message   : "gamification plug-in fucked up",
   codes     : [null, null, null] }
```

On the upside, it's good to know that my plug-in is now sending standardized JSON text. On the downside, I thought I set it not to send me messages anymore, and it shouldn't be sending null values, and I have no idea what error caused this message, and the Blue Whale is going to kill me if he finds out that I forgot to remove all the curse words from my error messages.

My ex wants to know how the trip is going. There are two identical texts from her, except the second one has three question marks instead of one. I tell her that it's going well. And she immediately asks whether she can video chat with the boy and I tell her that we're at the aquarium but we'll try later if the reception is decent. I feel like I'm lying, even though I'm not. I just omitted the we're-with-this-other-woman part.

My dad left me a voicemail telling me that religion is a kind of mental illness and we're living alongside a collection of ignorant Puritans. And then he asks me if I know that there was a hanging tree in his home town and whether that detail might be useful for my book. *They hung a Black man in my town for looking at a woman the wrong way*, he says. *This actually happened*, he says. *The tree is more important to history than my dad.* Then he says that he has an appointment with the cardiologist on Tuesday, even though he never told me about having any heart trouble. And then he asks my voicemail if it read the physics book he sent. And then he fails to hang up the phone for a minute as I listen to the phone shift around in his pocket, but I can't seem to hang up, even after I'm aware of what is going on, just because of the remote chance that he'll say one more thing, or that I'll miss the very last sounds from my dad.

#

When we get home from the aquarium, Kitty's hair is wet and she is brushing it. She looks good with long, wet brown hair. Almost good enough to forget about all the failures and violations.

Hello there! she says, more to my boy than to me.

Did you get some sleep? I ask.

No, she says. *But I went for a swim.* Her biceps are solid swimmer biceps, and they tighten as she brushes her hair.

Kitty! my boy yells at her. *We got you something!* He hands her the plastic bag.

Kitty pulls out the Dolphin Piggy Bank and immediately pulls it to her chest and squeezes.

It's a piggy bank! she says.

It actually is! It actually is! my boy yells. He is jumping as he talks.

Oh my God! she says. *I can't take this.* And she pries it away from her body and hands it to my boy, who refuses to take it back.

My boy has somehow learned a kind of generosity that is beyond anything that my ex and I have ever possessed or taught.

He insisted on buying it for you, I explain. We actually saw an octopus piggy bank that my boy wanted to get her, but I told him it would be weird to get her an octopus piggy bank when she gave him an octopus piggy bank, which is an argument he bought into, even though mostly I just thought about Kitty's octopus baby and what it would do to her to be around more octopuses.

My boy says, *I already put a quarter in it for you.* She shakes it and is surprised, like the quarter is even more valuable than the piggy bank.

How can I possibly accept this? she asks me. She's close to crying.

She kisses my boy on his head, and my boy is so pleased about this moment that it seems like he might also cry. And I want to cry thinking about my boy's heart getting broken by her.

You can totally possibly accept this, he says.

#

It's our last afternoon at the beach and it's cloudy and windy and rainy and I still feel weird in my stomach being around Kitty.

Instead of confronting the outside world, we all go to the Key West room, which is a community room where the only community is the three of us alone in a room that's full of sand-covered games, sand-covered puzzles, sand-covered couches, and a view of the sand-covered beach.

My boy grabs this board game called Zooreka!, where you create and build your ultimate zoo, or so the cover of the box claims. The object is to collect four animal habitats from a pile of different habitat tiles. My boy says, *We have GOT to play this game!* And he says it with so much intensity that the only thing to do is to sit on the sandy floor and play it.

Not bad, as far as beach games go. It's almost fun collecting enough bananas to buy new habitats. My boy is the first to get a habitat and he grabs Murky Depths of the Ocean, which has a one-eyed octopus on it.

He moves over to Kitty to sit on her lap. He rubs a hand gently up and down her arm. Just like that.

He looks at her arms and says, *You have stronger arms than Dada.*

She brushes her hand in his hair and then massages his head, and he closes his eyes like he likes it, like it's not risky to be around this woman who pours vodka into coffee mugs and takes things out of other people's backpacks and doesn't go to the aquarium with you when you want her to.

When he opens his eyes, he looks up at her and says, *Wasn't Dada's zebra mermaid story weird?*

It feels like that mermaid story was centuries ago. Long before Kitty annihilated my manuscript with her muscular arms, long before the time of the octopus baby, long before I asked Kitty to go to my wife's house with me. An eternity before we ever kissed.

Yeah, that story was weird, she says, and I'm not sure if she is teasing or flirting or neither, but I know that it doesn't feel great to see this woman and my kid on the opposite side of whatever side I'm on.

I throw the dice at Kitty. *Your turn*, I say.

Kitty scores the Otter Rock. My boy takes Coral Reef Touch Tank. I get Naked Mole Rat Maze.

When it's her turn again, Kitty looks over at my zoo. I say, *I notice you eyeing my naked mole rat*. But I can tell that she is squinting at the board like she is trying to look through it.

She says, *Your story is all wrong.*

What? I say.

Those pages in your backpack. I read all of them. You're making a mistake by writing your dad's story.

What the fuck kind of right does this woman have telling me about my mistakes after looking at my stuff without permission? Who breaks into your house and then stops to criticize your furniture?

The wind whips against the windows, and when I look outside I can't tell if it's really foggy out there or it's just that these windows are dirty. A family is walking miserably along the beach, into the wind, while holding onto their hats so nothing blows away.

Kitty is still looking at me, or through me, or in me. But instead of feeling naked in front of her, there's a new feeling. It's how this person is taking my book seriously. She's taking *me* seriously. My wife never looked at me this way. And I understand why my boy wants to sit on this woman's lap even when she was too hungover to go see an octopus with us.

I take a long breath and say to Kitty, *But it's not my dad's story. It's Papa's story.*

My boy says, *Isn't Papa your dad?*

No, I tell him. I hand him the dice. *I also called MY grandfather Papa, who would be your great-grandfather. Papa's dad.*

My boy's working out the math in his head.

Kitty says, *You need to write YOUR version of Papa's story. Not your dad's version. That's why your heart isn't in it. You need to bleed in there.*

Kitty takes the bat habitat and puts it on the board in an empty zoo.

Your blood, she says.

She puts the lion habitat next to the bats. *Your fears,* she says. And then the sloth. *Your wants.*

Like, she says, *how you were when you yammered to me last night about it. That was the real deal. That's how you REALLY feel.*

She grabs Insectarium and puts it with the others.

Just remember, she says, *your dad is your boy and you're just as messed up as Papa.*

How does she know I haven't bled in there? What kind of blood is she looking for? Even if it's nice being seen this way, she's still giving me criticism on something that I didn't ask for. Or want.

Worst of all: she may be right.

#

At bedtime, Kitty says, *Would you mind if I did the bedtime rituals tonight?*

Fine, I say, pretending to be upset, in order to cover up the real upsetness about how I'm not bleeding or whatever in my book.

She takes the complimentary hotel writing pad from the desk and brings it to the bed and starts telling a story about penguins while drawing things on the pad. I don't see the drawing, but I can tell that the boy loves it. Each time one of them adds an element to the story, like how the smallest penguin in this family has a big cowboy hat with pom-poms and seashells on it, she draws that thing on the piece of paper. Then she has him draw it. She tells him things like, *Just a few quick strokes is all you need.* And he listens and he draws and he is thrilled about it. Eventually, I say, *Maybe take a break from the drawing so you can fall asleep.*

He sighs and says, *Ohhh kayyy.*

Then Kitty sings some nonsense lullaby about mermaids and penguins and sloths, and the boy falls asleep.

Kitty gets up and tells me that she is exhausted and goes right to sleep on the floor. But before she goes to sleep, she kisses me on the cheek like we're family. She says, *You scored good with that fucking kid.*

#

While they sleep, I write. I write a short scene about Kitty—or Catty in this case—meeting Papa at his dry goods store. What would she do? What would he do? She tells him, *I know what your problem is.* And he says, *Azoy. Get in line. I have enough people telling me my problems. What I need is someone telling me where there aren't problems.*

He looks at her dress. Purple and feathery. He especially likes the tuches. Of course. *Gibacook*, he says. *Your dress is full of beautiful problems.*

I don't like where this story is going.

Catty says to Papa, *You're flirting up the wrong tree.* And leaves the store.

#

On the drive home, my boy passes out almost immediately. Kitty bought him a kite in the morning and they played with it for hours before the drive. In his hand, he's holding the drawing that they made together last night.

I can't believe I stayed offline the whole time, she says. *I'm totally dreading coming back to the real world. And to that collectibles convention.*

I can't believe I didn't work on my novel the whole time, I tell her. I choose not to mention that I stumbled into working on my novel through this Catty character. Then I say, *So what the hell is a collectibles convention?*

You know, it's a convention. Where people buy and sell collectibles.

That's as useful as a null response, I say.

Kitty says, *We should come up with a plan to disconnect even when we're back in Portland. Maybe like the first weekend of every month. Me, you, and the boy. He asked me to teach him how to draw zombies anyway.*

There's an uncomfortable tingle in my toes. Every time she mentions my boy I want to slam on the brakes.

My watch taps me and I glance at it to see that my gamification plug-in is still chatty. It says, *estimated time to complete social media assessment: 11,664,429,000 milliseconds.*

Which is weird because it really shouldn't be logging this information any longer. And I can't quite remember what I told it to do once it completes the assessment. I'll need to deal with this when I get back to town. I really don't need another gamification screw-up like before.

Kitty? I say.

Uh oh, she says. *I don't like the sound of that.*

Before thinking too hard, I say, *I'm sorry for screwing things up that night on the floor.*

That's funny, she says. Her feet are on the dashboard and they are cute skinny feet and because of them I feel like she has the upper hand in this debate. *I was about to say the same thing.*

Why? I say. *I'm the one who invited you to my fucking ex-wife's house.*

Yeah, she says, and she starts giggling. *That was amusing.* She giggles for a solid minute. *Can you picture Anne smacking her head in frustration with you?*

I've imagined it a thousand times already.

She giggles some more. I know she is laughing at me, but it doesn't feel bad at all. *I think I've fallen in love,* she says to me, and pauses for a real long time, *with your boy.*

There's this feeling of dread thinking how my boy has gotten too close to her.

I mean, she says. *This motherly instinct is taking over and I'm not sure how to handle it or what is best. It scares me. I'm still a mess. I'm a tornado on wheels. I don't know how things will go between us. I mean, I don't know what is good for a kid of divorced parents. If we didn't luck out by you saying that stupid line, we would've fucked by now. I shouldn't have taken that piggy bank gift. Or read your book without asking.*

I look back at my boy. He genuinely seems asleep, his little chest going in and out.

I activate my watch and say, *Add tornado on wheels to my grocery list.*

Kitty looks at me like I have just left the planet so I explain to her that I keep a list of cool phrases in my grocery list.

Of course, she says, *you wouldn't just use the grocery list for something as simple as groceries.*

Yeah, I admit, *some weeks, the grocery shopping is trickier than others.*

How would you rate this week?

I'm scared to answer. I count the cows. I count the telephone poles. I count the clouds that are impossible to count.

Kitty wiggles her toes and I try to interpret the wiggle pattern for signs. Maybe a great physicist has written a book on toe wiggle theory.

She says, *You're one of the least asshole-y guys I've met in a long time.*

Thank you, I tell her.

But you'll need to man up at some point.

I'll need to what? I say. I'm sure I don't hear her correctly. Did this strange woman just tell me to man up? Next thing you know, she'll call me a pussy.

And you're a bit of a pussy, she says.

What? I say, starting to get less confident that I'm mishearing things. *A pussy about what?*

Just in general, she says. *You're chicken.*

OK, I say. *I don't know if I can handle this many insults all at once. Can we just stick with one cruel metaphor at a time?*

She says, *What do you even stand for? What is Papa going to risk his life for? Why did you invite me on this trip?*

I let my foot off the accelerator and I let the car slow down as I pull over to the shoulder of the expressway.

I stare at her for a while.

What is it? she says, uncomfortable with my staring.

I look back at my boy. His head is in a crooked position against the door and I'm afraid it's going to give him a crick in his neck when he wakes up.

I turn back to this woman next to me who has effectively messed with my book, my boundaries, my backpack, and now me.

I appreciate you telling me all this shit. I suspect you're mostly on track with your long list of insults.

They're not insults, she says.

I raise my finger. *Let me finish*, I say. *I don't care what they are, but you've given me a good ten or fifty things to feel bad about. You know what I'd like?*

To feel less bad? she says.

No, I say. *What if instead of twenty things to feel bad about, you just dished out about five things? And then used the rest of the energy to help me work on those things. Be a spirit guide or a supportive friend instead of a shit upon-er. I've spent enough time in a relationship with someone criticizing me.*

She says, *I don't want to be a spirit guide.*

I get the car going again and pull back into traffic.

I like her so much it feels dangerous.

After a few minutes, I say, *How are you doing with the whole ex-husband cock-cutting stuff?*

Yeah, she says, like this was the most expected follow up question in the world. *It's up and down. When we were making out by Mount Kilimanjaro, I felt sure I was over him. But later that night, my whole world seemed full of hate and shame and regret and he was pressing on me like Hemingway's shotgun.*

This scares me. I feel bad for her. And selfishly, I get more worried for my boy. I say with complete hesitation, *Are you unsafe? Do you need help?*

Ha, she says. There is no humor in her Ha. It's a sad Ha.

She says, *I don't think I'm a harm to myself or others. Not any more than what you see here.*

Her toes are not moving at all.

She pulls out the copy of the book my father got me and I see that it is already worn out and I feel like this could be another way she is dangerous to my family.

Can I borrow this for a little longer? she asks.

Sure, I say, halfheartedly. *I would've thought you'd have finished it by now.*

Oh, she says. *I have. But I haven't read it a third time yet.*

You like it, I say, like I've encountered a fact that isn't obvious.

She wiggles her toes again. She fans the pages of the book at me. She says, *All the ridiculousness of God and the beauticulousness of the universe.*

I'm with a woman who can get away with calling me a pussy and with saying beauticulousness.

And I liked your book too, Saul. She's all whisper now.

My manuscript? I say, just to make sure.

Yeah. I didn't mean to shit upon it, as you say. It's good. But . . . There is an endless, painful pause, and then, *I can somehow see the even better book you're going to write when you figure it out.*

It's the exact kindness that I need right now. My wife never said the word *like* in connection to my writing. Ever. It tickles in my chest to hear this. I barely think about the implication that I still have so much more to figure out about the damn book and about relationships. I put my hand on her lap and I feel the jump she does inside her skin before relaxing again.

Thanks, I say.

My boy starts giggling and I look back in a panic, but he's still asleep. He starts mumbling in his sleep, which he often does. He says, *You can't bite into an octopus without chewing on the sea money.*

And as if my boy's sleep talking caused a change in her, she puts a hand on my hand, it's warm. She looks back to make extra sure that my boy is asleep, and then she says, *I'm glad we took this trip together. I fucking like you.*

```
"the trick to selling merchandise like a champ is
to think of the items you're selling like they're
your children. and you're just trying to get
rid of your children to smelly strangers with
disposable income. #bam" —@goodsalesmanbadparent
```

Chapter Seven: The Convention Center

The gamification plug-in keeps sending me weird messages, so even though I'm still on vacation for a few more days, I log in to the company's VPN to see what's up. Except they've locked me out of the main codebase repository.

So I send some direct messages to a developer dude. His name is Jessie—some smarty pants PhD we snapped up from Carnegie Mellon.

Me: *hey, I can't get onto our server to see the code. you still have admin rights?*

Jessie: *aren't you still on PTO?*

Me: *just wanna look at something. you got admin rights?*

Jessie: *after the last security breach, we've locked down the repository and moved some things onto a private server.*

Me: *can I get access? I need to check on a few things.*

Jessie: *whatcha need to check?*

Fucking Carnegie Mellon grads.

Me: *notice anything funny with the gamification plug-in?*

Jessie: *funny like how?*

He's right. I'm on vacation. I need to let go of it. And this dude will rip my neck off if I tell him where I grabbed this code from.

Me: *never mind. I can deal with it when I'm back next week. I shouldn't be wasting my life coding right now, I should be wasting my life writing . . . Just ignore me.*

Jessie: *k*

#

Kitty's thing is at the Portland Convention Center. Which means that enough people are interested in real, actual, physical collectibles to fill 255,000 square feet of contiguous exhibit space.

It takes ten minutes to find Kitty in this maze. I walk by booths for beer steins and salt and pepper shakers and ashtrays and music boxes and snow globes and even these creepy glass angel figurines sold by a skinny, pale, bald guy wearing angel wings. I normally hate big events, but it's weirdly comforting to be around these people—they're almost my people, these nerds, even though they're not book nerds and not computer nerds, which makes it even better because I don't have to worry about competing with anyone or promoting anything. I'm familiar with this solar system, even if it's not my planet.

Kitty is deep in the bowels of this convention, standing beside a small table that is full of piggy banks. Some of the objects look like they were just made, and some look a hundred years old. They're lined up in rows across the table. The front row has piggy banks of actual pigs, and then it goes to other animals, and then it goes to cars, and then houses and buildings, and the last row is people, a few of them naked.

Her booth isn't even a booth, it's just a table, without any banners and less advertising crap than anyone around her, but it's also one of the most crowded tables. When she spots me, we smile at each other, and she blushes while she continues talking to someone about *the quality of the clay in this vintage piggy bank from Mexico.*

When she's done, I approach her and say, *Wow, this place is crazy town.*

Shut up, she says, more defensive than I expect. It's so much work getting to know someone and their style—insane that humans keep doing this over and over again.

Oh, I say, *I mean this is a fascinating kind of crazy town.* That seems to satisfy her a little bit more.

What are you doing here anyway? she says. She straightens out her piggy banks while she talks.

I'm in the market for a piggy bank made of some fine Mexican clay.
Shut up, she says to me again.
I say, *I just came to see you, except my jokes aren't operational today.*
Oh, she says. *I'm a little on edge, I guess. These things are exhausting.*
Well, I'm impressed, I say. *People really like your stuff.*
I got a spot with great foot traffic.

I take a look around and realize that they designed this convention inefficiently, a flawed design that doesn't scale well—CollaborationHub faced a similar problem when customers started hitting the database more than a million times an hour.

A few more customers purchase a few more piggy banks. I'd expect the human piggy banks, especially the naked ones, to sell faster. But it's the plain old animals that people like. The whale piggy bank that I was eyeing for my boy gets snapped up by some old man in a French beret.

So why do you do this? I ask.
I don't know, she says. *I hate the fucking Convention Center.*
I mean why piggy banks?
Oh. They pay the bills.

Someone asks about a bank that Kitty explains is one of a hundred ceramic coin banks sold at Niagara Falls in 1957. The woman touches it all over before she says, *I love this*, and buys it. Kitty is so confident and comfortable talking to people about this stuff.

Kitty leans into me, puts a hand on my shoulder, and whispers, *So many things are not tangible in life. Every thought, every feeling—and the internet makes it even worse. The whole world is inside the bits or bytes or whatever.* She picks up a cast iron piggy bank of a lion and hugs it. *There's something magical about knowing that they start out empty and you fill them over time. It makes the hollow feeling feel . . . temporary.* She puts the piggy bank down and looks at me with a crooked head. *Is that the stupidest thing?*

Even though my whole life is inside the bits or bytes or whatever, I have so much affection for this woman and I love her explanation and I'm envious how she knows all this about herself. I say, *It's one of the not stupidest things I've heard all week.*

She's too busy for us to have a coherent conversation, but it's nice spending this time here. Not like a date, or a trip to the beach, just a little slice of life, maybe the first of many. And maybe after a bunch more slices we'll get so close that we'll get married. And then we can get so close that we'll get divorced.

I probably should get going, I say.

Did I scare you off or something? She seems disappointed.

Unfortunately, I say, *just the opposite.* I push my hips into her so she loses her balance more than I meant from this dumb gesture.

I don't hug her, I don't know why, I'm just too nervous about how to start the hug. But as I walk away, she says, *Wait, umm, thanks.*

For what? I didn't even buy anything.

For coming to see me. Other people—she pauses for a moment—*didn't care about this world of mine.*

I like this world of yours, I say.

There's her smile again.

She says, *If you still need someone to go to your ex-wife's house for dinner, let me know. You know, for protection.* And she puts up her fists.

I walk back and give her and her fists an awkward hug.

#

An hour before I have to take my boy to my wife's place, while my boy and I are each fiddling with devices, I get a notification that someone shared a picture with me. It is tough to look at on my phone—a lot of pinching and zooming—but over a few minutes, I get the gist of it.

Hey, I tell my boy. *Launch Dropbox on that iPad. I want to show you something.*

Aww, Dada, he says. *I'm in the middle of operating on a zombie's appendix.*

You're going to like this better than zombie surgery, I say. *Trust me.*

We open it up and my boy instantly says, *Wow!* I lock the orientation so my boy can rotate it in every direction and zoom in wherever he wants.

It is a ridiculously detailed colored drawing of The Octopod. As a piggy bank. But Kitty has done it so that it is a cross-section view of the fictional object and you can see inside and every character has a different room in this Octopod. She must have done a ton of research. It looks just like the one from the book and TV show, except that instead of a bubble engine, Tweak Bunny is controlling a coin engine, full of quarters and nickels and dimes and pennies. The colors are perfect. The style is just right. Even zooming in on the characters looks right. The more you zoom, the more details you notice. And she's made up these unique Kitty-like scenes. Tunip is working on rainbow kelp cakes. Dashi Dog is blow-drying her hair after an ocean swim. Kwazii Kitten and Peso Penguin are playing an intense game of Zooreka!. And Professor Inkling is working on a model of an Octopod piggy bank inside a glass bottle, and that little Octopod looks like a miniature version of the big Octopod.

At the bottom of the picture are simple words that are easy for my boy to read: *Warm thoughts.*

After five minutes of silent awe, my boy says, *I want to draw her a picture RIGHT NOW.* The level of immediacy is scary to hear, but I still set him up with the drawing app and hand him a stylus.

After a half hour, he asks me to send her this cute scene he drew of an octopus and a seahorse dancing underwater. He waits to hear the swoosh of the sent message before he moves back to his zombie surgery. It's sweet. And it terrifies me.

#

I really miss Mama, my boy tells me when I drive him back to my wife's house.

I say, *Do you think it'll work OK for you to switch once a week like this? I might get really miss-y at the end.*

I still don't know why he cries on the way to my house. Asking will be just as successful as asking him which kids are mean to him.

Maybe, I say, *we can make every day special when we're together. Like a sushi day or an arts and crafts day.*

He says, *Mom sings to me at night.* He presses his palm against the window and then takes it off and then inspects the handprints on the window.

I stare in the rearview at him for too long before focusing on the road, and then I have to swerve to get back in the correct lane.

Why, he says, *don't you miss Mama?*

Before I can answer, he says, *And don't say, it's complicated.*

I get a message from Anne and I let my car stereo dictate the message to avoid my kid's question. The car says, *I think you'll like this new role I'm scheming for you. Let's talk. Also, it won't kill you to blog about your trip.*

My boy says, *Don't let the car change the subject.*

CollaborationHub can even turn a vacation into work. What am I going to show in my blog, a picture of some vodka and a closet and a failed fuck? It's already Thursday and I'm going back to work on Monday, which feels like no time off at all.

I say to my boy, *I do miss your mom. I miss her a lot.* It's a relief to say this out loud. *But I also remember how we were not so happy when we lived together.* This part is not a relief to say. Those nights I spent awake, pacing in the attic, angry at her for things I'd forget about the next morning, cursing at the walls, trying to figure out why the sixth draft of my novel was worse than the fifth while entertaining these revenge fantasies where I'd finish my book and it would be successful and then she'd regret whatever it was I wanted her to regret. But even worse are those memories of how I didn't want to be a dad. Of hating her and that baby. And the guilt of it. Even now that I don't question my feelings for him, I feel guilty about it.

Well, he says. *You could just live with her part of the time. Like me.*

I don't think we have a part-of-the-time that works anymore.

My boy is now pushing both his hands on the window. He says, *How come you tell me to work things out with the not nice boys at school and then you don't work things out with Mama, who is almost always nice?*

I really didn't try to work things out, it's true. I just kept thinking *this is the year of the book.* Except every year was the year of the book and no year was *the year to fix the marriage.* Maybe Kitty's advice can help me. Maybe this can be the year of the book and the year of good relationships and the year to be a decent father all at the same time.

I say, *I don't know. It's just so . . . complicated.*

#

We get to her house and I walk him to the door. My back has been stiff ever since I threw my boy up in the air and I'm starting to think it might not magically get better. The door opens and the boy squeezes his mom even before I register that she has appeared from inside the house.

Mama, Mama, Mama, he says, in his baby voice that I try to get him not to use.

Baby, she says. She picks him up and hugs him and jumps around in a circle while hugging him.

I envy the strength of her back. She makes things look easy that aren't easy to me.

I missed you! my ex says to him.

Me too, he says. *Even though Kitty was nice and I really hope she likes my drawing.*

Who's Kitty? she says, and she looks down at the boy sweetly, but when my boy looks inside the house, she shoots me a nasty look.

But there's something else. Behind her anger, I think I see that her eyes are red and swollen. She has been crying. I know those red, glossy eyes. She can't cover up that look, even hours after she has cried.

Are you OK? I ask her. I almost reach for her hand. I want to touch her. Right here in this doorway. I imagine her lying on the couch with her head on my lap, like how it used to be. I would make up stories about horny wizards and devout alligators and ironic donuts until she was giggling too much to be sad about anything anymore. *What happened?* I say.

It's complicated, she says to me.

Oh boy, our kid says. *That dumb word again.* He kisses her on the cheek. *Can we sew something this weekend?*

She kisses him back. *Sure,* she says to him. *What do you want to sew?*

A zebra-striped pillow.

I say to her, *Do you want to talk . . . Can I maybe . . . ?*

No, she says. *You've done enough.*

I nod. And as she closes the door on me, I see so many things in that last expression on her face. There's the sadness from something that happened before we got here, and there's a happiness from getting to be with her boy who she missed, and then the frustration from how this man she once loved can inject mysterious Kittys into her life. Too many things to ever fit into a single blog post.

I stand there for about a minute.

I imagine Kitty calling me a chicken. A pussy.

I ring the doorbell again.

She looks at me with all that exhaustion and annoyance. *What? What is it?*

Those feelings from living in the attic come up all over again. I want to get separated all over again.

I say to her, *How about Kitty and I both come over for dinner this weekend?*

Kitty, she says, like she is trying to pronounce a word in another language.

Yeah, I say. *She's my girlfriend.* And I say "girlfriend" like it's also a word in another language.

Your girlfriend? she says. I hate how good it feels to see her disoriented like this.

I mean, I say, *if you still want me to come over and meet your fabulous guy.*

She takes a few seconds and then says, *Yeah, OK. Why don't you and . . . Kitty come over on Saturday.*

Perfect, I say, as if this situation could possibly be perfect.

#

That night, I sit down at my desk and I write. I'm tired of being weak and scared and worried.

Catty comes back to the store. She gets right up to the counter. Papa's wearing a not-so-clean, not-so-well-worn, not-so-blue blue tie. She pulls him by the tie towards her. She puts her lips against his. While their lips are touching she says, *You are one hell of a pussy.*

Papa wants to keep kissing this woman in the silky blue dress but instead of more kissing, he pushes her away.

Papa is scared. He is lonely. He misses his brother who died of the flu in 1918 when Papa was still in Poland with his family. Papa watched his older brother, the war hero, as his skin turned blue in the hospital. He remembers what it was like to be alone on that boat at age twelve. Almost every night, he wakes up in a sweat yelling for his mama, thinking he's still on that boat. He always remembers that boat. He knows the Nazis are coming for his family, even before the Nazis do what they do. He knows his wife will never be pleased with him. He knows his boy will always be ashamed of him. But Papa also knows his boy will do amazing things when he is older, and Papa is already proud of him. Even as he's fully aware that he can't help his boy. And so Papa drinks. And all of his charm and love leak out with the strangers who come into his store to talk to him about baseball and boxing. And he gives the boy with the hole in his pants a new pair of pants as if this will help his own boy. And thinks about shtupping the woman in the silky blue dress because it helps him forget the ache from how much he loves his family. This is his life. His mistakes are huge, but his love is even bigger.

I miss Papa.

I miss Bubbie.

I miss my boy.

I miss Kitty.

I miss my ex.

I miss my mom.

I miss my dad.

I even miss work.

So I get drunk.

Really drunk.

As in: I get so drunk that I log in to my work's collaboration system and drunk blog about my time away from the office. I talk about gups and Octopods and piggy banks and Mexican clay and naked mole rats. I talk about my boy at the beach. I misquote Hemingway several times as I say things like, *I mistrust all frank and simple people* and *you're a chicken if you don't enjoy wild boar pie.* I tell them about the octopus in the tank. And then I talk about being hot for Kitty. And the part where instead of fucking Kitty in the closet, I invite her to dinner at my ex's house.

I attempt to undo the post right after I publish it, but the undo doesn't work—a feature I really wish we'd fix. And then I pass out.

#

I dream that night of my mom and of all the blurry people who used to come visit us while my dad was at work. Not friend people. Odd people. People that looked weird like on TV. Long cheekbones. Scar on the neck. Reeked of smoke. One glass eye. One kept saying the word *cantankerous*. One dragged a cane behind her when she walked. Had a plastic arm. Transparent purse. Tattoo across the chest. I don't remember any names. I don't remember any conversations. I just remember that they would come over. One at a time. And they didn't say much. And my mom didn't say much. They would sit at the kitchen table next to my mom as I played with Legos in the living room. No matter how big and scary these people might've seemed outside of the house—inside our kitchen they were small and fragile.

When I first told my (trying to be ex) wife about it, she said, *Did your dad even know? Was she cheating on him? That is some creepy shit.*

It made me sad how much the story creeped her out.

I never thought of it as creepy. I loved these visits. My mom was so calm around these people. These fragile mystery people, they calmed her. And they were beautiful.

#

When I wake up the next morning, which turns out to be one in the afternoon, I've received 321 Likes on my blog post. It is getting more attention than anything I've ever blogged before. It has even more Likes than any of my boss's posts. In fact, all but six of our employees have liked this post. I don't even know if the CEO could achieve this level of Like-ability. The Impact Metrics plug-in gives me a global reach score of 98 percent and a

Sentiment of "Wowzers!". My gamification plug-in was designed to expo-
nentially award a high level of exposure, regardless of content, quality, or
appropriateness. So I should be rolling in points from this.

I get a message from the gamification plug-in that says *new keywords
added to collaboration database: ex-wife, closet, chicken.*

The messages are getting more frequent. I'll need to find a way to access
the codebase as soon as I get back.

I send Anne a message: *are you still thinking about my career or did my
blog post render me unemployable?*

It's a joke but I really do feel nervous and nauseous about posting that
stuff.

Anne: *You're not big on taking the shortest path, are you?*

Me: *due to the theory of relativity, the shortest path isn't always a straight
line.*

Anne: *The line at the unemployment office does not bend to Einstein's
theories.*

Me: *so are you going to finally tell me about this new job you have for me?*

Anne: *I'll tell you when you're back. But you'll have to step up and start
working for real again. Can you do that?*

I close my eyes and try to block out images of what Papa might say . . .
If I step up, you know I will just fall back down on my tuches.

I send Anne a gif of Tevye from *Fiddler on the Roof* lifting his shoulders and saying, *I don't know.*

Anne: *You'll be dotted line to me.*

Me: *dotted what?*

Anne: *You'll report to me for now . . . and about that blog post of yours . . .
the execs actually liked it!*

Me: *how do you know about the fucking execs?*

Anne: *Because I meet with them. They know we need more humanity in
our collaboration. And your post was . . . let's just say it was alarmingly full
of humanity.*

Even by text, she sounds so much a part of the company. It's eerie to
see it, especially when I feel so detached from the company. I *think* I like

the idea of reporting to her, but it also scares me because now there are more ways I can disappoint my friend.

Anne: *Let's talk about it on Monday . . . How are you and Kitty?*

Me: *going out with her tonight.*

Anne: *Don't fuck it up!*

Me: *the job or the girl?*

"the secret to hosting a successful dinner:
avocados, wine, and a time machine that lets you
go back in time and kill the guests."
—@dinnermuncher

Chapter Eight: Dinner @ Wife

Kitty's feet are on my dashboard again, except this time she's wearing heels. And she seems to be digging her heels into the dash.

I know this is awkward, I say. *But my wife, she's—*

Your wife? Kitty says.

It's impossible for me to explain it. I still can't quite call her an ex even though she's basically an ex.

Did you tell Anne? she says.

No, I say. *I was scared. Did you?*

No, she says. *I was scared for you.*

Thanks, I say.

At least I get to see your boy, she says. She rubs her hands together, like either she's cold or she has a sneaky plan. *His drawing was the most fabulous thing in the world.*

Even though it's a warm August evening, I turn up the heat in the car.

He'll be so keen to see you, I say.

Keen? Did you just use the word KEEN?

What? The cool kids don't use that word?

The cool kids, she says as she digs her heels hard enough into the dashboard that I fear the airbag will release, *do not go on dates with the past.*

I hope this doesn't make you want to cut off my cock.

Well, she says, *we need to have evidence that you have a cock in the first place.*

The sweetness from the Convention Center has worn off, and the messiness of my rotten marriage is rotting into this world with Kitty.

I get a text from Anne that says, *Have a blast tonight. I want to hear all about it at work.*

Remind me, Kitty says. *They don't live together. Right?*

I don't think so, I say.

How long have they been together?

I don't know, I say.

So what DO you know?

I say, *I know that* The Empire Strikes Back *is a movie that brings up some complex family dynamics that are not explored as fully as I had hoped in* Return of the Jedi.

Kitty takes her feet off the dash, and she seems to get small in her seat. She whispers, *This is harder than I expected.*

I put my hand on her lap, and even through her corduroy pants, I can feel that her skin is warm.

Look, I say. *I know this is really weird. I shouldn't have brought you into this mess. But I like you. And I'm glad to be going to this thing with you.*

She gets small and shy and she says without any sassiness, *Thank you.*

I rub her warm pants. Somehow she makes brown corduroy pants sexy. Even in August, which seems like a totally illegal time to wear corduroy. *You look really good tonight*, I say.

We're quiet for the rest of the drive over there. We have a lot of feelings bottled up inside of us. And we don't talk about them directly. Hemingway would be proud.

#

As we walk up to the front door, Kitty says, *I love Craftsman homes. What year was this built?*

I have no idea, I tell her, annoyed because she's complimenting my ex-house.

I get a message—on a Saturday evening!—from Carnegie Mellon Jessie that says, *Your code's a mess! Hasn't anyone taught you to avoid the pro-*

gramming pyramid of doom? You code like my grandpa. You gotta learn how to write decent JavaScript code!

My boy opens the door to greet us. He's wearing a purple tie and a new pair of jeans.

Kitty grabs the boy and picks him up. She says, *You look like a movie star.*

The boy smiles and tries to hug us both at the same time, but he can't quite reach his arm around me. He whispers to us: *I have a surprise for you.* We put the boy down and he runs into the house to announce that we're here.

And then, before we step into the house, into this pyramid of relationship doom, Kitty whispers to me, *The universe is the way it is, whether we like it or not.*

#

My ex is looking great, unfortunately. She's wearing a black dress that I don't recognize and a necklace with a blue rock at the center that I'm sure my son knows exactly what it is.

She kisses me on the cheek and then nods and smiles at Kitty.

My boy points up at Kitty like she's a statue to worship. He says, *Mama, Mama, Mama! She's the one who took me to the beach and drew that drawing and is going to teach me how to draw zombies and seahorses.*

Yes, my ex says. *I'm piecing things together.* Her smile is polite, controlled, tolerant.

We walk into the living room, and there is the great boyfriend I've been hearing about. My ex puts one hand on his shoulder and squeezes as she smiles at him. She says, *This is Daniel.*

Daniel turns out to be even better looking than I expected. He is wearing black leather shoes and an untucked white oxford. He oozes with I'm-a-Professional. And he looks young compared to the rest of us. Probably in his thirties. A nice, healthy head of thick brown hair, unscarred by divorce.

Great to finally meet you, he says as he approaches me. I prepare to shake his hand but he ignores my hand and goes for a hug.

A hug!

I mistakenly poke him with my hand in his gut as we hug, a gut that isn't a gut at all, but a thing with actual abdominal muscles.

Who is this muscular asshole?

And also: Finally? To *finally* meet me? How long has this thing been going on?

I look over at Kitty and it takes some time before I notice that she's giving me the universal gesture for introduce-me-before-I-kick-your-ass.

Oh, I say. *This is Catty, I mean, Kitty.*

Levels one, two, and three failed.

They shake hands and linger a little too long as their hands slowly separate, and it comes off more intimate than my hug.

Wine? Daniel says to us.

Before the word has time to enter my brain, Kitty has already said, *Yes, please!*

#

We all sit in the living room—my old living room. Daniel pours everyone wine and Kitty grabs her glass first and takes a big gulp.

My boy says he's going to get something from his room and disappears.

The place looks a lot nicer than when I lived here. There are new paintings on the walls. Abstract art that looks scary and expensive.

Daniel's arm goes around my ex, and my ex gives Daniel a kiss on the lips. The kiss is too long and too wet.

I gulp from my wine and then I get it over with right away: *Why exactly did you want me to come over anyhow?*

Well, my ex says. She wipes her lips and scratches her nose. *I thought it would be nice for you to meet Daniel.*

Daniel rubs her back. I never rubbed her back like that. My ex looks over at Kitty and then back at me.

So we've met, I say. *What now?* I can feel the frustration bubbling in me like during those last fights.

My ex says, *And we can meet your beach friend, too.* And she looks right at me. Like Kitty and Daniel don't exist.

But they do exist. And I know this because I hear the gulping of Pinot noir. And Kitty pouring herself another one. She pours another one for Daniel, too.

I grab my glass and point towards Daniel, and some of the wine spills onto the coffee table. I say, *So where did your dude come from?*

Excuse me? Daniel says. He puts his hand to his chest with a pretend sort of pride. *Cool! I'm cool enough to be considered a dude.*

I almost appreciate that he's trying to make things lighthearted, but I could blow him away with self-effacing humor if that's a game he wants to play.

My ex wipes the table with a few cocktail napkins. When I lived here, we never had cocktail napkins. She shakes the wad of napkins at me and says, *I am allowed to be happy.*

It burns to hear her say this even though I can't find a way to argue.

I get a message from the gamification plug-in:

```
{ status      : "assessing intimacy rating
                before the hit fits the shan",
  good_quotes : ["are we having fun yet?",
                "autoerotic asphyxiation",
                "impeach them all"] }
```

I don't know what the fuck this means—and these aren't my words. But there are only so many messes I can deal with at once.

Any minute our boy is going to come downstairs. And to what? It seems impossible to keep the bugs out of this system.

Kitty leans forward and rests her hand on my ex's knee. *Your boy is a lovely kid*, she says.

My ex tries to smile, but it is a strained, painful smile. And then Kitty pulls her hand away.

I want to hug Kitty. I want to apologize. I want a normal date with her.

I want to awkwardly stick my hand inside her warm pants pocket and I want her to laugh about it. And at the same time, I want to apologize to my ex. I want to rewind the tape all the way to the point when we were allies. Trying to raise this boy together. When we ordered takeout and argued sweetly about what to watch on TV. When we went to bed together. When we didn't know about separations.

And then Kitty stands up. She walks over to a double-doored closet just through the door to the dining room and opens it up. Just like when I lived here, it's filled with arts and craft supplies. My ex watches Kitty's movements like she's going to attack her at any minute.

Kitty closes the door. *Oh My God*, she says. *This closet used to be a built-in hutch, didn't it?*

Daniel immediately stands up. He marches right over to Kitty and I close my eyes while waiting for the attack.

But there is no attack. Daniel opens the closet door again and says, *Yep.* He taps on the wall inside the closet. *The top part was shelves for dishes and the bottom was a bureau for linens.*

So who changed it? Kitty asks while she inspects the closet.

Daniel says, *We think the last owners did.*

Fuckers! Kitty says.

I know, right! They're nearly hugging each other at this point. *We're hoping to restore it soon.*

Kitty is nodding all the way. *I just love Craftsman houses!* Kitty and Daniel are now like best friends. I'm surprised she doesn't volunteer to help restore the stupid thing.

And what is all this WE talk? This guy is acting more settled in this house than I ever was. I say under my breath, *We.* And then my ex leans over and slaps my knee as a way to tell me to shut up. She used to do that all the time when we were married. I kind of liked it and I kind of hated it.

#

The four of us sit at the dinner table. Two more bottles of wine. My wife made brisket, couscous, and a salad. Not what my Midwestern wife would've made when we first met. It is one triumph of our marriage.

Just when I'm about to ask about the boy, he comes downstairs. He is wearing a peacock costume and he is holding four red cardboard boxes in his hands. They are little jewelry boxes.

Wow, I say. The peacock costume has bright feathers all around his waist, colorful plumage, iridescent. A headband with a peacock feather on it. He looks beautiful.

He spins around with pride. *I'm a boy peacock.*

As if Daniel and my boy are part of the same performance, Daniel says, *The boy is the most colorful peacock.* And my boy nods at Daniel in a very satisfied way.

Thinking about the hell my boy might catch if he goes outside in a peacock costume worries me. A thousand new complicated things enter my head.

What are in the boxes? I say to my boy.

Oh, he says. He looks down at them like he momentarily forgot. *I have a present for each one of you.*

He walks around the table and gives us each a box with our name on it. When he goes by Kitty, she squeezes his arm and says, *You look perfect.* He smiles and giggles and kisses Kitty on the cheek. Their affection for each other is heartwarming. And it bothers the hell out of me.

I watch my wife at this moment and she actually closes her eyes and winces. She's jealous of our boy's relationship with Kitty.

When he drops the present off with Daniel, Daniel winks at him and my boy smiles again and I try to gauge whether I'm jealous too. I don't even know what the feeling is watching them, but it is a bad feeling and I want it gone. Daniel seems sweet with him. But he's too nice and supportive, like he's hiding something. You can't trust a man who isn't balding.

Can we open it, sweetie? Kitty asks.

My boy says, *No, you have to wait until you go home.* He says it like he already made some kind of secret plan with his mom.

OK. I'll be patient, Kitty says. And we leave the little boxes on the table, longing to know what's inside.

#

The food is great, and even though the adults don't know how to proceed in the conversation, my boy, clearly the most well-adjusted creature among us, carries the torch by reciting peculiar facts during most of dinner. He also stands up occasionally to straighten his peacock outfit.

My boy says, *You know, Kitty and Daniel are exactly the same height.* They look at each other. Like teammates.

My boy says, *You know, Mama and Dada are exactly the same age.* We look at each other. Like a divorced couple.

My boy says, *You know, we all live in the same time zone.*

I say to him, *Eat your brisket,* because we're all eating while he keeps talking.

He says, *You know, Mama's house was built in 1912 and Dada's apartment was built in 1993.*

I rub my boy on the head. *How the hell do you know all that?*

Dada, stop! he says. He fixes his hair and his peacock feather. *I looked it up on a real estate website.*

Kitty seems so impressed with my kid. She leans over to me and says in a fake whisper, *You should let this kid help you find a decent place to live,* even though she has only seen my place for about two minutes, just before heading over to my ex-house.

My boy says, *I know, right?* like he's my exasperated real estate agent all of a sudden. And I hear my wife chuckle.

Kitty pours herself the last of the bottle of wine. Daniel grabs the empty bottle from the table and says, *Should I open another one?*

Kitty nods.

My ex looks over at Kitty and then at Daniel and says, *I think we've had enough.*

I have so many fucked-up feelings right now. I like this woman who is my date, and it seems like I should be happy that my boy likes her. But her drinking is just too much for me. And I'm ashamed of her in front of this other woman who gave up trying to raise a kid with me, I feel like all my flaws are on display. Somehow I resent my date for the failures of my marriage, and I resent my wife for the failures in my dating life.

In my head, there's a screwed-up blend of Kitty's physics quotes and coding metaphors and a judgmental Hemingway, all saying to me: *The first draft of the universe is a pyramid of shit.*

#

After dinner, Daniel tells Kitty to follow him. Daniel says, *If you like Craftsman homes, you are going to be HORRIFIED by how they destroyed what used to be the dumbwaiter.*

Kitty downs the rest of her wine and follows Daniel out the door. She mutters something like, *I have GOT to see this*, like anyone could possibly care about a dumb dumbwaiter in this moment.

I can tell that my wife doesn't enjoy this new bond either, which should make me feel like I'm on the same side as her, but I'm on nobody's side right now.

And then it's just me, my boy, and my ex. All in the room together.

I pretend that this is my simple, happy life. Right here. With these two other people next to me. Man, woman, child. A nice little family dinner.

But then I look around. The half-eaten plates. The empty bottles of wine. The way that Kitty and Daniel suspiciously disappeared.

My wife says to me, *Your friend is nice.*

My boy says, *She's great. She knows everything about piggy banks. And she can draw things perfect, even tiny things. Just ask her.*

I hate how my ex is acting all polite and proper. I say to my ex, *Your friend seems pretty young. When did he graduate high school?*

My boy says, *He graduated in exactly the year 2000. And he got his*, he pauses and thinks for a minute before continuing, *he got his crier-practice degree in 2008.*

It takes me a while to do the math to figure out that he's about ten years younger than us.

My ex says, *He's a great chiropractor.*

My boy says, *I asked him because I'm doing a family tree. Isn't that cool?*

The idea of this Daniel quack being on the same tree as us is unacceptable. He's not even in the same forest.

I lean over to my boy and say, *Would you mind leaving me and mom alone for just a bit?* I say it so sweetly and innocently that it sounds so obviously not-sweet and not-innocent.

Why? he says.

Honey, my ex says to him. And somehow her nonexplanation is more persuasive to our child, who makes one sigh, and then walks away.

She waits until the creaks from our boys' steps are a safe-enough distance away and then she says, *I would prefer if you told me next time before taking our kid on any trips with women who are so . . . spirited.*

I say, *Listen. I'm sick of you acting all mature and proper when you're just as stupid as the rest of us.*

She has that smug look like I'm not making any sense. *How am I acting exactly?*

You know, the way you're showing off your dumb boyfriend and how you act like you're so much better than me.

I don't know for sure that any of these things are true, but it gets to her, I see the crease on her forehead and the tremble in her lips and the way she's taking deep breaths.

She says, *I love you,* and she pauses for so long that it hurts me because it's obvious what word is going to come next. *But,* she says, *it was so exhausting watching you worry about everything except being right here with us. I couldn't raise my little boy in that world.*

She looks down at her lap. I've never heard her talk like that before. I've never seen her look this vulnerable. And I wonder if I'm ever that vulnerable. What would I say if I didn't hide behind all my exhausting bullshit? I look down at my lap, pretending like there's something interesting there.

I say without thinking: *I still hate you for leaving me.*

We both look up at each other. She says, *I know.*

I reach out my hand and try to touch her hand, but she pulls away fast, as if shocked. And then she wipes my touch off of her hand.

I say, *Our universe is the way it is, whether we like it or not.*

#

When we get back to my apartment that was apparently built in 1993, Kitty goes right to the couch and sits down with the boxes that my boy gave us. I don't want to follow her, but she seems so driven that I sit down next to her. She hands me my present.

She holds her box up and says, *I'll show you mine if you show me yours.*

I can smell her sweat and the alcohol off her breath. Even though I'm also a little drunk, I'm so annoyed with her for over-drinking tonight. Not a single part of me is attracted to her right now. So I focus on what my kid gave me.

He sewed me an iPad from a sock, with the app icons sewn in there and everything.

As she opens the box, she says, *God damn. God damn. God damn.* And she says it like she just got a call that her dad was dead. I knew that my boy was getting into sewing with his mom, but I didn't know he was this good. It is a stuffed octopus with a zebra pattern. A card falls out of the box, and Kitty puts the octopus on the couch, right over the crack between her cushion and my cushion, and then picks up the card and looks at it for a while.

What's it say? I say, impatient with her.

Her voice cracks when she reads it. *Dear Kitty, I sewed a quarter inside it, so it's kind of like one of your piggy banks.*

She hugs me real tight, one of those awkward couch side hugs, and she says, *I haven't felt this way about a kiddo since . . .* and she doesn't finish the sentence. She keeps hugging me and she whispers, *I love your boy so much.*

When she says this, I push her off of me. Fast.

She gives me a quick look to figure out what just happened. She says, *What the fuck was that?*

I stand up and look down at her and say, *You don't love him so much. You barely know him.*

Oh, she says, finally noticing my state of mind. *I just mean that I have some affection for him.*

The same way you have affection for Daniel when he showed you the dumbwaiter?

Now she stands up. She's wobbly on her feet. *What?*

Well you did drink a lot and then seem to get off about Daniel showing you the dumbwaiter.

Excuse me?

I sit back down. *I don't know.* I put my face in my hands and wait for her to sit down next to me, but the expected readjustment of the weight on the couch does not happen.

I'm leaving, she says. I look up and I see just how angry she is. Her face is red and her look is as cold and as cruel as I've seen from her. *I'm sorry for drinking and for liking your fucking kid.*

Every time she mentions my kid, I get even more frustrated. I don't understand what it is. This feeling.

She is still shaky as she grabs her purse and orders a Lyft from her phone.

She says, *I told myself I was done with men who are assholes. It's so exhausting being around their bullshit.* There's that word, exhausting, the same word my wife used. Kitty says, *I can't believe I agreed to go to her fucking house.*

I say, *It is a bad house*, which is all I can manage to say because I totally regret this moment, but I also don't have what it takes to fix it.

On the way to the door, I notice how she looks back at me one last time, like she's trying to figure it all out, to see if there's any possible window back to a good place, and then that window closes, we turn to pillars of salt or however that Bible story goes that we don't believe in. And then she's gone.

#

After popping some Advil and drinking a whole lot of water, I get in bed and close my eyes. I try not to think about the disastrous dinner or about Kitty and my crappy dating skills or about my boy and my failure to keep him safe from bullies (and from Kitty), or about my mom and whether I have a gene for drinking too much. Or for dating people who drink too much.

When I was my boy's age and my mom kissed me goodnight, reeking of cigarette smoke, she'd have this pained look in her eyes, like she didn't want me to go to sleep, and her lullabies were these half-song, half-stories about being alone in the forest. They scared me more than they comforted me, but it was also the only time of day when my mom seemed like she was focused on me, like there was somebody real there behind her eyes, for a change, even if it felt like it was this scared little girl, it felt real in there, so I never told her how scary her songs were, maybe I even told her they comforted me. I thought it was just love. Afterwards, when I was in my early twenties and she relapsed, I stayed safely 2,500 miles away while talking to her and my dad on the phone. I was more angry about her drinking than I was sympathetic. Pain, comfort, fear, anger, sympathy. All these messy feelings pushing up against each other.

"all successful careers begin with hard work,
discipline, and a paranoid coworker with a
glass eye who goes by the name of sir jujubutt.
#eyeboy" —@careerishtips

Chapter Nine: Back 2 Work

It sure doesn't feel good to walk back into CollaborationHub. I make sure not to go into the building until Anne has explicitly texted me to say that she is at the office. The cactus that was between us on the desk is now gone. In its place is a white brick-shaped device with antennas shooting out in four directions. There's a yellow Post-it on the device that says "wifi extender #5." There's still a bit of soil on the table from the missing plant.

Anne wrote a blog post welcoming me back, and there are thirty-seven comments on that post already. I smile a lot—both in real life, and with emoticons :), and even with emojis, as much as I hate emojis. I send a few GIFs of Kermit the Frog and Samuel L. Jackson and Oprah and Taylor Swift and Bender Bending Rodriguez. I Like everyone's comments, even the snarky ones that suggest I shouldn't get extra vacation days just because I blew up the gamification plug-in (which turns into a digression in the comments about our unlimited vacation policy and how it's a farce). I even laugh along when people joke about inviting Kitty to dinner with my ex-wife—I should write a plug-in that gives you a breathalyzer before allowing you to publish anything . . . or before you take your not-quite-girlfriend to your not-quite-ex-wife's house.

It feels like I've been away from work for a month, but it's just been one long crazy week, a lot of moping, some drinking, a beach trip, a piggy bank convention, and a disastrous dinner. I should have spent some time thinking about whether I'm ready to be happy at work, like the Blue Whale told me to do, but I forgot about that part until walking back into the office. I try to think of an answer before confronting him. How can I be happy at work when I can't be happy on vacation?

It's weird that the Blue Whale hasn't said anything about my return yet, not even a Like.

Anne sends me a message on an ephemeral channel: *When you're ready, come to the Millennium Falcon. Let's talk about your career.*

My boy sends me a video from my ex's phone with him fixing his hair for the first ten seconds of it, and then he says, *Dada and Kitty, did you guys like my presents?* and then a big, finger-drawn question mark appears over his face, and then he fiddles around for a few seconds trying to stop the video.

I write back a text that says, *LOVE LOVE LOVE*, all caps, of course. Along with emojis of a heart, a peacock, and an octopus.

And then I go mope in the bathroom.

#

When you're sitting in a bathroom stall pretending to take a shit and your boss knows you are pretending to take a shit and your head throbs and you have in front of you a story with a fictionalized version of a woman who doesn't even qualify as your ex-girlfriend but is somehow sitting on your fictional grandfather's dry goods counter with a notepad from a real hotel, it is difficult to relax. If Kitty is out of my life, then Catty should be out of Papa's life too. Right?

But she won't leave.

#

The Millennium Falcon is a peculiar conference room because the employees have decided that this is the place to send their broken office chairs. And so even though there are three or four functional office chairs around the small conference room table, there are about ten other chairs packed into the corners of the room—some with broken arms, some that don't spring up, some whose backs don't ever lock in place. One that just has a hole straight through the middle of the seat in a way that I don't even want to think about. It is office chair purgatory.

Anne is quiet for long enough that I don't like it.

You know, I say. *I think I liked it a lot better when you were criticizing me for my failed writing life and my failed love life. I'm not sure I'm emotionally prepared for you to trash me about my failed career.*

She starts smiling.

I say, *Is this some kind of death by smiling?*

Sorry, she says. And she straightens out her skirt. I've never seen her wear a skirt before. It is bright red like the color of a heart emoji and long so that it only exposes her ankles. It works on her.

Her face gets serious now. Here it comes.

She says, *The Blue Whale left the company.*

I cover my mouth. *Oh no*, I say.

I have this terror that my rogue gamification plug-in—which is still sending me updates on its social media research—somehow caused his departure.

Was it my fault?

Don't be ridiculous, she says, like I'm obviously not important enough for whale-sized matters. *You didn't read his goodbye blog post?*

It's odd that I missed the post. I wrote a plug-in that automatically notifies me whenever anyone writes a goodbye blog post. Those are my favorite of all the blog rituals we have at our company. Because inside a goodbye blog post, you can get a little window into a person's humanity. It's not easy. Most of the post will be a bunch of RAH RAH RAH, I love this company, I love the people, and a bunch of other crap. But if you look hard enough, you'll see the sentence—or even just the phrase, or even just an unusual bit of punctuation—that reflects the heartache and frustration.

Should I read it now? I ask Anne.

No, you can read it later. What you need to know is that he left for another startup. He told me to tell you he'd reach out on LinkedIn.

I deleted my LinkedIn profile, I tell Anne.

You did not! she says in shock.

I did, I say apologetically. *I got sick of the daily endorsements I was getting from my contacts.*

Saul, she says. *You should be flattered by your endorsements.*

It was like having my friends vomiting on me. And then I felt guilty that I wasn't vomiting right back at them.

Well there's a perspective I've never heard.

I decide not to tell her that instead of actually deleting my profile, I renamed it to Tinkle Von Tinkleface because my boy used to giggle for hours when I pretended that was my name, back when we were potty training him. My ex hated the joke. My boy quickly outgrew the joke. But I didn't. Von Tinkleface lives in Tinkletown, Tennessee, and is a urologist.

Anyway, Anne says, *he's the fourth person to leave for another startup this week.*

I know, I say. *Don't you remember I'm the one who wrote the plug-in that tracks quitters and gives them 50,000 points during their last hours?*

She laughs, finally. *The execs hate that one.*

Yep, I say.

Anne says, *So let's stop sniffing each other's butts and get right to the point.*

I sit up. I don't quite understand how the metaphor applies, but it still gets my attention.

She says, *Here's the deal. For one, you're miserable here. And also, it seems our customers are struggling to use the software the way we mean them to use it. And even though that's a problem with our UX, we're just not nimble enough to fix it as fast as we need to. And now, we're losing important people from this company.*

Um, I say. *Aren't you supposed to be the optimist? You've got me wanting to slit the company's wrists.*

Shut up, Saul, she says with a smile. *So let me review. You're on a path to destruction. This company is on a path to destruction. Our customers are on a path to destruction. And who is going to save the day?*

Spiderman? I say. I always liked Spiderman. And his miserable backstory.

No, she says.

I glance down at my phone. Another gamification message.

Want to guess again? Anne says.

You? I say. Even though I regard Anne very highly—even more highly since she told me to shut up—this also doesn't sound right.

No, she says.

I give up, I say, getting impatient with this game.

Then she says, *You. You are going to be the new company evangelist.*

Um, I say. I take a deep breath. And then I pass out.

#

When I come to, I have an ache on my forehead where I hit the table. Anne is rubbing my back, and I have some weird reflective blanket around my body.

She pushes an open pack of Fig Newtons towards me. *Here,* she says. *Eat. Did you forget to eat again?*

I stuff the cookies in my mouth. I choose not to tell her that in addition to forgetting to eat, I spent my Sunday drinking vodka tonics and moping about Kitty.

Easy tiger, she says to me, and pulls the pack of cookies away.

Her rubbing my back is so damn comforting. I should've considered rubbing my ex's back more often. When she was upset. When we were married.

With her hand on my back, she says, *Do you know much about the city of Corinth?*

This is a part of Anne that I never knew. Is she a real believer, or just a recovered Sunday school goer?

I take the blanket off of me. *Is that the setting for Corinthians? And its sequel?*

Anne is not impressed. *In ancient times, it was a city famous for fine ceramic and clay pots. But things changed. It got harder to find a good pot. It got harder to find an honest merchant.*

I'm getting impatient with Anne's crooked approach here. *Are we going to start selling ancient pots online?*

She ignores me. *But there was this one man who never wavered from the right way to make or sell a pot.*

Was this Jesus? I ask.

No! she says, she swats her hand in my direction like I'm a Georgia gnat. *Of course not. Anyway, this merchant was eventually murdered. But the point is—*

Wait a minute. The pot guy was murdered?

Look, she says. *The fact is that this man made a lot of money doing the right thing.*

Until he was murdered, I clarify.

Shut up, Saul. She reaches out and grabs my two hands in a sweeter way than her "shut up." She says, *We need more quality pots around here. And until then, you're going to work with companies who bought our shitty pots and teach them how to use them. Less shittily. Basically we're going to pay you to bitch about how people are not doing things right, like you do anyway.*

Like a murdered Corinthian merchant?

Like a GOOD Corinthian merchant, she says. *The point is that I think we can use your critical thinking in a positive and honest way that will also help CollaborationHub. Sometimes doing the right thing is also the profitable thing. What worked on the streets of Corinth can work for online collaboration.*

I don't know how this happens, but her ridiculous story with a giant plot hole has given me some hope. *Anne,* I say. *If I'm understanding things, this job is more like an anti-evangelist. A de-evangelist. A devangelist. Right? I can tell them whatever they need to know, be honest? What if their collaboration problems don't have to do with our software but how there are terrible people running the company?*

She looks over at the broken chairs in the room and says, *Give whatever guidance you think can help.*

What if they don't want to hear what I have to say?

Then they ignore you.

What if I can't do this job?

You can.

What if I make them regret buying our software?

She lets go of my hands and she stands up and looks down at me. *We'll cross that bridge when you burn it down. But if you want to stay with Col-labHub, you can't do what you've been doing lately. Let's just say that your old job no longer exists.*

It's like I'm on another planet, hearing murder stories from a bible that is somehow supposed to motivate me. And what makes this even more ridiculous, it's working. I'm motivated. I want this new job. I want this career. I can use the money. I need the distraction. But I'm not sure I can pull it off. It seems like more of a jobby job.

I say, *Can I think about it?*

OK, she says in an impatient way. *Sleep on it. Let's talk again tomorrow.*

I say, *So if I did take you up on this psychotic idea, where would I start?*

She sits back down. Right next to me. Her shoulders go hunch. Somehow deflated by this simple question. And she says to all the broken chairs, *Start with us.*

#

I sit at my desk and try to figure out why this code keeps sending me kooky messages and whether anyone else is receiving this crazy shit. But it's harder to find the root cause than I expected and I'm feeling slower than usual. Maybe it is time for me to move into a different realm. Anne made it pretty clear that something has to give. I either need to devangelize or get off the CollabHub toilet. In the regular world, I'm not really that old, but in internet years, I'm a dead man walking. Or limping, in my case. I remember the internet when it was a bunch of computer science geeks making ASCII text-based art of Abe Lincoln and naked people and we didn't worry about 256-bit encryption or zero-day vulnerabilities. I feel more and more unfit for this digital world.

I envy how Kitty gets to deal with real-world things that you can touch and shake.

Kitty.

It's still so confusing to think about her. I hate thinking about her drinking. I hate thinking about how much my boy likes her. I hate thinking of my ex and Kitty in the room together. I hate thinking of how I got jealous of Kitty disappearing with Daniel. But when I think about that look on her face when she left my apartment at the end of the night, it's a feeling much warmer than hate.

I send her a text, *So maybe I was a schmuck the other night.*

It's less than a minute when I see her typing dots appear in our conversation. Even these dumb dots give me relief, to know she's on the other side.

Kitty: *You were a schmuck.*

Me: *So what now?*

Kitty: *Now I'm going to a one-month sober arts meditation retreat.*

I start to text her a whole pile of questions about what the hell she just said to me, but then I get this message from her: *Don't text me anymore.*

I give up on figuring out the code.

Nobody's mentioned these scary gamification texts, so I must be the only one getting them.

I need to move on.

What the fuck is a sober arts meditation retreat?

While sitting in this noisy office, I close my eyes. I put on my noise-cancelling headphones but don't play any music. I try to remember the meditation that I learned that one time I took an intro to Zen meditation.

It's almost peaceful. I can almost forget the Kitty and ex-wife ache. I imagine the blood going through my arteries. I imagine my lungs expanding and contracting. I imagine the planets rotating around the sun. I imagine the sun imploding. And the solar system going dark.

It's comforting. To the point that nothing else—work, Kitty, my dad, my boy getting bullied—matters one iota.

And then the haptic feedback system on my watch applies a force on my wrist in an unfamiliar pattern. Tap Tap Buzz Tap. Tap Tap Buzz Tap.

I try to keep faux-meditating. Flying through the Milky Way.

I try to pretend that the taps and buzzes are part of the meditation process. Signals from other stars.

But I can't.

I look at the stupid watch. It says that my wife would like me to install something called the Divorce Proceedings App on my phone. It says that she has already created a profile for me on their system. It claims that the app is updated for the latest revision of the operating system, provides a choice of fifteen beautiful backgrounds, will legally hold up in a court of law in forty-three states, supports watch notifications, and allows you to sign your divorce papers using face recognition.

Fuck.

One part of me wants to burn down the building where they wrote that app. Another part of me is really curious to see those beautiful backgrounds.

I have no faith that my wife and I can ever make things work out. We've let things get too sour for too long. When I think about her, I think hurt, I think pain, I think arguments, criticism, loneliness. I think of all the ways she doesn't accept me and I don't accept her. She doesn't like my book, she doesn't like my friends, she doesn't like my jokes. It's an impossible future that we have.

But I don't want to let it go.

My wife and our history are part of me. I don't know how I'll live after cutting out this organ.

And then there is the boy.

I don't want permanent. I want to hover inside this blurry in-between world forever.

The app makes me agree to so many end user license agreements that I question whether the app has any content to it at all. Just some lawyers drinking too much vodka. And then the screen fills up with something called a Petition for a Simplified Dissolution of Marriage. With an animated tree going through all the seasons in the background. The animation ends in winter with all the leaves gone. It's cold and beautiful.

I delete the app and leave the office.

"when online #dating, remember to bring your
charm, your grace, your Advil, your Xanax, your
Ambien, and your huddled ass yearning to breathe
free. #ladyassliberty" —@onlinedates4dogs

Chapter Ten: Quirk

When I go to pick up my boy, my ex looks concerned. She invites me in
and even though I try to think of an excuse, no excuse appears.

Sit down, she says. *Sit down.* She is a little too excited about me sitting
down.

I sit on the chair beside the couch where she sits and I stare at that
dumb closet that during our marriage was always a dumb closet and now
all I can think about is that dumb-hutch or dumbwaiter or dumb-some-
thing, whatever it's called. A thing that Kitty could recognize in a matter
of seconds and I couldn't see across an entire marriage.

My ex-wife calls to Daniel and Daniel doesn't sit next to my ex on the
couch but on the chair across from me.

I'm annoyed to see Daniel. If I'm alone, she should be too.

I've been doing a lot of meditation lately, is how she starts the conversation.

I want to tell her that I was also trying to do meditation, but it fell
apart when I got the notification of her trying to divorce me.

I look at her and look at Daniel and look at the hutch and then back at
my ex. I say, *The good kind of meditation or the bad kind?*

She laughs. That big laugh of hers when she is surprised by my humor.

Then the laugh disappears completely. *Did you get my online request to
do the dissolution?*

I believe I did, I say.

What do you think?

I dissolved the app.

You what? Why?

If we're going to do this, we're going to do it in person.

She laughs through her nose. *Of all people,* she says, *I figured you'd most appreciate this way of doing it.*

I like communicating online when it comes to friends, I say.

So what are we exactly? she says, sadly.

I don't have an answer for her.

She says, *I've been angry at you for a while. I kept wanting you to be somebody else.* She takes a deep breath. *But I'm not angry anymore. At least not as much.* She nods at me and at Daniel. Clearly, she has practiced this with her little chiropractor friend. *You've always been a good father. I should trust your judgment. With the boy and with your . . . friends.*

I say, *Kitty and I are no longer a thing.*

My ex says, *Oh.* She looks up the stairs, where our son should be coming down from. I don't know what is turning through her mind, but something is.

While she's not looking, I glance at my watch to see the latest weird message: *communication_error: "payload sent using the wrong format"*

She says, *What happened?*

A lot of things, I tell her, which feels dishonest, but also feels accurate because I don't know if it was me being a schmuck or her drinking or my drinking or her divorce or my nondivorce.

She says, *How are you going to tell him?*

Yeah, I say. *That.* I put my head into my hands and try to focus. I tear up a little, but I rub my eyes to stop it from happening.

I say, *I think I might tell him that she got abducted by aliens.*

No, she says, *be serious.*

Maybe I'll tell him that she chose piggy banks over me.

You've got to be straight with him.

Daniel is being very quiet, but I see him nod.

I say, *What if I don't honestly know what happened?*

My ex nods. *I don't want to pry or put words in your mouth, but you could tell him that even though she's a good person, the two of you couldn't find a way to be together.*

It's weird. Even after all the arguing and animosity, I trust her about this. She knows the boy and she knows me and she's the only other person in the entire world who cares as much about him as I do. This is what I lose by dissolving our marriage.

She leans forward, almost like she is going to rub her hand on my leg, but she doesn't. She says, *Are you sure you don't want to give it another chance?*

Isn't my ex supposed to want to cut this spirited woman off from our boy? What about the jealousy? I mean, I want this Daniel out of the picture. Why doesn't she hate Kitty?

Daniel stands up, like in reaction to my thoughts, and he says, *I'll go upstairs and get the boy ready.*

Look, my ex says, *this is something for you to work through yourself. But spend some time reflecting on this.* She opens her eyes wide. She stands up. She puts her hand out for me to grab. *You seemed happy around her. It's good for our boy to see you happy.*

I stand up and put my hand out to her and I hug her and I feel her flesh against my body and it feels nice.

I step back and play around with my phone for long enough that she says, *Umm, what are you doing?*

I finish up with the phone, wait for the face recognition algorithm to confirm my existence, and then say, *We're officially divorced. In person. Pending digital lawyer approval.* And I put my phone away.

She smiles and then whispers, *Thank you,* with a voice as sweet as when we first were courting. I want to kiss her.

My boy comes down the stairs.

Dada! he yells. I stand up to greet him, and he runs over to hug me.

#

The first thing my boy asks me when we get in the car is if Kitty is around.

It breaks my heart to hear this. As much as I've thought about her and as much as I've thought about how it would affect my boy and what to say to him, I still can't seem to get anything out of my mouth.

Eventually he says, *Earth to Dada, Earth to Dada, come in Dada.*

No, sorry kid. She might not be around. Me and her, we just ran into some trouble.

Trouble like how? Trouble like the teacher caught you daydreaming, or trouble like you don't want to go to recess because they make fun of you and will beat you up if you play on the monkey bars?

Who beats you up? I say.

Don't change the subject, Dada.

I smack the steering wheel. I need to talk to his teachers. I hate not knowing.

I say, *Do you remember when me and Mama split up? How sad we were and how hard it was to talk about?*

No, he says.

Well it's kind of like that right now with me and Kitty.

He's quiet for a while. Then he says, *Did she like my present?*

What present?

Dad! You know. The zebra that I stitched for Kitty.

Oh, I say. *Yeah. She loved it.*

So she has it to keep her safe? I see tears on his face that he quietly rubs away.

Yes, I say. *She has it.*

Sometimes I forget how young he is. This belief that a sacred object can keep someone safe like a lifetime of pain and suffering can be reversed with some afternoon arts and craft project.

Jeremy and Sam, he says. *They said that they'll give me a wedgie if I get near the monkey bars. And I'm pretty sure a wedgie is bad, even if it's not as bad as an atomic wedgie.*

I squeeze tight on the steering wheel. I quietly say, *Why?*

They are buttheads, he says. *And I kind of called them ignore-anus-heads in class.*

Where did you learn that word?

The iPad, he says.

That's it. On Monday, I'm going to go talk to the teachers.

Please don't, Dada. It'll make it worse. It's not bad like you think. I double triple promise.

Let me think about it, I say. Which is one of the most comforting things to say when parenting. Then I say, *I know you really liked Kitty, and I really liked her too. But we couldn't find a way to be together right now.*

Can I still see her?

I say, *She needs to work on things by herself. Her divorce was pretty recent.*

Then maybe she needs us more than ever.

#

That night, we play a game of *Heads Up!* on my iPhone. He loves when I go first and have to put the phone on my head. He is supposed to help me guess the word or picture showing without saying that specific thing. I suspect he doesn't give me the best hints because he likes to watch me guess wildly wrong answers or maybe because he is still upset with me about Kitty.

When the game starts counting the last ten seconds, he loves to just yell the answer in a panic without any sort of hint. *This one is the Grand Canyon! Just say the Grand Canyon right now!*

The Grand Canyon?

Yes! You got it!

We then watch the video it took of us playing the game. This is the most brilliant part of the game. The ability to watch and re-watch videos of yourself being an idiot.

While I'm trying to help my kid guess that Abraham Lincoln is displayed on his forehead, I see a message from Anne flash by on his forehead. *What the hell did you do to Kitty?*

Hush! I say to my boy's forehead.

What? my boy says to me.

Oh, I'm sorry, I say, trying to focus on Lincoln again. *This president was shot in the theater.*

Babar the Elephant's dad?! my boy yells, with so much hope.

Pass! I say.

#

After I put my boy to sleep, I start to feel lonely in the apartment. I can't shake it. I want to be around someone. I want to feel somebody's body.

I'm cleaning the dishes in the kitchen and squeezing that old stinky sponge full of hot soapy water and that burn goes up my arm and into my heart and I feel lonelier than I've ever felt before.

I am divorced. I am a divorcé. I have an ex-wife, who is living with another man and probably laughing at me and my stupid, drunk ex-not-really-ever-a-girlfriend.

I want some armor to protect me from this feeling. I should grow a nice, tough divorcé beard. I want to run out of the claustrophobic kitchen and get a thousand miles away from this loneliness. I want to go to a bar and drink. But I can't. I have the boy.

I keep the iPad he sewed for me on my desk. I squeeze it when I write. Or when I try to write.

I drink two shots of gin, I squeeze the sock iPad, and then I get to it.

I've accepted that I can't get rid of Catty. She comes to Papa's store every day. She hops on the counter and tells Papa that he has to write a book, and she's holding a complimentary hotel notepad. My real life is oozing into this story in a way that I'm having trouble controlling. Catty shakes the notebook and tells Papa that he has to bleed in there, even though Papa is the kind of man who passes out when he sees blood. She hands him a pen, full of red ink, and the notepad. She says, *Write*.

Papa writes like his life depends on it. Or more importantly, like other people's lives depend on it. He tells about how he loves his boy but doesn't know how to connect with him, he talks about how he loves his wife but can't stop thinking of shtupping shiksas, how he hides from himself with the drinking, and with the sports page, how he hides like how the jumping spider hides in the Spanish moss hanging from the trees.

I drink two more shots. I need a break.

I install the Tinder app on my iPhone and use it to look for women who are nearby. I find a woman who looks a little bit like Kitty and my ex and my mother all combined, and I think the situation through. What would happen next? I would bring a woman to this house and mess around with her while the boy is sleeping thirty feet away? And then what? We fuck? And then we eat breakfast with my boy and he sews her an octopus with a quarter in it?

I delete the app.

I drink another shot.

I exercise enough restraint to avoid drunk blogging.

I install a less hip dating app called Quirk. I think about how Kitty said she hated her husband calling her quirky. So in a crooked, nonsensical way, I feel like I'm getting back at Kitty by downloading this word she hates.

The app isn't even updated for the latest version of the mobile operating system. The buttons on the app have big shadows on them. Doesn't it know that shadowing was out five years ago? And the background is the texture of blue velvet. Who uses textured backgrounds anymore? And the resolution is all wrong. Its average rating is a half-star out of five. And the app has all kinds of bugs with the software. Like when I set up my profile, it asks me what values are most important to me, and there is a big text field for me to fill in my answer, except it only brings up a numerical keyboard. So I enter 42.

Then it asks me for all the "gory details" about my most recent breakup. It says it will keep this information confidential. So I write about Kitty. I talk about how angry I am at her. How much I didn't like her drinking and how I had a mother who drank too much. But how I also miss Kitty. How it hurts to know that my boy misses her. How I yell at her while taking a shower. How bad it burns to be divorced. How many things I regret, right down to the crappy sponge I'm using, with a stink that won't go away.

It feels so good to write this . . . to ooze all the good and the messy feelings. I want to laugh and to cry, and it reminds me of the feeling I had when I first started writing fiction. How freeing it felt.

Once I complete this section, the app says in a computer voice: *Don't feel bad. Everyone is lonely and miserable.* And then the app crashes.

Some weird, buggy, audacious shit.

Papa's head is down on the counter, exhausted from the writing. And a little drunk. Catty picks up the notepad. She reads what he wrote. She says, *It's not the worst thing I've ever read. There's no blood, but it's a start. It's time for you to wake up. You hide behind the sports page and your drinking. Meanwhile, your son hides under the table. You don't attend to your wife. You have to face this stuff head on.*

Before the night is over, Quirk sends me a push notification. It says, *We've reviewed your record and determined that you are not fit for a mate. Good luck in your loneliness. Please rate this app five stars!*

#

On the way to work, I take a detour to Powell's Books. I just want a little comfort browsing the rows and rows of novels, but I spot one of my ex's friends in the fiction room, so I wander over to the comics and graphic novels to avoid confronting a human who reminds me of another human.

This is a genre that I've never explored. I start opening books and reading through them.

And they are incredible.

What amazes me is how few words it requires for them to convey something powerful. The pictures are not necessarily so complex either. But together, the pictures and the words can do amazing things. And when the words are more spare, or when the picture is more simplistic, the story leans on the other element. They play off each other. I'm giddy from this new world. I get absorbed in a Hawkeye comic because the guy keeps getting beat up and screwing up and his love life is a mess and I have so much affection for the dude.

Then I get a message from the gamification plug-in:

```
{ title      : "almost done with analysis",
  next_step  : "you don't wanna know" }
```

This stuff still scares me. I don't know how to fix it. Maybe I just need to finally escalate this problem.

Then I get a notification about being @ mentioned in a blog post about me being the first devangelist at the company. And I see twenty congratulation comments before shutting off my fucking phone.

I did NOT tell Anne that I would take this job.

On my way back to the office, I see that I missed a text from my dad, which is weird because my dad doesn't text. But then I read it more closely. It says, *This is the nurse. Call Piedmont Hospital.*

#

Dangerously high blood pressure. That's what they tell me. They also say that they suspect a clot in some artery that sounds important.

When they connect me to his room, he says, *Don't worry about me. I'll be out of here before you can say tuches face.*

Tuches face.

Well, he says, and he coughs into the phone, *maybe not that fast.*

Dad, I say. *I'm coming to see you.*

Don't be ridiculous. I'm fine.

I book two refundable tickets while we talk.

#

I walk up to Anne's desk and tell her that I want to speak with her in a conference room.

She says, *I'm busy. I could book one for this afternoon.*

I say, *I won't be here this afternoon.*

When we get into the Serenity conference room, I begin pacing back and forth.

My dad is sick, I say. *I have a bad feeling and I'm flying out there.*

Oh no. She presses her hand to her chest.

I don't like that you decided about the devangelist thing without me, I tell her. I'm feeling dizzy again. I want to press my head against Anne's chest and have her tell me that it'll all be OK.

And then, as if it came to me from up above, or from down below, or just by Wi-Fi, I know exactly what I need to tell this woman. I say, *If you can wait until I get back from this trip, I'd like to do this devangelist thing. It might save me. And it might not. Either way, while I do it, I don't want you to treat me like a child who can't make decisions on their own.*

She's a little defensive when she says, *And what if you act like a child?*

I say, *Then treat me like an adult even if you need to tell me that I'm acting like a child.*

OK, she says.

Anne looks at me up and down like they do in those movies her husband obsessively watches. She is looking for evidence about whether I'm being for real with her.

She nods. I can tell she's not yet confident in my newfound confidence.

I'm sorry about your dad. And I'm sorry about how it went with Kitty. You are like family to me, she says. Her eyes go wet and her lips shake a little.

Sometimes I think about a word so much that I can't recognize it. I can only see the individual letters and the word looks like nonsense.

Family. Fam. Ily. Fa. Mi. Ly. F. Am I ly?

I nod but I can't seem to talk because I'm about to cry myself. So I hug Anne, and while I hug, my watch taps me. I glance at it just in case it's my dad. But it's not. And it's not my rogue gamification plug-in either. It's the school principal. She says, *I've got your boy in my office. He got in a fight over recess. Call when you can.*

#

Unfortunately, my boy chose to punch the kid of the biggest financial contributor to the school. He punched this kid in the throat and with a little bit more force, could have caused real harm. My boy would not utter a word to anybody about why he did it. I tried to tell the principal that I suspect he is being bullied, but I had no concrete ground to stand on and my boy didn't help at all. We agreed that he'd take a few days off. A polite way to say suspended. I tell the principal that my dad is sick and I'm planning on taking my boy to Atlanta with me anyway. She nods, like getting the kid out of town is a good thing. Like he's dangerous.

When I get my boy in the car, I try to get the real story.

What did he do?

He is quiet.

Where did you learn to punch like that?

He is quiet.

I can't stand his silence. I say, *I'm going to check in with your teacher every day. I need to understand what is going on.*

After a few seconds, he says, *They called me a fairy because I like peacocks.*

Why didn't you talk to a teacher?

Kitty said you should poke your characters. And fairies have nothing to do with peacocks. That's just stupid.

She didn't say to punch a kid in the throat.

I was trying for the carotid sinus, he says. *That's what the video on YouTube told me.*

I drive too fast on the highway. I say, *If you want to learn self-defense, I can sign you up for a class. But you need to first talk to the teachers if there's a problem. You only punch people in the throat if you are in danger. Were you in danger?*

He says, *The carotid sinus, Dada.*

Whatever, I yell back to him.

He mumbles, *Kitty would understand me if she were here.*

He's got his arms crossed like he is angry at me. And now I'm angry at him, too.

I slow down the car and say, *Listen. Papa is sick. I'm going to visit him. I'd love you to come with me. But I checked with Mama and you can stay with her if you want.*

He is quiet for pretty long. And then he says, *Does Mama know about what happened today?*

Not yet, I say.

Are you going to tell her?

Yes, I say. *She needs to know.*

Can I talk to Kitty about it?

No, I say. *Not now.*

How do you know if you haven't talked to her? A good person checks on their friends.

Listen, I say, with a voice that is too gentle to be raised, but too raised to be gentle. *Right now, I'm worried about Papa. He is family. And he is sick.*

Could Papa die?

Yes, I say. And it hurts to say this, like I just realized it myself.

Could he live?

Yes. I really don't know. He is eighty-eight.

And that is pretty old?

Yes, I say. I reach to the backseat of the car and try to pat him on the leg but I miss his leg and pat something sticky like maybe an unfinished lollipop.

You know, Dada, he says. *Some bowhead whales live more than 115 years.*

Well, human heads are lucky to live to eighty-eight.

Dada? my kid says, in a way that is so sweet it hurts me.

Yes, matzoh ball?

I didn't mean to hurt him like that. They don't like peacocks. Even boy peacocks. I wanted him to stop being mean about peacocks, and I was afraid it would be a weak punch so I pretended like I needed to punch through a brick wall. That's what the video said to do. Except his neck was a lot softer than a brick wall.

I'm glad he can't see my face. Or my tears. I tighten my hands on the steering wheel and hold my breath. *I'm glad you stuck up for yourself. I just want to make sure you only use violence when you've tried other things. You really hurt that boy.*

I can't stop thinking about what happened at school. I prepared for all kinds of other speeches. We still haven't had a proper birds and bees speech. He probably understands more about how peacocks mate than humans. But I didn't anticipate this. Should I be more proud of my kid? I've been worried about bullying for a while. And today, he stopped the bullies. But he went from zero to carotid sinus awfully fast. Why isn't he getting help from the adults? What is the best way to handle this? What the fuck is a carotid sinus?

"always treat your dad with respect. he raised
you (maybe). he loves you (conditionally). and
who else is going to give you a meandering
speech about canvas bags at six in the morning?
#fathersdaybagmonologue" —@darthdad19

Chapter Eleven: Fathers

It's too early in the morning, but sitting at our gate in the airport is kind of nice. For a moment, I forget about my dad and about bullying and just enjoy that my son and I are eating delicious, artery-clogging bacon, egg, and cheese biscuits.

My boy reads an *Octonauts* book and I catch up on messages. Anne tells me that she hopes my father gets better. She also tells me that I shouldn't worry about work while I'm away.

I start reviewing my Papa story. Even though I like the idea of Papa and Catty writing a story together, Papa still needs to step up. Even if he fails, I'd like to see him try to be a hero.

Dada? my boy says. *Do you think this flight will be turbulenty?*

I don't know, I say. *It is hard to know.* Turbulence scares me far more than it scares the boy, but when I fly with him, my terror takes a backseat to protecting him. And with him, I am able to use statistics for a calming effect, even though they don't do a damn thing to calm me down. *You know that planes don't crash because of turbulence. They're designed to handle a huge amount of turbulence. Driving is more dangerous.*

I know, he says. *It's just that it tickles my penis when the plane bounces like that.*

Hmm, I say, which is really the only thing a parent can say in response to that.

#

When we land in Atlanta, my boy is resting on my arm. His eyes closed. An iPad with a dead battery on his lap. He's drooling. There's a thunderstorm outside.

I didn't think about the fact that we have no ride from the airport. Usually, my dad picks us up. Or we take the subway to the stop near their house. His house. But this time, he's in the hospital. And I failed to make arrangements with anyone else.

I tell my boy that we're going to Lyft it.

He says, *Can we rent a Tesla instead?*

Where did you hear about Teslas?

Dada! Everybody knows about Teslas. We could get a red one.

My boy is fascinated by the thunder since we don't get much of that in Portland. He says, *Do you think we might get electrocuted?* He says it like that's a good thing.

#

When we get to the house, it's sad to open the front door ourselves and have nobody home. It smells like emptiness. My boy looks exhausted, so I let him go to sleep even though I realize we'll miss visiting hours. I didn't calculate the issue of being with a kid and having nobody to watch him.

I get another creepy message from the gamification plug-in:

```
{ title      : "entering experimental phase",
  next_step  : "stay calm. or call 911." }
```

I call the hospital and the nurse says that my dad is sleeping and stable, whatever that means.

And then I send Jessie a direct message.

Me: *Would you mind doing a search in the code for "call 911"?*

Jessie: *Are you shitting me?*

Me: *No shit. Search.*

Jessie: *brb*

This house is creaky. It's not an old house—nothing like my Craftsman ex-house. Just a shitty cookie cutter house in the suburbs of Atlanta that my folks bought after I went to college. But it creaks like an old house. There are ghosts in here just the same.

Jessie: *Nothing.*

Me: *Are you shitting me?*

Jessie: *What's the deal here?*

Me: *Any chance you'd give me access to the code?*

Jessie: *Codebase locked down. Plus, we're doing a security audit. Isn't your father sick?*

Me: *One last thing. Can you check out GamificationPluginController. java and let me know if anything in that file looks funny?*

Jessie: *Funny?*

Jessie: *brb*

Jessie: *it seems OK. there's a loop that is O(n^2) that could be O(n). want me to fix?*

Fucking Carnegie Mellon grads.

Me: *No, that's OK. thx.*

Jessie: *np*

Well that didn't help worth a damn. I'm torn between being worried about the alarming messages and not taking them seriously because it's probably just some bullshit info that only I'm getting and I can easily rip out later when I get the chance. It feels like everything is this way—either it's nothing, or it's a disaster.

Jessie sends a GIF of The Dude from *The Big Lebowski* drinking milk in a robe at a grocery store with the words "The dude abides" on the picture.

#

It's weird trying to write in my parents' house without my parents. I find a desk in my dad's office. The walls of the office are covered with collages of my father's publications. There are awards and diagrams of chemical compounds and pictures of him alongside his colleagues. I want these things to mean something to me, but they just don't.

In my story, Papa has gotten really obsessed with writing the story of his family. Not only is he scribbling his story on page after page of the notebook, he has also started drawing pictures of each scene. But when Catty walks in, she's no longer pleased with his progress. She scans over the pages and tells him that he should quit this bullshit and get himself a rifle to prepare for the angry mob that is coming to close down his store. But Papa is too absorbed in his story of a lost man trying to connect with his son. Catty says, *You know that writing a graphic novel isn't a practical way to survive in this world.*

What the hell is a graphic novel? Papa says.

And that is when I stop writing about Papa and Catty, because graphic novels don't exist in 1938, and I don't know why Catty isn't being more supportive, and I don't feel comfortable in my dad's office, and I don't know what the hell to do with my story anymore.

#

My dad lives one mile from one of the best hospitals south of the Mason Dixon line. They have the best cardiology team around.

And this brilliant cardiology team doesn't know what's wrong with him. But something is wrong. His blood pressure is not safe and will not go down.

I ask my boy to stay in the waiting room and I give him the iPad. Before I leave, he says, *Dada! There's even a zombie hospital!*

Of course, I say, as I walk away, feeling like a zombie myself.

Last night, I watched all 175 minutes of *The Godfather* on my iPad. Anne's Hubby would be proud of me. I remember thinking this movie was about the Mafia. Now I see that the whole thing is about family.

#

My dad's arms are like old leather. And the skin on his face seems to be obsessed with gravity (even if he'd call it a scientifically false force). He is fragile, with the IV coming out of his arm and the way the smock is too big and the hospital socks are too long. I'm scared to see him this way.

Without turning his head, he says, *I figured you'd disobey me.*

I was in the area on business, I say.

I put my hand around his wrist and squeeze. He's cold.

Do you need another blanket? I ask.

No, he says. *I'm hot.* He turns slowly towards me. *Did you bring the boy?* His voice doesn't actually sound sick, or even weak. But it sounds resigned. Like he knows something I don't want to know yet.

I don't answer. Too absorbed in him and his body. The IV bag is so slow to drip.

Bring him here, he says. He waves the arm with the IV in it.

#

What's it all about? my dad says to my boy.

This is something Papa used to say to customers who'd come in the store. It's not a phrase of my father's, it's *his* father's line.

My boy shrugs his shoulders. *What's what all about?* he says.

My dad looks at the iPad in my boy's hand and he says, *You like that computer?*

It's an iPad, Papa.

My dad says, *That sounds like a feminine hygiene product.* His laugh is more like a grunt and then a cough.

Like pink Listerine? my boy asks.

My dad laughs and points to the IV. *You see this?* he says.

My boy nods.

This is magic juice. It's like apple juice that goes right to my heart.

Is it dangerous? my boy says. *Apple juice is bad for your teeth.*

I've got news for you, son. Breathing is dangerous. He rubs his IV hand on my boy's head. *Can I give you a kiss?*

My boy looks at me. He wants out. He wants my help.

I lift one finger in a way that he can see but my dad can't.

One kiss on the head, my boy agrees. *But not two.*

My dad gives him the agreed-upon kiss and then my boy asks if he can leave the room. On the way out, he turns around and he says, *I hope you live longer than a bowhead whale, Papa.*

After my boy leaves, my dad says, *I scare the shit out of him, don't I?*

Sort of, I say.

It's good for him. He'll remember me years later and he'll remember how I loved him.

It's hard to hear him talk in the past tense. Like the way my book about Papa is in the past tense. Or at least it used to be until Catty walked in and screwed things up.

What are the doctors saying? I ask.

They think I'll die any minute. Or else it's nothing.

What do you think?

I think both are true.

It's weird, my dad keeps staring at his hand—the one on the arm not connected to the IV—and keeps turning his hand back and forth. Like he's never seen it before, or like he'll never see it again.

Dad, I want to say. *What is it? What's wrong? What's it all about?* But this moment feels too big to talk about.

And then he stops staring at his hand and looks at me. He says, *I sent you* The God Delusion, *but you fucked up by coming to visit while it's in transit.*

It's weird hearing him say the word *fuck.*

Aren't you supposed to get closer to God as you get closer to death? It hurts to mention death. I'd rather talk about pink Listerine.

I wish, he says. *What did you think about the other book I sent you?*

Oh, I say. The book that Kitty stole from me and never returned. I say, *I'm not quite finished with it yet.*

He coughs a bunch. And a nurse comes in to check on him. And she checks his vitals. *Am I still alive, Mary?* he asks her. She giggles without answering him, like they're old lovers. Except *they* are not old, just him. She puts her hand on his arm for a few seconds without performing any sort of check. She leaves without a word.

What's the deal? he says. And I think he is talking about his health. But then he says, *I know you didn't read that book. I'm trying to connect with you. An old fart like me can't be doing all the work here.*

What do you mean all the work? I say. *I flew out here to see you.* I get dizzy while I talk.

Guilt trip, he says. He opens and closes his fist on the arm with the IV. He's got bruises around the spot where the IV goes in.

You know, I say, *it's hard to forget.* The words come out before I mean to say them. *You were gone most of my childhood.* I hold on to my chair and I try to breathe regularly. I guess we're doing this.

What the hell do you mean? he says. *I was busy earning money to give you a good life. I gave you a good life, didn't I?* His voice is loud, it is angry, too loud and too angry for a man in his situation.

I want to undo this whole moment, I feel so childish and so selfish bringing this up, especially right now. My own father, my only father, he is sick and I need to take care of him, that is all that matters, it is time to take care of him.

I feel like I'm failing to be an adult, like I'm failing to be his son. I hate this feeling. And on top of this feeling, there's this anger that he has the nerve to age on me.

I say, *I could have used more of you, Dad.* The tears are small, he won't notice them, I don't even need to wipe them. *You know what it was like being alone with Mom all the time?*

Yes, he says, like he's talking about something entirely different than me.

We're quiet for a minute. Then he says, *So what do you want from me? Did your therapist tell you I'm responsible for all your problems?*

I say, *Can you understand that you were absent?*

He looks up at the ceiling. Not just in one spot. But in four or five spots. Multiple times each. And he softens as he does this. I see it in his forehead. He goes from strong and angry to weak and sad.

No, he says. He says it with a tone so quiet and so resigned. *I tried to be the father mine never was for me.*

I get close and kiss his head like he kissed my boy's head and whisper, *When we die, what stars do we create?*

My father watches me like maybe I'm not real. Like I'm just a dream of his. I say, *You wrote that in the copy of the book you sent me.*

He smiles and his eyes close like he just got very tired, and the muscles across his face relax just a little bit more.

I hold his hand. The skin is clammy.

#

My boy's standing in a wide stance in the waiting room. He's moving his arms around slowly in something that looks like little kid Tai Chi.

Dada, my boy says. *Do you think Kitty knows how to do the judo?*

I don't like hearing him say her name.

I say, *Do you want me to sign you up for something? Maybe we can both learn.*

What do you think Kitty would think?

What do YOU think?

I don't know. I think Kitty would know. She just gets me.

Sometimes these phrases come out of his mouth and it hits me like a blow to the throat that my boy is getting older. And that I have less and less control over his world. And the more I try to push us away from something, the more he pushes towards it.

I say, *How are you feeling about . . . what happened in school?*

My boy says, *Half of me wants to punch him again. And half of me doesn't care. And half of me wants to explain to him about peacocks and why they're great.*

I'm comforted by his confusion. It's a human confusion. Though his understanding of statistics needs work.

I nod. *What about being around Papa?*

He has to think about an answer. And then he says, *I'm glad I came to see him.*

He goes back to his iPad and I go back to my iPhone.

The conversation with my dad is still inside of me. The man has been trying to reach out to me, in his own crooked way, and I have been keeping him out.

I wanted my dad to be more involved in my world when I was a kid, but maybe I'm getting *too* involved trying to protect my boy's world. I'm doing the same thing by doing the opposite thing.

I also wish I could reach out to Kitty right now. I also think that she *gets me*. She gets me so well that she doesn't want to talk to me anymore.

#

We spend a few more hours in the room with my dad. People keep checking on his temperature and his blood pressure and heart rate. But they don't seem interested in the results. He's drowsy from the medication they gave him and so not much talking happens.

I feel Papa inside me when I'm here. I don't even remember if I visited the hospital when he died of pneumonia at the end, but with my boy and my dad here, they blend into my Papa.

Papa, I want to say. *What's it all about?*

Looking over my writing, it occurs to me that my book is turning into something beyond just the words. I've even started doodling in the margins, trying to bring stick figures to life. But stick figures are not enough. Decent illustrations would add another layer to this story.

I fall asleep listening to my dad snore. I dream that we're living in an Octopod in the ocean—me, and my boy, and Kitty, and my father, and my ex-wife, and Daniel, and my mother, and Papa. In awake life, this sounds like a nightmare. But in dream life, it's beautiful.

My watch taps me awake with some more nonsense from the gamification plug-in:

```
{ communication_error :
    "relationship corrupted.
     destroying nodes and starting over." }
```

#

I remember waking up from a nightmare, back when I was a very little kid, still in a crib. I had a high fever, I remember that. And I remember the nightmare: Ernie and Bert were standing on the ceiling, looking down at me, and telling me that I was a bad kid. I woke up yelling and screaming and my mom ran into the room. She picked me up, she held me against her side, like she could hold me up forever. With me on her hip, she got me a cup of water, and I drank it carefully like I wasn't sure if my body could handle it.

She said, *Hush now, hush now, little one.* I didn't explain to her a thing about my nightmare—I just kept looking up at the ceiling to make sure they were gone—but she spoke to me as if she knew everything: *Don't listen to those crazy voices. They don't know what they're talking about. You're OK. Just remember that. We're perfectly OK.*

#

I step out of the room and call my ex on my phone while pacing the hospital hallway.

I say, *I need to talk to you about—*

She says, *I already spoke with the principal.*

You did? I say. *How did you know?*

A little birdy. Good for him that he kicked that kid's ass.

Did you know about him?

About Jeremy? she says. *Of course.*

Oh.

She says, *Let's get him into a self-defense class. If he is going to protect himself, let's make sure he knows what he's doing.*

I agree. But we need to speak with the teachers too. Make sure he knows how to speak up before punching a kid in the throat.

The carotid sinus, she corrects.

Yes, I say. *That thing too.*

How's your dad?

He's OK. He's stable even though they don't know what caused it.

The boy handling things OK?

Yeah, I say. *He's a champ.*

She's so good at having an efficient and practical conversation when the situation calls for it. It's refreshing how easy it is with her. And hard to imagine how it could be like this with anyone else.

I'm glad you got a chance to spend time with your dad.

Thanks, I say. She always appreciated that I had a connection to my dad—something she never had with her own father.

#

The flight back is exhausting. Even though it seems shorter because you're going against the time zones, it is an hour longer in actual time because of the headwind. And that extra hour takes an eternity.

My boy spends an insane number of hours drawing the seascape. In addition to an intricate coral reef, he has drawn all his favorite sea creatures—including the snot sea cucumber—and there is Kitty sleeping with the fish. Not in a Luca-Brasi-sleeps-with-the-fishes sort of way, but in a Kitty-the-mermaid-napping-with-the-fishes sort of way. A beautiful mermaid with a blue tail.

Somewhere along the way, he learned how to draw well enough to give the impression of depth. He definitely didn't learn it from me. When I compliment him, he says, *I just wish I could draw better.* I'm bummed that he is frustrated with his lovely little drawing. He keeps using the undo button in the app to undo his mistakes, which don't seem like mistakes to me.

What do you think? my boy says, and he shows me his picture.

It is beautiful, I say.

Can I see her, Dada?

Who? Kitty? No, not right now.

Then when? he says.

I don't know.

He sighs and then goes into his zombie game.

I watch a mom and daughter sitting across from us. The daughter is squeezing a doll real tightly. So tightly that it is hard to make out any of the doll's features. And the mom is buried in her iPhone.

My boy says, *Even though Papa was sick, it was a fun trip. I think I'm a better drawer when I'm in a hospital. Do you think that's possible?*

I tell him that sometimes it is easier to be creative when you're in a place where people are feeling a lot of things.

Will you cry when Papa dies?

I can't seem to answer him.

You should cry, he tells me. *It will help you.*

"to succeed in any business, you have to be
extremely empathetic. Or better yet, a psychotic
narcissist with bipolar disorder." —@biz_fail_tips

Chapter Twelve: Devangelism

The well-dressed executives are all sitting unhappily on one end of the table—all twelve of them—and I sit at the other end, next to Anne. It is as awkward as it sounds. I've always said "Hi" to them when I see them in the elevator, but I've never actually had a work-related meeting with them.

Here's the situation, I say to the execs, who are all men. *We lack focus. We let users create blog posts, discussions, documents, status updates, trophies, virtual awards, virtual pints, virtual spanks, instant messages, text messages, direct messages, indirect messages, ephemeral messages, ethereal messages, action items, inaction items, groups, projects, spaces, places, bases. We're making it too hard on ourselves. Our collaboration has turned into a maze that is terrifying for the newcomer and tedious to the veteran. Every day I have to sift through too many confusing types of messages.*

I've got their attention now.

Exec #1 says, *But we have to eat our own dog food. It's the only way to make sure we understand the product before we give it to others.*

I say, *If your dog food told you to jump off a building, would you play ball?*

The execs look at each other in confusion. Anne looks at me with serious discomfort. If she could text me the emoji of Munch's *The Scream* without the execs being offended, she'd do it.

Let me try again, I say. *I guess it's fine that we eat our own dog food, but why the hell do we have so many closets full of dog food? We are using every old closet from every past dysfunctional relationship. And we're scared to clean those closets. And we're not really imagining what this thing could be for a new generation of more diverse worker bees.* I'm a little horrified by how many metaphors are spewing out of me.

Exec #2 says, *OK, big shot. So what do you think we should do?*

Well, I say. *Simplify. Even a basic discussion is no longer a great experience. Why not just make one thing great and not try to do so many things just because it seemed like a good idea three years ago and we're scared to get rid of it now?*

I have this confidence that came from I don't know where. It's like I've got all the bullshitting powers of Papa with all the career authority of my father and all the creative powers of my son.

Exec #3 says, *What makes our product amazing is that we work with just about everything. We are the king of integrations.*

Is that really true? I say.

Exec #4 and #5 say, *Yes.*

I say, *I thought our product was amazing because it makes collaboration a delight.*

Exec #6 writes that down.

Exec #7 says, *Where did you hear that?*

My phone vibrates, and against my serious-guy-in-serious-job judgment, I look at the dumb thing. The push-notification gods punish me with a notification from the gamification plug-in:

```
{ company_rating    : "sucks balls",
  next_step         : "strap on spare underwear,
                       or flip existing underwear
                       inside out!" }
```

Exec #7 says, *Excuse me. I'm sorry to bother you during your precious text message, but where did you hear that bit about collaboration being a delight?*

Oh, I say, *I just made it up.*

Anne would send a furious poop emoji right now if she could.

Exec #8 says, *Do you have anything to say that didn't come from your ass?*

He's wearing an orange band around his wrist, and I try to remember what it symbolizes. Maybe some kind of cancer or mood disorder. I already feel bad for not donating to this orange cause.

I say, *Someone more nimble and more compelling will destroy us.*

Exec #9 says, *What will they do that we can't do better?*

I say, *Do you even pay attention to what the kids are using these days? Their chats don't even involve text anymore. They're pictures, they're videos, they're scribbles, they're stickers, they're pulses on the wrist.*

Exec #10 makes an arrogant chuckle and says, *Our customers are not children.*

I say, *They aren't?* I look around at all twelve of them. *When is the next round of layoffs? And why do we have so many executives? And why is Anne the only woman in this room?*

Anne's face turns red. Exec #11 looks at his ten counterparts like they're all wondering how long it would take for IT to disable my account. (The answer is: less than a hundred milliseconds.)

Exec #12 says, *Why the hell should we listen to you?*

I spend a few seconds thinking about it. They don't have many obvious reasons to trust me. I don't know if I can do this job. But I don't want to lose it either. I'm angry at Anne for having faith in me.

I say to the execs, *You don't have to listen to me. But I think our software is a confusing piece of shit. And even though I'd rather sit on the toilet and write my novel than give someone a Virtual Pint of Beer, I still think about these problems a lot. And maybe I'm one of the crazy assholes you need to think about if you want to make this thing compelling to everyone. Knowing our product as intimately as I do, I'm not convinced with what I see today.*

I'm a little dizzy from talking and so I pause and take in a deep breath. And then I say this last thing really slowly because it feels like the only thing I need to say today: *When we advertise that we take collaboration to the next level, trademark, we need to ask ourselves if we're actually taking things to a better level. The next level has got to help us feel more connected to each other.*

I stand up. I spread my arms out. I say, *I'm talking about an actual human connection.*

Execs #1 through #12 all stare at me, and I'm honestly not sure if they are horrified or amazed. I feel like I'm naked for a moment, but even stranger, it's not so bad. I feel strong.

#

I don't hear from Anne or the execs the next few days after the devangelism meeting. I focus on researching other companies that Anne wants me to assess. I scour their CollabHub databases for hints about company health. It's kind of fun—to snoop in on how corporate assholes behave online and think about how to fine-tune their CollabHub systems for less asshole-y behavior. I don't know if they'll want to hear what I have to say, but for now, I practically enjoy the work.

I use my false sense of work-related authority to drive over to Kitty's apartment. I run up the stairs and knock on the door quickly before I can think too hard about what I'm doing.

A grumpy, sleepy voice says, *Hang on.* I didn't even consider that it might be too early to be knocking. I check my watch. It is seven thirty in the morning. I just dropped off my boy at school.

It's been a month since I've seen her. I don't know if it's the devangelism or the book or the boy or the time with my dad, or just time, but I missed her, and I felt like this time it might be different than before. She told me not to text, but she didn't say I couldn't visit.

She's wearing a man's oxford on top, and baby blue sweatpants.

Oh, she says, when she sees me.

Oh, I say. *I'm sorry. It is too early. I should have called. Are you alone? I'm sorry. Should I go? Is this wrong?*

She waves her hand at me and blinks her eyes in a very fake sexy way. *You probably say that to all the women.*

I've missed her humor. And her fake sexy is actually sexy.

She says, *It is too early. You should have called. I am alone. You shouldn't go. This may be wrong. Come inside.*

#

The mantle above Kitty's fireplace contains farm animal piggy banks. Her bookshelf is half-full of books that seem to be about science and religion (like she stole everything my father has ever sent me), and half full of piggy banks. One piggy bank looks like headphones and one like a book and there's one of a volcano and one that's like a fourth-generation iPhone and one that's a hand grenade and one of an Uzi. And there are others, too, all over the place. A sideboard (which is a term my ex-wife made me use when I kept calling something in our house a furniture thingy) is covered with piggy banks. A toilet piggy bank. An ear piggy bank right next to a Van Gogh *Starry Night* piggy bank. Sexy, dancing girl piggy banks. The planets.

On the coffee table, there's a naked-man-covering-his-schmeckel piggy bank. Right next to a naked man *not* covering his schmeckel.

Next to these schmeckels, I see the science book my dad gave me. And beside that book, I see a copy of my first book. My only published book. It is well-worn and a big dog-eared mess in a way that does my heart good. Until I get a flash of fear, realizing that now she knows too much about me. The book is face-down and she has scribbled all over the back cover. Tiny sketches that I instantly recognize as the fragile little characters from my book—characters who once consumed me completely and now feel like they're from a different lifetime.

Here's the craziest thing about her place: there is a boom arm hanging from the ceiling, but instead of a microphone on the end, there is a giant monitor on it, just hovering above the coffee table, and all this Etsy and eBay information is shooting by on the screen with an app that's like a digital ticker tape. On the coffee table is a wireless keyboard and a wireless mouse in the shape of a pig.

Holy shit, I say.

Are you going to insult me? Make a dumb joke? She pushes the floating monitor to the side as we sit down. And then she plays with a top button on her shirt, opening and closing it, and I don't know if it's impatience or insecurity or flirtation.

I've never seen anything like this, I say. *Did you set this all up yourself?*

Nobody else here to help me, she says.

I'm awestruck. But it's more than awe. I'm jealous. All my activities are so intangible—code for work, words for the novel.

Just wow, I say. I pick up the naked guys on the table.

Take a final look at them because I have to send them off today.

How much? I ask. *If that's not too personal.*

It's not personal, she says. *It's business. Thirty dollars for the guy showing his cock. Seventy dollars for the guy covering up.*

Piggy porn, I say. She doesn't smile. Her eyes are greener than I remembered.

The fee, she says, *for barging in on me is breakfast.*

#

While she packages up the schmeckel banks, I dig through her under-stocked kitchen, trying to make an omelet.

I'm sad about how she doesn't seem excited to see me. I mean, I know I'm barging in unannounced, but I had a fantasy that we would click more easily. Maybe it's just me being lonely, but I haven't been able to stop thinking about her.

It turns out that I make a kick-ass omelet. A fallout from divorce. I'm an expert at making a depressed divorcé breakfast that doubles as a single parent / only child breakfast (and triples as a dinner when you forget to eat breakfast and lunch). Her kitchen is pretty barren, but I make do with garlic, bell peppers, tortilla chips, cheddar cheese, potatoes, molasses, and cayenne. I bring it over to her as she's finishing up her work and put it on the coffee table. I tell her that I made her my special Sicilian omelet.

I didn't peg you as a Sicilian, she says, still not fully present with me in this room.

I'm not, I say.

So what makes it Sicilian?

I say, *It's just that I can't stop watching* The Godfather *ever since Anne's husband started talking about it.*

Wow. Weird. She takes a few bites. *Yummy, but weird.*

Maybe she's warming up to me. Maybe she was just hungry. But still,

I want to get a better feel for how she's doing. I say, *So how are you doing really?*

She pushes her hair away from her face. *OK*, she says. *Working through the muck.*

How was the meditation retreat thing?

The thing was pretty good. I mean, I actually can meditate now without yelling about how meditation is stupid while I'm trying to meditate. And I learned to draw with the right side of the brain.

That sounds great, I say. *Yelling and meditation don't mix so well.*

She smiles, but she still looks so serious. She looks older. Not her body, which looks even more vibrant than before, but something inside her body. There's a calm about her. And her calm makes me nervous.

She leans over and whispers, *I really needed it.*

I'm not sure why she is whispering, but I like that she's getting closer to me. I say, *What do you think was the magic of it?*

I don't know exactly, she says. *I mean, maybe it was the meditation and getting clean. But also it was the time away. It was the art. It was the people.* She looks up at the ceiling and says, *I really liked the people. They even liked my jokes.*

I say, *Who wouldn't like your jokes?*

She gives me a kind look. I get shy and look down at the copy of my book next to the piggy banks. I wonder if Kitty knows how autobiographical that book is. My ex hated how I wrote her into the story.

She says, *I feel more comfortable.* Then she puts one hand to her chest and says, *With me being me.*

Wow, I say. *I'm so glad to hear this, Kitty.* It's true that I am happy for her. But there's also a part of me that's jealous that she's had this experience. It's like she skipped a few grades and I'm still looking at her from my rickety desk way back in middle school. She's all mature and cool and beautiful, and I'm still brooding about that girl who didn't want to go with me to the dance.

Yeah, she says. She picks up a piggy bank. *I just needed some time to look inside myself, I guess.* And she puts the thing down.

Wait a second, I say, and I grab a piggy bank. *How do you get the money out from inside this thing?* I turn it all around, looking for a slot to uncork.

She looks at me for a while to verify I'm that dumb, which I suspect I am.

You break the thing. Duh!

You destroy this beautiful, unkosher pig?

Well, you do if you want to treat the piggy bank like a piggy bank.

That's so sad, I say.

It's beautiful, she says, and she really means it, even though I don't fully understand why.

We sit there quietly for a little while.

How is your boy doing? She puts her hands to her heart. Her eyes get watery. *I miss him.*

He's good. He's good. He's gotten into drawing things. It's nice.

She's perfectly lovely, and my boy is totally crazy about her, but all this gives me a heartache from the risk of it all. One of the things about being divorced with a kid is not being able to share this crazy love for your kid. And when you see someone's affection for your kid, you feel that longing to share the love, but you also know that whatever this person feels, it's never going to be enough.

She says to me, *I could help him get even better at drawing. He already has so many great instincts.*

I nod again, I think maybe I'm smiling, but I don't say anything. My boy keeps asking when we can see Kitty and I keep stalling, hoping he'll forget.

Her piggy bank monitor makes a few melodic beeps and she looks up at it and then looks back at me. *How is work?* she says.

It's weird. I kind of have a new job at my job. I actually like it. I think I'm good at it. If I don't get fired first.

Kitty's a good listener. Those eyes track me closely and I know that I can't bullshit her about what I'm doing here.

Listen, I say, *I want to apologize to you.*

About what?

That night at my ex-wife's.

You don't need to apologize. We both weren't in the right place.

I don't know how to be. A part of me wants to dive right in and take in all that she is, and another part keeps running back to the other she, my ex-wife, the mother of my kid, a woman who already knows exactly what to like and what to dislike about me. But my ex is my ex, and this woman is right here, closing and opening the button on her shirt.

Whose shirt is that? I ask.

My ex's, she says.

How the fuck are we ever going to get past our past?

I reach out to touch Kitty's collar and rub my thumb against it. *It's a nice fabric. What is this? Like a five-hundred thread count?*

She looks up at me, real shy. *Um,* she says. *I think you are mixing me up with bedsheets.*

I pull her and her shirt closer to me, and then kiss her.

#

You've learned a few things from the Sicilians, she says to me.

We're both naked in her bed and spooning, her on the inside, my lips against the back of her neck. She is so warm, and it is so comfortable.

Even though my ringer is off, my phone vibrates from wherever it is, and based on the vibration pattern, I know it's from the fucking gamification plug-in. This continual reminder of my previous sins that I can't seem to undo.

Before this happened, she says, pressing her ass back into me, *I was going to ask if you'd like to try hanging out again. And also maybe drawing lessons for your boy.*

Umm, I say. *Can we reverse back into that place we were at an hour ago?*

Not really, she says.

As good as it felt to have sex with Kitty, I wish we hadn't. I feel like we cheated the system, like when you play a game of Chutes and Ladders and you land on one of those ridiculous ladders and skip over way too many steps and you know you're going to pay a price with the next chute.

I say, *I was worried that I couldn't pull it off with, you know, someone different.*

Kitty sits up quickly. I love her breasts.

Is that what this is? she says. I realize she is annoyed with me. *Is this a can-I-fuck-someone-other-than-my-ex test? A rebound fuck?*

No, I say. *No.*

Kitty puts her shirt back on. She doesn't look at me when she says, *Tell me this. Are you over your ex-wife or are you still stuck on her?*

The woman who just put on her ex's shirt is asking me if I'm stuck on my ex. I want to say NO—I'm even legally divorced now!—but the answer is more complicated than that. I may not be wearing my ex's shirt, but I'm wearing the years anyway, all those arguments, life with her and the boy, the burden of the novel, the custody discussions, memories of lying in bed together on a Saturday morning, walking across the Hawthorne Bridge, us holding hands, both a little drunk as we make fun of romantic comedies that we love anyway.

I say to Kitty, *I don't know if I'm stuck.*

I don't hear from you in a month and you come over to fuck me and you don't know if you're over your ex?

Kitty stands up and looks down at me. When I was lying in bed last night thinking about Kitty and this visit, I was all in. I wanted her. Not just her body, but her mind, her wit, her vicious honesty. I had all the confidence of my devangelism in me and I was ready to win her over. To come here and say to her, *Here I am! Here you are! Let's do this thing!* But that man is gone now, and I'm scared all over again.

I say, *Let me explain,* and I reach out to grab her, but she moves away so fast and so fierce that I fall off the bed and smash into the ground, right on my ass bone.

I'm on the floor in pain and she stands above me without saying anything. I don't say anything either. My back burns like hell and my toes tingle.

Then Kitty says, *I think I want you to leave.*

I stand up quickly even though my back aches and my legs aren't yet fully under my control.

I say, *Can't we try this again?* It takes me forever to get my legs in my pants.

She grabs my dad's science book and hands it to me. She says, *I have a thing to do.*

Are you sure? I say. *If you give me a do over, I might be 57 percent less awkward.*

She closes her eyes and breathes in a way that I suspect is meditation-retreat breathing. When she opens her eyes, she says to me, *I just need more time.*

She walks me to the door. She opens the door and says, *Next time, text me before dropping in.*

I step out of her apartment and as I'm about to try one last repair attempt, the door closes.

Chapter Thirteen: Sacred Objects

Luckily, this new job thing is keeping me pretty occupied even if I feel a new sort of pressure to succeed. But my back is on fire after the Kitty incident. And I haven't checked in on my dad in a few days—he's doing better, but I'm struggling to call him, with so many things in my life in flux. I leave for lunch a little bit early and grab a burger and a gin and tonic at the McMenamin's pub near my office so I can bask in the comfort of mediocre food and mediocre service but in a cozy atmosphere where I can exist unjudged and unpressured for a half hour.

I write with a pad and pen I find sitting at the bar. The only thing on the page are the words "Stuff To Do" and nothing else.

The gin doesn't work, and my back starts aching worse and worse. In fact, the pain is so bad that I occasionally have to close my eyes and tighten all the muscles in my torso as I tear up from the pain.

Fucking Kitty.

Some drunk next to me burps on my page, and I smell the tater tots and bourbon. He says, *Whatcha doing with that homework over there?*

I say, *It's not homework.*

He coughs a few times, and he swallows another shot of bourbon and drinks half a beer and then burps again and says, *Then what's the point?*

I try to move my body around to make it hurt less but the pain is so sharp down my leg that I say, *Fuck me*, and there's a spasm in my back and I fall off the stool.

The tater tot drunk helps me up. He is incredibly forceful and also incredibly careful with me like he knows exactly where it hurts and what I need. I thank him.

You gotta take better care of yourself, he tells me.

Instead of going back to work, I call my wife. Ex-wife.

#

Are you being straight with me? she asks.

Yeah, I say. *I swear to you.*

Why don't you contact one of your friends about this?

I look around the bar, at the sleepy bartender and at the tater tot drunk who just ordered another round of tater tots and beer.

She sighs, as ex-wives are prone to do. *OK,* she says, and then digitally shares contact information for Daniel's chiropractic office.

#

Daniel's office is a Craftsman home on Division Street that somehow dodged the great rebuilding of the street into generic multi-use developments. Inside, the floors creak, and the living room is the front desk and waiting room. He uses the two bedrooms for his adjustment rooms. X-rays are done in the kitchen. There is a working dumbwaiter that is used for laundry. I learned all this by reading his pamphlet while getting an x-ray in the kitchen from one of his assistants.

What is it with this guy and dumbwaiters?

Daniel seems very pleased to see me, like maybe this is his chance to crush me. I walk into his bedroom office with a feeling of failure. More than usual.

Daniel says, *OK. Let me try to understand this.* He is looking at the x-ray of my lower back, my vertebra glowing brightly against the lighting. *This happened because you got tossed around in bed?*

Well, not exactly in bed, I say. *Off bed, you could say.*

His curious expression shifts from all business, to not-quite-all-business.

Forgive me for asking, he says, *but I thought you weren't dating Kitty anymore?*

I'm not.

I see, he says. And he's looking at me so closely, like he is trying to figure me out, he almost falls off his little doctor stool looking at me.

He sniffs the air. *Have you been drinking?*

Listen, I say, and I point at my x-ray, and even the motion of my arm stings in my back. *Is it OK to work on that messed-up part of me before we work through my other parts?*

Sorry, he says. *I probably should have been a therapist instead of a chiropractor.* He shakes out of it and then stands up and looks at the x-ray for a bit longer.

His hair is so shiny. He's a walking shampoo commercial.

While looking at the x-ray, he says, *Your L5 is slipped forward.*

Am I going to die, doc?

He turns around to look at me. *What?* he says. *Oh. No. Not from this.* He nearly walks over to pat me on the shoulder. Nearly.

I'm just kidding, I say, sad for my ex who is dating this humorless man.

He points up and down the x-ray. *It's not because of the bed thing. This problem is an old one. You've had it for decades. Probably a genetic defect. It's just that various*—he makes a rolling gesture with his hand that really does remind me of falling off that bed—*activities . . . cause the area to swell up, pinching some of the nerves in that area.*

It burns from my back down to my toes to hear him say this. I say, *What do I do about it now? Lie on the couch and mope about the shitty things I inherited from my parents?*

That is one solution. This man treats my suggestion as an actual suggestion.

And . . . another solution?

Well, an MD would jack you up on anti-inflammatories for years until you rot a hole in your stomach or kidney.

And you'd suggest what exactly?

Well, he says, *it wouldn't be bad to take some anti-inflammatories for a few days to take the edge off, but you'll need to do some serious core-strength-ening exercises to keep this thing from giving you troubles the rest of your life.*

You're not going to adjust me?

I could if it would make you feel better.

What about surgery?

Well, that's messy business. Those muscles and nerves are connected to every other part of your body. You can't mess around with one thing without messing with everything.

I see, I say. *So how long do I need to do these exercises?*

The rest of your life. He takes a long, heavy breath. *That is, if you decide you care about your spinal cord.*

I'll have to think about that, I say. *It hasn't done much for me lately.*

And you have to make sure that you have good ergonomics at your desk, at what's that company, collaboration something or other?

CollaborationHub, I say.

Yeah, right, they take collaboration to a special level or something like that, right? He's trying to remember the slogan in such a genuine and annoying way.

They take collaboration to the next level, I say.

Right, yeah, he says, more satisfied with the slogan than I am. *You don't seem like you believe in their motto.*

I don't believe in much right now, I say.

Listen Saul, do you actually want to get better?

I say, *Are you like this with my wife?*

Ex-wife, he corrects.

Or with my boy?

You want me to be honest with you, Saul?

I don't answer him.

He says, *I don't like you. But I like your ex-wife. And I like your boy. And because of them, I want you to get better. But I have to wonder: why won't you take yourself seriously?*

How seriously do I need to take myself? I'm not sure I want to be as serious as you.

He stares at me for a long time, with his glasses on this time. And I try not to look away. In my head, I start counting by threes to distract myself from the discomfort.

When I get to thirty-nine, Daniel bursts out laughing.

And then I laugh too. I don't know why. But we both laugh so hard together, to the point that I have to help him stay standing.

I give it to him unfiltered and unfunny: *Doc, I'm scared of change. Even good change. But I'm almost willing to accept that things need to change.*

He hands me five pages of exercises and these exercises don't just have to do with my back, but with muscles all over my body. Which scares me. Why do we have to bring other muscles into this mess? Can't we cherry-pick the important stuff?

He says as if he knows me better than me: *Saul, I am sure you can stumble your way onto the right path if you want to. But when I look at you*—he looks at me for too long, and he sniffs the air again—*when I look at you, I'm not sure I see a man who wants to be on the right path.*

#

Outside Daniel's office there's a homeless guy in a flannel blanket walking down the sidewalk yelling about how the fucking barista didn't understand his fucking situation. And walking the opposite direction on the same sidewalk is a man in a suit with Bluetooth earpods yelling about what time he fucking wants them to reschedule the fucking meeting. Both these Portland men scare me, so I pretend to focus on the pages in my hand until they pass.

It's so odd and so perfectly Daniel-working-from-a-Craftsman-home that he'd give me actual, physical pages for my exercises. They are even bad xeroxed copies of exercises. Of course, I'll snap a shot of them with my phone, run them through an optical character recognition system, and recycle the pages, but at the moment, it's kind of nice to have a real physical thing to hold for my real physical pain. My genetic defect.

#

On the way to pick up my boy from school, I call my dad. When I ask him how he is doing, he says, *I'm just suffering from old.*

But you're feeling OK? I ask. *Your blood pressure is OK?*

It's still too high. But what the hell do these doctors know? They are more like failed mechanics than scientists.

How's the atheism going? I ask him.

It's not a thing that comes and goes, he says.

#

At school, my kid immediately notices how hard it is for me to get back into the car.

What's wrong, Dada?

Every time I imagine Kitty throwing me off the bed, my back does another spasm and I tear up.

Oh, I say. *It's nothing. I just slept funny last night.*

That's weird, he says. *You didn't walk like that in the morning.*

As if woken up by our conversation, my car stereo recites a gamification message:

```
communication error  : data irretrievable
```

#

We get back home, and as my boy goes to the couch, he says, *What's that thing?*

What's what thing?

His hand is digging between the cushions, a place where there is always danger lurking.

When he pulls his hand out, he is holding onto the zebra octopus he sewed from a sock. The present he gave Kitty that night.

His face goes from confused to sad. Tears in the corners of his eyes.

Then he looks at me and his expression turns to something else. When I cheated on a girlfriend a long time ago, I remember when telling her about it, her face started out in a kind of pain, like an organ inside her was not functioning right, but then I saw the switch flip in her eyes, and the emotion went outward, it went angry, and I could feel the danger of being in her sights, it felt more dangerous right then than when she slapped me a second later, which was somehow a relief. My boy's face looks like that anger.

My boy yells, *You promised me! You told me! You said so!*

The heat is so hot and so big and I still do not know why.

The spasm in my back shoots up to my neck and down to my left toes and I squeeze my eyes shut and tighten my abs and I squeeze out the words: *What is it? What did I promise?*

You told me that Kitty had this. He shakes the zebra octopus with each syllable. *This was su-pposed to be for Ki-tty.*

Relax, I say. *She must have forgotten it.*

No, he says. *You told me she had it. You lied to me. All this time. You said it was with her.* He squeezes the object so hard that you can see the shape of the quarter he sewed inside it. *You lied to me!*

Hey! I say in a raised voice that even surprises me. *Don't talk to me that way!*

He's breathing real big and angry and his forehead is so tight.

I've never seen him so upset. I've never felt this kind of weakness before. I want to do anything to make it stop. But I have no idea what to do.

He says, *I hate you,* and races to his bedroom with the octopus.

#

He stays in his room for hours. I brood about whether to knock, or open the door, or bust down the door, or beg, or yell, or cry. Or run away.

It is such an enormous ache in me that he feels this way. I hate the powerlessness of it. I hate Kitty for leaving this octopus with me. I toy with getting plastered but decide to hold off in case I need to be at my best if he comes out of his room.

Except the pain in my back is so bad. I gulp down two shots of vodka and four Advil.

I grab the sock iPad that he sewed for me and I squeeze onto it as I prepare myself to knock on his door. I want to show him that I have treasured the thing he made me and maybe that should make things OK between us, but I know it won't. It doesn't help her.

I say, *You need to eat dinner.*

I have a stomach ache, he says through the door.

Is it serious?

I don't need a doctor, he says to me. *I just want to be alone.*

I can just slip something under the door.

A moment passes. I hear a few footsteps. And then: *A plate wouldn't fit under the door.*

I'm sorry, I say. *I should have made sure she got the octopus.*

He is quiet for long enough that I consider saying it again. But then he says, *It's OK.* Even though I know it's not.

#

I hold onto the sock iPad during the night. I don't really sleep. I just wait for the seconds to pass until morning.

Not only did my boy take the time to sew apps into this thing, he sewed the exact apps that I like to use. All the stupid messaging and collaboration and writing crap that I have on there—he got all the colors and shapes just right.

I write a little to kill some time. I used to like writing in the middle of the night when everyone else was sleeping, but it doesn't feel good tonight. The story feels as stuck as my life. Papa is drunk and sitting under the table at his store, the spot where his boy normally plays. The rifle is next to Papa even though he does not know how to use it. Papa connects with his son in the graphic novel he is writing but does not know how to connect in real life. The Klan is coming for him. If this were an actual graphic novel, you'd be able to make out the torches in the distance out of the storefront window.

#

Normally my kid is up early, but I wait until 7:15 a.m. and then knock on his door.

I say, *You need to get moving. We'll be late for school.*

There's no answer.

I open the door. The window is open. My boy is gone.

"#transitions are essential for growth. but
keep in mind that you'll probably die first, so
transitions don't mean shit." —@buddhabum14

Chapter Fourteen: Serenity Later

My ex-wife gets to my apartment in minutes. She's in tears, quiet tears going down her face that she wipes away quickly with her hand, and she's sitting on the couch next to me as we talk to the cop who just arrived. My boy has been gone almost an hour at this point, and maybe for longer. She's already set up a phone tree with her friends in the neighborhood who are looking for him right now. This is why people maintain friendships. Real friendships with real people who you talk to in real life and help when there are real problems. I get it now. And it's a good thing at least one of us knows how to do this. While the cop asks questions, she keeps grabbing onto my leg and squeezing. I put my hand on hers. Divorce is not a thing right now.

I say to the cop, *He has never done anything like this.*

I hate being indoors right now. I'm claustrophobic in here. I want to be out there. Searching for him.

The cop says, *But you had a fight with him last night, right?* He has a deep voice and he's chunky, fits fully in his uniform, and he seems to have no emotion about this situation. He didn't lose his boy. There are too many different things on his belt. I can't distinguish the gun from the taser from the pepper spray from the flashlight. He's not even taking notes. He's sucking on a cough drop or something with a horrible artificial lemon smell that makes me want to vomit.

I shouldn't have called the police.

I pace the room, trying to think about where he could be.

My wife explains on her phone to the tenth person that our boy ran away while he was on my watch.

The cop says, *Does your boy have a name?*

What? I say.

He says, *Your boy. His name.*

Oh, yes, of course. August. August Baum. We call him Auggie.

The cop coughs. He says to me, *So what exactly did you argue about?*

I take a breath. I say, *He found something in this couch.*

The cop pulls out a notepad, finally, from who knows where. *What did he find?* His pen is out, and now he is looking at me like maybe I hid my son. Like maybe I did it. Like maybe it is all my fault.

I say, *A zebra octopus.*

A what what?

I say, *An octopus with zebra stripes.*

Is that even a thing?

Yes, I say. *I mean, no. It was something that he sewed for my girlfriend.*

My ex looks up from her phone when I say this.

The cop says, *So did you contact your girlfriend?*

Oh, I say. *I'm not talking to her. She's not my girlfriend.*

My ex goes back to searching her digital Rolodex.

The cop keeps staring at me. *Where does your girlfriend live?*

I say to the cop, *The boy is seven for Christ's sake. He has no idea where Kitty lives. She's not even my girlfriend anymore.*

The cop says, *Where does this Kitty live?*

I say, *About a half mile from here. On Stark. But he's never been there.*

And then it hits me. My iPad. It's not in the living room bookshelf in that area Auggie calls *the iPad nest* and it's not on the coffee table and it's not under the coffee table in that spot he calls *the iPad hideout* and it's not in my backpack and it's not in his backpack or on the kitchen table or on my bed or on his bed.

While I'm scouring the apartment, the cop is slowly following me, turning around and around again as I swoop through the house in my completely inefficient way. Eventually, the man says, *Um, sir?*

I feel an incredible relief in not finding the device. Auggie's got it. I can search for the iPad with my phone. I've never been so appreciative of buying the stupid model with a stupid GPS.

It takes five seconds to pinpoint the location. I say, *It's at Kitty's! He's at Kitty's!*

My ex stands up fast. She has her hand to her chest and she looks right at me and she says with such a slow big force, *Are. You. Sure?*

I grab my phone and I see that I already have a voicemail. The message has been sitting there for eight minutes and I didn't realize it. From Kitty. I missed it. Because I'm an idiot.

The voicemail says, *He's here. He's OK. He's fine. Come.* Her voice is a whisper, but it's loud, and it's intimate.

I look at my wife. *Yes. He's OK.*

My ex says, *Thank God!* We hug. She wipes the snot from her nose on my shirt and this all feels so good.

The cop shakes his head and breathes out a big lemon breath in my direction.

I say to the cop as a way to apologize for ignoring his suggestion that turned out to be exactly correct: *It's funny, I guess he learned how to use the map app quicker than I thought he would.*

Funny, the cop says without a smile.

He tells me that child protective services may want to speak with me about this. I say, *Of course,* even though I'm thinking, what the fuck do they want from me?

I convince my wife to let me get him alone. She'll wait here. She'll call off the search party. And I promise to come straight home as fast as I can. *No funny business,* she says to me, and I have no idea what she means, except I wonder what details Daniel told her about my visit to his office.

I say to my wife, *Nothing is funny.*

#

I race to Kitty's door and blast it open without knocking and there is my boy on the couch with an enormous glass of milk.

It's a weird sight. He looks older—not that he is any bigger—but he holds onto that glass of milk with the confidence of how my dad holds onto a martini, like everything in the world was unbearable until receiving this beverage that makes everything OK again. It's red around his eyes and they're swollen and his hair is too messy and he's wearing yesterday's clothes and his ears are red.

Dada, he says holding his milk martini, *you should knock next time.*

Auggie! I yell, and I hug him so tightly, and he says, *It hurts*, and I say, *I know*, and I keep hugging him, and then he says, *No, you're hurting me*, and I say, *Oh*, and let him go and see that he spilled some milk on my pants.

Kitty's floating TV that once was showing eBay auctions is now playing *The Octonauts.*

The sewn zebra octopus is on the coffee table. On top of my battered book.

Kitty walks in like she's been hosting my kid for a year. She hands him a bowl of blueberries and he says, *Thanks.*

She's wearing her ex's shirt again and leggings that show off those leg muscles. She smiles sweetly at me, like this is how it is supposed to go. I have this mixture of joy and hatred at seeing her so at ease.

Honey, she says to him. *I'm going to speak with your dad in the other room.*

He nods at us, holding a handful of blueberries. Not a hint of anger inside him.

#

She sits down on her bed. And I sit down a foot away from her. And neither of us talks.

This bed where we fucked and then I crashed to the floor and then she kicked me out.

I shake my finger at her. *What did you tell him? Did you promise him anything? Why isn't he mad at me?*

Relax, she says. *He asked if I could teach him to draw better and I just told him that I'd talk to you about it. No promises.*

No, I say. I smack my hand on my thigh. *I don't like this.*

I'd be very reliable about this. You can trust me on this.

I say it slow and loud: *I don't like this.*

Saul, she says. *I know you want to protect him, but you can't protect him the way you think you can protect him.*

She puts her hand on my leg like my last failed visit never happened, and I tense up all over. And for the first time since Auggie ran away, I'm aware of how fucked up my back is. It explodes through me so I can't tell if it's muscle or nerve or bone or blood. I don't know where it starts or ends. It just hurts.

My watch taps me and even though I don't look at it, Kitty looks at my watch face and then says, *What the hell does this mean?* She pushes my wrist towards my face:

```
{ communication_error :
    "flushing invalid gamification data.
     messing with data structure until it works.
     hopefully. ouch." }
```

I double over and vomit on her floor.

It feels like everything inside of me comes out.

Kitty drops to the floor quickly, like reflex, like she wants to be ready to catch me if I fall off the bed, like she's not scared to be near my vomit. She puts both her hands against my legs and says, *Relax. It's OK.*

But—

She interrupts me. *Relax. Lie down.* Then she stands up and has me lie down on her bed. She handles my back carefully as if she knows exactly where it hurts. Somehow she can get me lying down without a lick of pain.

She leaves the room and I hear her tell Auggie to give us a few more minutes and I wonder how in the world everything can get fixed in a few minutes and I close my eyes and pretend that I can rewind the world to a point where things didn't seem complicated, I rewind past today, past yesterday, before my boy got mad at me, before sex with Kitty, before the aquarium, before gelato, before divorce, before the boy, before Mom died, before I had to pretend to be an adult, before it all. I don't know where to stop.

Kitty comes back to the room with a warm washcloth that she pats around my face.

The warmth is such a relief.

Are you OK? she asks. More softly and more patiently than I feel like I deserve.

I nod.

She cleans up my vomit, like it's just a routine thing, like she's cleaning the kitchen, even humming a tune while she does it.

I'm sorry, I say.

Hush, she tells me.

Her sweetness is so comforting to be around when everything feels like a mess inside of me. My ex turned to annoyance much faster in these situations.

Auggie says, *Dad?* from the other room. It's a perfectly normal voice he's using and it feels like he is calling me for a perfectly normal need.

My ex-wife is waiting for us at home and has probably sent me a hundred messages by now.

I sit myself up, which is a lot more painful than when Kitty got me down. I reach out to touch her hair, but when I touch it, I don't know what to do next and so I let go. We both look at each other and then look away.

I say to Kitty, *We should go.*

Of course, she whispers. She nods fast. I see it in her—she doesn't want us to go, even though I just vomited all over her floor. She still likes me after everything that's happened and I don't know why.

#

He's quiet all the way home. And I can't quite get words out myself.

When we park the car, he starts walking back to my apartment and he's moving too fast and I'm limping. I say, *Wait!* I yell it by mistake.

He turns with a scare.

I say, *I need you to promise me that you won't run away.*

He doesn't say anything.

I know it's sometimes hard with me. And I'm sorry that I didn't know that Kitty didn't have your octopus. And I know you don't understand why we can't see Kitty more often. But I'm scared.

He says, *She's the least scary person we know.*

Two things. I hold up a few fingers. *First of all, it is very hard to have a romantic relationship when two people are working on personal problems. And second of all, I don't want you to get hurt if she comes into our lives and then has to go away again.*

Dad? he says.

What? I say. Trying really hard not to cry.

You're holding up three fingers.

I look at my fingers and of course he's right. *Oh,* I say.

So what's the third thing?

Three, I say. *It's pretty darn complicated being a dad.*

Somehow, this last thing, this thing that is about the stupidest thing a dad can say to a little kid is the thing. His tears start coming down fast, faster than he can wipe them, and I run over to him, and even though I feel the pain in my back it doesn't stop me. I pick him up and I hug him and he says to me, *That third thing is not even a thing.*

My wife races out of my apartment and yells out *Auggie!* and she comes over and hugs him and me and we're all in this awkward ridiculous hug thing together and it feels like everything.

#

We agree that Auggie can go to my wife's place even though he's technically supposed to stay with me for two more days. It's hard to allow this, but the look of longing on my wife's face is even more fierce than what I feel, and I feel a feeling as fierce as I can possibly imagine.

I also want my ex out of here because I'm feeling something weird inside me going from Kitty's place to here and I could use some time alone.

I give Auggie a super duper hug, as he calls them, and I twirl him around even though my body hates the feeling of it and I tell him I love him.

He doesn't ask me about whether he can visit Kitty and I'm appreciative to at least have some time to think about it.

#

That night, I get a text from my wife: *so what are you going to do about Auggie and Kitty?*

It's weird seeing these two names together.

I say: *What do you think I should do?*

She says: *It's your call. I trust your judgment.*

That makes one of us.

Be serious.

Sorry. Let me sit on it for a few days.

OK.

I say: *Merry dreams, Julia.*

She says: *What did you just say?*

I say: *Merry dreams? I just wanted to screw up the cliché.*

She says: *No. The Julia part. It's nice to hear you call me by my name for a change.*

I have a craving to drink. I don't know if it's different than normal, but I'm more aware of the bottle of gin in the cupboard, the pimento olives in the fridge, the vodka at my writing desk. I want to sip on something that burns on the way down, something that touches me in many different spots and reminds me of all the feelings inside of me.

I grab the bottle of vodka and I get the exercise instructions that Daniel gave me. With these crappy xeroxed pages and the half empty bottle, I get down on the floor, and do my exercises. I don't drink anything. I use the bottle instead of the foam roller suggested by the exercises. To roll up and down my quadriceps.

While I'm rolling out my tight muscles, I remember this thing my mom used to say to me: *You gotta stop banging your damn head against the wall even if it feels good to do it.* I never understood what the hell she was talking about, which wasn't so unusual—she said a lot of stuff I didn't understand. Back then I didn't get why it would feel good. But now it makes more sense. It's time to move on with my life even if I somehow get some comfort from banging my head against the wall.

I'm lying on the floor after stretching and I'm staring up at the bottom of my wooden coffee table and I think about my story of Papa and my father, and now, Catty. I can picture Papa with his boy, both of them sitting underneath the storeroom table that is covered with bolts of cloth. Papa and his boy are down there working on the graphic novel while Catty is standing nearby, annoyed, trying to get Papa to learn how to shoot that gun, to prepare him for the mob coming to burn down his store.

I think I finally know why Catty is there. I mean, at first, sure, it was just because I was hot for Kitty and didn't want to admit it. But now it's different. She is there to push Papa forward, even if Papa goes a different direction than where she's pushing. When you push someone, they don't always go in the direction you expect.

Maybe Catty is right that learning to shoot a gun could save his life, but this moment under the table with his boy will save his soul.

PART THREE

"remember those horrible, awkward, terrifying
moments in middle school? Well i got news
for you: those were your best moments. it's
disappointment turtles all the way down."
—@your_consciousness

Chapter Fifteen: To Be Uncomfortable

Anne sends me a message that says, *Serenity Now* the first second I walk in the office, so I get my butt over there even before my morning bathroom ritual.

She doesn't look good, sitting there in the Serenity conference room. Her eyes are red when she pulls her hands away from her face.

What is it? I say. And I worry that the execs didn't take to how I criticized them, or worse, that this is about the rogue gamification plug-in. It's amazing the way family crises can make you forget about career crises.

Am I getting fired?

She shakes her head. *Actually*, she says. *You didn't do anything wrong this time.* Then Anne covers her eyes.

Really? I say.

Didn't you see my post today? We're going to run with your suggestions to focus on the essentials. We're following your lead.

Really? I say. *But I was bullshitting.*

You actually weren't, she says. *You were right. Plus, I started an external CollabHub group called Geeky Girls for women in tech and 125 women have signed up already.*

Great! I say. *So why are you upset?*

It's nothing, she says. *It's Rick.*

Who?

My husband.

Oh, I say. *Hubby.* It takes me some seconds to make this context shift. *What is wrong? Did he cheat on you?*

No, she says.

Is it cancer?

No, she says.

Then what?

She covers her face again and I can tell she is weeping by how her head shakes so much. She says, *He wants to make an app!*

An app? I didn't know he was a programmer.

He isn't. But he wants to use our date nights to figure out how to write an app that helps you pair movies with the right beer.

He's doing what now? I sit down right next to her and lean in so I can hear her better.

He's ruining our date nights! she says. And she grabs my hands and squeezes them.

What's the app going to do exactly? I say, feeling her warm fingers.

It'll help you pick an old movie and a local beer that go together.

I laugh and say, *Well there's a niche. What platforms is he going to support?*

It's not funny, she says. *This is my life. I don't want to be the one bringing in the money while he does some idiotic project, gets stoned, and never takes me out again. I've done that before. I did that for years. I hate it.*

I know about her last relationship. The guy was a bum and she hated taking care of him. He would sit on the couch and get stoned while complaining about how everything was stupid except for his great ideas, which he was always too lazy to do anything about.

Wait, I say. *Let me understand. Is he planning on quitting his job?*

She pulls her hands away from me and takes a few breaths. *Not yet. But he's already created an LLC with the dumbest name for a company I've ever heard. He even made a website with Squarespace!* She starts crying again.

Hubby isn't the same, I say.

Who's Hubby?

Sorry. Rick. Rick isn't the same as that bum who got stoned on your couch.

How do you know? You barely know him.

She's right. I sort of wish I knew him, too. He seems like a decent guy. And I haven't honestly had a guy friend in a while. My novel has become my social life, which maybe hasn't been the best thing.

I stand up and pat her on the back a few times. Then I kiss her on the head like I do with my boy when he is upset. It is all a very awkward thing, but I keep trying to find a way to comfort her.

In this moment, my back ache and my Kitty ache and my boy ache and my novel ache all disappear. They're nothing right now. I look at this aching woman in front of me and I want to help her.

I say, *I know enough to know that Rick is not a lazy, irresponsible asshole.*

It was hard enough to spend quality time with him before this whole thing started. How is it going to be now?

What's the name? I say.

What?

The company name. You said it sucked.

Oh. A-Hops-on-Your-Lips Now. And it's written in the same style as the title on the movie poster for Apocalypse Now *that's hanging in the garage.*

Ouch, I say. *That is pretty bad. It's not even grammatically correct.*

Anne gets even more upset by my response.

I sit down next to her. I grab her arms. *Hey! It's OK. What's in a name?* I can't remember what Juliet meant when she said that line about the rose, but I hope it doesn't totally contradict my point.

I ask, *So what are you most worried about?*

She doesn't answer.

Is it the bad name?

No, she whispers.

Is it the fact that he's learning how to write an app?

No.

Are you afraid he'll quit his job anytime soon?

Not really.

Are you afraid of losing time with your man?

She looks right at me and nods her head.

OK, I say. *Do you think he still wants to spend time with you?*

Yes, she says.

Good. We can deal with this problem. I see she is skeptical. But I'm not. I know exactly how to help my friend. I go up to the whiteboard. I grab the eraser. I point at all the bullshit work diagrams on the board—drawings of clouds and servers and databases and stupid stick figures. *Do you need any of these bullshit diagrams?*

No, she says.

She's totally confused by this sense of authority that I've never exhibited at work.

I erase the whole board. I ask, *Where are the dry-erase markers?*

She points to the other side of the table where there is one black marker. *Not enough*, I say. I run to the other conference room, where I interrupt a meeting with a bunch of execs. I mouth the word, "sorry," and then swipe all their markers.

OK, I say to Anne. *Tell me your schedule.*

Here's the deal. Julia and I were expert schedulers when we were married. We're even good at it divorced. I might have failed emotionally. I might have hidden inside my damn book and destroyed our intimacy. But I knew how to schedule our lives. Emotional honesty is terrifying. I was a mess. But I could plan our week like a Mega Super Bad Ass Senior Project Manager. How to track our day jobs, taking care of our baby, our side projects, our (really just her) social life, our eating schedule. The fact that Anne and Hubby don't even have a kid to worry about—not even a pet or a niece!—makes this task feel like child's play. But, you know, without the child part.

In twenty-five minutes, I have a color-coded schedule on the board that represents an average week in the Anne/Hubby household. Purple is used for day job hours. Blue is used for sleep. Green is when Hubby works on his app, on his beer, and watches his movies. It is also the time slot where Anne finds a new hobby so she can have her own thing that is not Hubby and definitely NOT CollaborationHub. And finally, red is the quality time that they spend together. Easy peasy, cliché freezy. In black, I make a short list to the side about the things they will have to sacrifice or discuss further. She will stop playing *Cooking Fever* on her iPad. She will talk to him about taking a weekly walk around the block together. And they will have their groceries delivered to them via Instacart for a small fee. I snap a shot of the whiteboard with my phone. I launch an app to convert the drawing into a schedule, send Anne the calendar using the ICS file format, and then erase the board. I tell her to share the calendar with the man.

Does that help? I ask Anne.

Anne licks her lips for uncomfortably long. Her phone beeps—probably my message I just sent her. She looks at it and then looks back up at me.

Amazing, she says. And she gets up to hug me so quickly and so tightly that I stab her with the blue marker that doesn't have a cover on it yet, and she doesn't even loosen her grip when she becomes aware of the stabbing.

I remember why I love doing this kind of thing. It turns overwhelming things into small pieces that you can comprehend. You can see it in a picture. Even the big scary things become less scary this way. I don't have to worry about the failed relationship ten years from now or what Auggie is going to be like at age eighteen, I just have to worry about how the next two hours are going to go. The complicated becomes uncomplicated.

Thank you, I say to Anne, because this has helped me more than her.

#

As we drive over to Kitty's apartment, I say to Auggie, *Use the iPad to contact me if you need ANYTHING.*

Dad! he says. *For the googolplex time, you don't need to worry. It's just Kitty. I'll be fine.* His voice right now reminds me of his mother, more exasperated than angry.

I drive into the apartment parking lot and there is Kitty sitting at the bottom of the stairway to her apartment. Her hair is back in a pretty ponytail and she's in a tank top and her biceps really show. I don't understand how she can make herself seem so big and so small at the same time.

She's wearing the same brown corduroys from that night we went over to Julia's.

She gets up and then waves to us as we park.

I can't explain exactly why I don't like this. I just don't want Auggie to get hurt. Is she using my boy as an octopus replacement? Is my boy using her as some sort of mother replacement? Are we all just using each other as replacements for something else?

I drive past a few empty parking spots looking for one in the shade. Auggie says, *Dad! You missed a bunch of closer spots.*

I can feel his giddiness and impatience as he wiggles in the backseat.

OK, I say. *Hang on.*

When I finally park, Kitty is right there next to us and she opens the door for Auggie.

He grabs and hugs Kitty. *I missed you!* he says.

I shake Kitty's hand, looking down at her pants the whole time.

What? What is it? she says, suspicious of my staring.

Oh, I say, feeling light-headed. *You wore those pants that night we went over to Julia's for dinner.*

She says, *It's true that I wear pants more than once.*

My boy looks up at her trying to figure out if she's telling a joke or if it's something more serious. And I look at her with that same curiosity. Even pants chatter is confusing and risky.

I say to her, *I should pick him up in two hours?*

She says, *Yes*, and they go up to her apartment.

#

I close my eyes and press my head against the steering wheel.

This isn't how it's supposed to go. On a Saturday morning, I should be with my boy and my wife and we should all be going on a hike together and we should be teaching my boy how to distinguish the edible mushrooms from the poisonous ones.

But in this alternate reality, it's poisonous mushrooms all the way down.

So I sit in the car and I wait and I hate that she has my boy captive.

I also know that I need to give my boy space.

I look in the rearview mirror at the stairs on the way to Kitty's apartment.

Nothing there.

I get a particularly unhinged gamification message:

```
You want to know how to social media? You can't
handle social media! Son, we live in a world
with walls. Are you talking to me?! Well I'm
the only one here. Who the fuck do you think
you're talking to? Conjecture jester, what's
your hectare?! Turn on, Wi-Fi in, drop the sig-
nal. To be everywhere is to be nowhere. Death
and dying are my two favorite subjects.
```

My head pushes on the steering wheel too hard and my car honks and I lift my head up to make sure no one's watching. I stay put for two hours.

I heard about my mom's death while I was in the car. The call was from a friend of hers from AA who called me. I had just pulled over on the side of the highway.

The caller ID on that old cellphone registered it as Unknown and I sensed immediately that it was a known unknown.

The woman said to me, *I know this doesn't help much, but she died instantly from the aneurism. She didn't feel a thing.*

Thank you, I said to this woman. And I hung up. It didn't help to hear that my mom didn't feel a thing, because I wanted her to feel more things throughout my whole life.

#

When he gets in the car, Auggie says with surprise, *You parked in the exact same spot!*

Yes, I say. *It's crazy pants.*

How was it? I ask, hoping my voice sounds normal.

It was exactly awesome, he says. *Kitty taught me to draw submarines and narwhals and zombies and even zombie narwhals.*

Kitty's standing by the car next to him and she's buckling him into the car seat—something that he'd never let me do without saying, *I'm old enough to buckle myself.*

He hands me a page of his art. It's a narwhal-shaped submarine. With a horn. And there are other animals peeking out the submarine windows and some zombie humans and sea creatures on top of the sub.

You drew this? I ask.

Yes sir ree bob, he says with too much enthusiasm. *Do you know the secret to zombies?*

What?

She looks up at Kitty and says, *Can I tell him?* She nods. And he says, *The secret is that you have to show broken parts on the skin so everyone can see what they are.*

I look at the drawing again and see all their broken parts and I say, *Ow,* instead of wow.

Kitty gives him a kiss on his head. She says, *I had a lovely time.*

She checks that he is buckled tightly and then closes the door gently.

Then she comes up to the driver side window and says, *We had a great time.*

I'm happy that he gets to spend time with you. I experiment with a smile that probably looks like a zombie smile.

She leans in and puts a hand on my arm, which is holding onto the steering wheel. She says, *Hopefully next time you can leave the f-ing parking lot.*

Auggie giggles about the hidden curse word. He likes hidden curse words even better than real ones.

Baby steps, I say.

She leans in and gives me a kiss on the head just like she did with Auggie.

#

The principal has reassured me that they're keeping their eyes out for inappropriate behavior around Auggie. I told her that he won't punch anyone in the throat again unless he feels he is in danger.

Auggie has been taking a taekwondo class too. He says he likes it because he likes to use his legs for things.

Dad, Auggie says when he gets in the car after school, *I think I understand what Kitty means to poke your characters.*

Oh yeah? I ask, scared to hear what he's about to say.

Yeah, he says. *She means that it's interesting when someone is uncomfortable.*

How do you figure?

Jeremy is uncomfortable around me now that I know taekwondo.

OK, I say. *Just tell me if you ever feel uncomfortable.*

My car stereo interrupts us to say: *Message from Anne: Have you got all your ducks in a row for tomorrow's meeting?*

My kid says, *What are ducks in a row?*

I say, *It's just a dumb metaphor that means I have more work to do tonight before work tomorrow.*

I don't think it's dumb, he says. *But why do the ducks need to be in a row?*

I have no idea. This devangelism stuff has been getting more intense lately. I actually like doing it, which is an unexpected thing not to loathe my work. But it is eating into too much time at night when I should be with my kid, or writing, or sleeping. If we were still using sea creatures for the gamification plug-in, I'd be way past Goldfish by now.

My boy says, *When is my next time with Kitty?*

This weekend.

Why don't you have a playdate with Kitty? It's weird that you drop me off, but you don't go in.

You'd like me to come inside?

Yeah, he says. *You should put your ducks on this row. Even if it makes you uncomfortable.*

#

One night when Auggie is with his mom, I head over to Anne's house. I haven't been over there since the infamous blind date. Anne is totally surprised to see me, and not the good kind of surprise either.

What the hell are you doing here? she asks. She's in sweatpants. Not "I just went on a run" sweatpants, but more like "I'm not expecting to see anybody for hours" sweatpants. Not a big deal, she looks perfectly fine, but it's surprising to me just because of how formally she dresses for CollabHub.

Rick didn't tell you? I say. *I'm going to drink a few brews and talk about his app and then watch* Taxi Driver *in the garage.*

You're shitting me? she says, and she looks me up and down like what I said couldn't possibly be accurate.

Saul! I hear from Hubby in the other room. *Get your ass in here.*

You see, I say to Anne. Somehow loving how disorienting this is to her. *My ass has been invited inside.*

I pat her on the shoulder and step inside.

Rick hands me a beer just as I get into the kitchen. He says, *Here. This stout has more shit in it than we have in the kitchen right now.*

I take a sip, and I can't say I like it, but I don't hate it. And after I gulp some down, I say, *Damn good,* and then I look over at Anne and I wink at her.

Hubby puts his arm around me and walks me to the door into the garage.

Saul, he says as he opens the door, *welcome to the man cave.*

Chapter Sixteen: Actually Getting Close

This particular company uses our software to collaborate on making software that helps other companies make software. The head of HR is a small woman with a deep voice. She says, *What else do you have for us?*

Their office is on one of the top floors of Big Pink, which is a big building by Portland standards. I used this building to teach Auggie about how a parallelogram can have no right angles—something that really bored him until the lesson involved ordering fresh-out-of-the-oven cookies on the top floor of this building.

This company's conference room has a great view of the fog of the city, and staring at the fog makes it easier to say what I need to say to this woman from this broken company, a broken company that I spent half the night researching in preparation for this meeting.

I say, *Your CEO is a passive aggressive asshole and your employees will never be able to use our software to communicate properly until he leaves or gets some serious therapy.*

The woman doesn't even flinch. She says, *Assuming what you say is roughly correct, are there any ways we can improve collaboration without the therapy part?*

Well, I say. *I did create a plug-in that allows users to post anonymously. That might help. Not even the admins will be able to track who wrote what. But that can also cause people to become inconsiderate assholes. And you already have a misogynistic tone to the conversations online. You need to hire more women. And bring in more diverse hires. Not just these white guys. I can point you to some resources to help you hire differently. Where do you find new employees?*

My watch taps my wrist every twenty minutes to remind me to do my core-strengthening exercises, and so I say, *Excuse me for a moment.* I stand up to do a few stretches and stare through the fog at the river below us. And then I sit down again.

So that was strange, she says to me.

I say, *We can tune the system so that it encourages people who haven't been friendly to be more friendly. But you'll still need to give the team some actual training from professionals. Nothing can replace in-person team-building.*

I ask the HR lady whether she thinks she can get the designers to document their design process inside CollabHub.

She thinks about it and says, *It's possible. They already do it on the Wiki.*

Good, I say. *I'll have someone send y'all the settings to get you started.*

Thank you, she says. *Will this actually work?*

It's possible, I say. *If the employees can step up to be the best version of themselves, it will work.*

#

How's the back?

It's actually good, I say.

Daniel takes off his glasses and looks at me for a long time. Why do people do that? You wear glasses for a reason. Taking them off won't make the world any clearer.

So you're actually doing the exercises, he says to me, with an actual smile.

Yeah, I say. Even though the man has no funny bone in his body, there's something refreshing about not being able to use humor. It forces me to dig a little deeper before I say something, even if that something sounds like a gross Hallmark card message. I say, *I guess I'd like to thank you for having faith in me.*

But now the man laughs, like I told a joke. *To be honest,* he says, *I didn't think you'd pull it off.*

Really? I say. *What was all that talk of being sure that I could stumble my way onto the right path?*

Oh, he says. *I did say that, didn't I?* He chews on the tip of his glasses as he thinks about it. *I guess I thought you could, but I didn't think you would.*

Daniel has me lie on his chiropractic table, face down, with my face jammed into that uncomfortable face cradle. I stick my face in there and look through the hole in the cloth, like I'm peeking through a mask. My nose stuffs up immediately and the pattern on the rug, which was originally just abstract lines and shapes, now I swear it looks like a volcano laughing at me. And while the volcano laughs at me, Daniel starts walking his fingers up and down my spine in a way that both tickles and hurts.

He says, *How's the book coming along?*

It's a trick question. Doctors don't want to know about your damn book. Even more so—ex-wives' boyfriends don't want to know about your damn book. But I'm helpless in this position. I can't stop myself from answering. I say to the volcano, *I think I'm actually getting close.*

Now he has me lie on my side, bottom leg straight, top leg bent, arms wrapped around my chest. I feel like one of those crazy crooked trees in our backyard when I was a kid that I'd climb up until I got too scared and then yell for my mom to help me come down. Daniel asks me to move towards him, closer to the edge of the table. I scooch. Then he says, *Closer.* I scooch. *Closer.* I don't like the way he's got me hugging myself. I feel too fragile this way. He leans against me. He says, *Don't worry, you won't fall.*

Daniel leans down and squeezes me. He says, *Take a deep breath.* He grabs me even tighter. *I want you to exhale. Blow it all out.*

And I do.

He whispers, *You're getting close to what exactly?*

Well, I say, with no air left in my lungs. Without waiting for me to finish, he presses into me. It hurts. He's too close. I smell his breath. Olives and garlic. My back hurts even worse in this position.

And then, crack. There's a tingle down in my toes, something rushes out of my lungs, and then the pain in my back turns into just the memory of the feeling.

He doesn't ask me if I'm feeling any better, just goes back to his stool and starts taking notes in his clipboard.

I lie there, stunned, until he says I can sit up.

I sit up and it doesn't hurt to change positions. I say, *In my story, I'm getting close to the answer.*

He's still looking down at his notes, but he laughs.

What? I say.

Finally, Daniel looks up at me. *You do know that every one of your answers has a new set of bigger questions lurking behind it. Right?*

I keep getting thrown off by Daniel, not sure if he's shallow and full of shit, or he's the real deal and has something profound to pass on.

What are you? I say. *Some kind of life coach?*

He says, *I'm sorry.* He's not offended at all. Still with that boyish sort of curiosity. *So tell me. What's the question? You said you're close to the answer. But first I'm curious about the question.*

Oh, I say. This is exactly why it's important to shut up about your book while you're writing your book. *Well,* I try, *it's about how to be a dad. Or maybe it's about where I came from. I'm trying to understand my grandfather. I guess the question is . . .* but then I don't know how to finish the sentence.

He's just sitting there, staring at me, waiting for me, with a half smile, and I'm wondering if he is amused that I'm about to succeed, or that I'm bound to fail. When I look down at the floor, I can no longer make out the laughing volcano, it's just a bunch of shapes and lines in a rug.

OK, I say. The tingle in my toes is still there from the adjustment, but the spine feels strong, I feel more centered than before. *How about this: It's about a man who saves himself because of his connection to his family and to the people in his community. The question is, can he protect himself with love and good will instead of with money or a gun?*

He makes those about-to-laugh sounds and it's annoying because I'd rather he continue to not understand my jokes than laugh at my nonjokes. I say to him, *What? What is it?*

I guess, Daniel says as he tries to straighten his smile, *you could say that your hero takes collaboration to the next level.*

Oh, I say. *I guess that's true.*

I'm impressed. Not because his joke is so brilliant—it's not—but for the first time, Daniel got me to think past all the clichés and all the business speak to consider what this might mean in a world that is free of bullshit. And it's actually kind of beautiful.

#

After I finish a draft of the book, I give Kitty a call. I mean like an actual phone call—not with a landline (I'm not a caveman!), but still.

She answers the call with an unrevealing *Hello?* which doesn't give me much to work with.

I say to her, *My mom used to say to me, "Don't do a damn thing until you're ready to do a damn thing and then do the damn thing with all the damn strength that you got."*

Kitty snorts on the other line. *Really?* she says. *I can't decide if that is good advice or horrible advice.*

It's both. Like everything my mom said. I get a tickle inside of my chest thinking about her.

I assume this is your way of saying hello?

Yeah, I say. *I'm sorry. I was hoping to check in with you if you have time.*

She is silent on the other line. I wish I had a cord to play with while I spoke with her. Wireless Bluetooth earbuds should come with a fake, tangled cord for this purpose.

I say, *First of all, I want to thank you for your time with Auggie. The highlight of his week is his date with you. It's fabulous, even if it still scares me a little.*

Before I finish, she says, *I love spending time with him. He's so bright and curious and sweet.*

We're silent again. I can't decide if this conversation is awkward or it's just that we're not acclimated to the format. Regardless, it's mostly OK for me to hear these kind words about Auggie.

I say, *Next of all, I've tried to deny it, but my book could use pictures as much as it needs words. And I can't draw worth a damn. But you can draw worth many damns. And I think you'd know what to do with this thing. I think this latest draft is close . . . or closer. Do you think you'd consider looking at it to see if you're willing to do some illustrations?*

More silence.

I say, *You totally don't have to. And only do it if you actually like it. And feel free to suggest changes. It is just a draft. But I thought maybe we could work together.*

Hmm, she says.

Uh oh, I say.

No, it's not a bad thing, she says. *But can I think about how this fits into . . . how things are right now? Would you mind sending me a copy?*

Oh, I say. *I like that answer. OK. Thank you.*

You know, she says, *you don't talk about your mother much. Funny to hear you quote her instead of a hello.*

Yeah, I say. *It's a thing I need to confront. Some day that is not today.*

She says, *I'm familiar with the feeling.*

I have so many isolated memories of my mom, but I've never been able to build those memories into a clear feeling or story about her. I don't know if it's love or resentment or anger or something else. It's just warm and getting warmer over time. It used to be easier for me to write her off as a drunk. Over the years, I think I'm starting to love her more for the burden she carried.

I say, *So who are your parents?*

Oh, she says. *They're Max and Sadie.*

I mean, who are Max and Sadie?

Oh, she says. *They're Mom and Dad.*

I don't laugh. She doesn't laugh.

And then she says, *I'll tell you about them. Some day that is not today.*

At the risk of her hanging up on me, I choose a painful, corporate expression. I say, *Can you give me the fifty-thousand-foot view?*

Oh, she says. *At fifty thousand feet, they look like ants.*

I don't laugh. She doesn't laugh.

And then she says, *OK. How about this: my dad was an abusive asshole and left us when I was five and my mom raised me and she was angry and lovely and broken like everyone else and she is still alive and in Boulder and*

I talk to her on the phone every Sunday afternoon even though I haven't seen her in five years and she even knows about you and about Auggie. How is that for an answer?

Wow, I say. *That was great.*

Are you messing with me?

I mean it, I say. *That was the most efficient relationship summary I've ever heard. It's like you sold me on the movie trailer and now I want to see the whole movie.*

Good, she says. *I'm glad to be efficient.* Though I can tell that she is somewhere else. She's not on the phone with me, she is floating above the cellular towers, maybe thinking about her mom or her dad or about ants at fifty thousand feet.

My phone shows a gamification notification while we speak:

```
{ next_step : "too late for underwear, now you'll
    need neon balls" }
```

She says, *They caught the VHS burglar.*

They did what now? I say.

You know, she says. *The burglar in Surburbaville where I used to live. The guy who left VHS tapes at his victims' houses.*

Oh! I say, trying to focus on her words and how much I like that we're talking in such a friendly and simple way. *That guy. How did they catch him?*

Duh! she says. *From his VHS tapes.*

I say, *I'm kind of sorry they got him.*

Why? she says. *He wanted to get caught. He told the cops that he was mad that it took them fifteen burglaries to find him.*

Still, I'm sad to hear this news. I love how he was stuck in this VHS-focused past. I wanted it to go on forever. But of course nothing can go that way.

OK, I say. *One last thing before you have to go to your meeting.*

I don't have meetings, she says.

Well, the thing I'm going to ask you before that looming, high-pressure meeting is if you're willing to go out to dinner with me next week. No exes, no kids, no work, no beds, no muck. Just me . . . And, well, ideally you'd be there, too.

#

My dad says, *I don't think I like you looking at me like this.*

I sent him an iPad with a very clear explanation (printed-out pictures with big red arrows for instructions) of how to accept a video call from me. His finger sometimes covers up the camera as he moves the iPad around in a better position, the reception is a little sketchy, he is pixelated, but it's still nice to see him.

I hope this didn't cost you much, he says. *I don't know what to do with this computing contraption.*

Auggie runs into my room. *Don't worry, Papa,* he yells out. *Dada got us the newest iPad and gave Kitty our old iPad and then sent you Kitty's old one.*

Auggie touches the iPad on the stand. He whispers to me, *Dada, can I play* Zombie World *on that?* He points at my dad on the video stream.

I say, *Give me some private time with Papa.*

How many minutes? he says.

Bye, I say to him.

Like ten minutes?

Bye, I say to him.

Auggie leaves the room and says in a disheartened voice, *Bye, Papa.*

Bye, my dad says. *Wherever you are!*

I'm surprised my dad can hear all of this so well. I expected to have to repeat everything multiple times.

Good kid, my dad says. *You raise him well. Except for the zombie part.*

How are the doctors? I ask.

They're still a pain in the ass. He points to one ear and says, *But they're making me wear these damn hearing aids.*

Oh, I say. *They're working.*

If you ask me, he says. *They're working too well. I don't want to hear so much bullshit. So tell me about this Kitty cat. Is she the babysitter or your lover?*

Well, I say. *Neither.*

What is it with your generation? Scared to call a spade a spade.

I say to my dad, *What's a spade?*

What? he says. *Your TweetBook doesn't help you understand real words?*

She's just a friend, I say. *Auggie loves Kitty and Kitty enjoys spending time with him.*

Azoy, he says, which is a word I'll never know the depths of. *How's your book?*

I'm practically feeling good about it, I say.

Really? he says. *Did you put in that part about the hanging tree?*

Sort of, I say. *But I had a slightly different story to tell.*

My father is silent for a while. The connection is glitchy and it's tricky to know how he feels about what I said.

I say, *How is the blood pressure?*

Oh, he says. *Too high. But it goes down when I drink two martinis.*

You still drink two martinis at night?

Yep, he says. *For my health. My cardiologist told me not to drink, so I stopped seeing my cardiologist. That guy was giving me these horrible drugs that didn't help my pressure one bit. Meanwhile I have the perfect remedy right here in this little bottle.* He shows the camera the bottle of Beefeater.

I don't tell him that I've quit drinking. It feels like something I'd rather tell him in person. I say, *Did you and mom ever have nice drinking time before the—you know?*

No, he says. *She was never a good drinker. She was either too drunk or too sober.*

I say, *Why do you think she relapsed?*

Because of you, my dad says.

All my narcissistic fears momentarily come true. I'm responsible for everything. For a split second, I can fit every emoticon inside this feeling.

Really? I say. *Me?*

Really, he says. *It was amazing she was able to be sober the whole time she raised you. That poor woman was miserable for those eighteen years.*

This is all news to me. I knew my mom was miserable. I resented her for years because she seemed depressed and detached all the time. I thought she didn't love me. My friends were scared of her. There was lots of therapy in my twenties, but it mostly involved letting go of my disappointment and my hurt. It didn't involve trying to understand her better. This idea that she stopped herself drinking just because of me turns her into a different woman. Her misery came from her love.

He says, *I'm surprised she lived another ten years after you left the house. Why did y'all email each other?* I ask.

Oh, he says. *We were using the*, he snaps his fingers in the air to remember, *the America Online. She wanted to email me while she was at that recovery place.* He snaps his fingers in the air again, but never remembers the name. And I don't either.

Wow, nontechnical people sending emails in 1998, I say. *That is true love.*

It was the nicest time we ever had. I got to know her in a way I never did before. Somehow doing it by the email broke down all these walls. Seems like it would go the opposite way. But I quit being so disappointed that she wasn't behaving the way I wanted her to behave. And she was able to speak about all her fears and worries and shame as if they did not make her a terrible person. America Online saved us.

I'd never heard him talk about it before. And I never heard my mom talk about her fears. A whole side of her that AOL knows better than I do.

I don't feel like I ever knew Mom, I say.

My dad shakes his head and puts his hand on his forehead. I think he has forgotten how clearly I can see him.

What? I say.

Saul, he says. He shakes his finger at the iPad. *In the end, you probably knew her better than anyone.*

Really? I say. I always felt like she was so far away, but maybe what I saw was a very close view of her feeling so far away from the world.

He says, *You know what I learned about relationships in eighty-eight years?*

What? I say. I'm disturbingly hopeful that he'll say something brilliant right now.

Relationships are pretty fucking complicated and if you think you know what's going on, you're either senile or a con artist or a drunk or a religious man or a soft scientist or a failed mathematician. Or all three.

#

```
{ communication_error:
                "socket closed. protocol failed.
                all channels unavailable.
                communication impossible.",
    next_step : "sending message anyway"}
```

"never write a story with buffalo wing gunk on
your fingers—it's a waste of buffalo wing gunk."
—@badwriter883

Chapter Seventeen: Whiskey Soda Lounge

I take Kitty to the Whiskey Soda Lounge, which sounds terrible since we're both not drinking alcohol, but she loves wings. I know this because Auggie told me. And this place has great Vietnamese fish sauce wings, and yummy nonalcoholic drinking vinegars, which taste better than they sound.

When the waiter comes by, I order a rhubarb vinegar drink and Kitty orders a celery vinegar drink. And of course the wings.

I say, *You don't have to order a virgin drink just because of me.*

She reaches out her hand and touches my hand.

I'm trying to cut back on the stuff myself, she says. She pulls her hand away and looks down at her fingers. It's a sad look, like her fingers aren't the way they should be, and it reminds me of the way my dad looked down at his fingers when he was in the hospital.

It's been two months without a sip of alcohol.

I can't wait for the wings, I say. *They give me vicious heartburn so I only let myself eat them once every few months.*

Humans do the stupidest things to their bodies, she says.

I imagine our bodies will be more resilient in heaven. It's a throwaway line, just a dumb joke I regret saying immediately, but I can see in how she watches me that she's somewhere else.

The universe, she says, *has a much greater imagination than we do.*

For someone who isn't religious and isn't a scientist, I say, *you have a lot to say about the universe.* My words are just not working right. In front of her, at this moment, all my lines feel like throwaway lines.

She says to me with a little defensiveness: *I don't have to be a scientist to believe in the scientific method.*

Sorry, I say to my rhubarb beverage that just arrived.

She grabs my hand again, and she says, *I have an amazing book for your father. Can you give me his address?*

You mean his actual snail mail address? I say. *For an actual physical book?* I say.

She gives me that look. Half unfazed, half amused. Half annoyed. And I like all 150 percent of it.

I say, *It might require going back to my therapist if you get close to all my family members before me.*

My insecure friend, she says, and smiles while she stirs the little cocktail straw in her vinegar drink.

I blush. I'm flattered.

She opens up her purse and pulls out an envelope with my manuscript. It is bent up and covered in coffee mug rings. She also pulls out a pencil like she wants to be prepared to make more marks.

Wow, I say.

She says, *Don't wow until you look.*

I pull the pages out from the war-torn envelope with this fear that never occurred to me before: What if I don't like it? What if these pictures totally misunderstand what I'm trying to do? What if I hate what I see?

The pages are totally worn out—both my writing and her drawings are absurdly aged. It feels like the pages traveled to 1938 and back.

And then I look.

She has drawn it in such beautiful detail. The store is great, sure, but Papa is so carefully drawn even in just a few strokes. Dozens of drawings. His expressions are perfect. But it's a completely different book with her drawings in them. I want to cry. These drawings feel more like Papa than the actual photos I have of Papa. Somehow her drawings make my memories of him more vivid.

Wow.

Kitty says, *I think you pulled it off.* She shakes the pencil at me like it's a bad thing.

I say, *Did I bleed in there?*

Somebody's blood is in there.

I get that rush of something. Maybe pride or excitement or something else I can't name, except that it's definitely not shame. It's one of those rare gifts a writer gets every now and again if they bang their head against a wall long enough and hard enough to have a moment where it almost feels magical.

Even better than magic—worthwhile.

I say, *I guess now we've both bled in there.*

Kitty taps the pencil on the envelope between us. She says, *You know, the women are oddly absent in here.*

And suddenly the magic disappears. And what replaces it is a terror that maybe everything I've ever done is bad. It is the cost of playing with magic. *Is that bad?*

I don't think so. It's just the nature of this story.

There's an ache inside me like I swallowed a brick that is trying to get through my body. I say, *I miss my mom.* I swallow a few times to get the ache to go away, but it won't disappear. I tell Kitty, *I never appreciated what she was going through, even though I saw that she suffered, even when I was too young to understand it, I felt it, the way she stared at herself in the bathroom mirror hoping to see something different. But I didn't appreciate what she carried. Not while she was sober. Not while she was drunk. Not even when she died. She made me who I am and I gave her nothing.* I press my tongue to the roof of my mouth to hold back the feeling.

Kitty rubs her hand up and down my forearm and her touch is warm. Even comforting. She says, *I'm sure you gave her a lot. You just don't know what you gave her. I'd like to hear more about her someday.*

The way she says "someday" is a kind of kindness. It makes me feel like we can be patient in the midst of this mess we're in.

Kitty pulls her arm away from me and leans back in her chair. *Speaking of blood*, she says, *my dreams have been . . .* and then she trails off. She does this thing with the pencil in her hand where she spins it around on the knuckle of her thumb and catches it again after it's done a 360. I can't decide if it's a tic or a talent.

She continues: *They're vivid. Vivid like watching* The Godfather *in 3D.* Did I tell her about my obsession with *The Godfather?*

It's my octopus baby, she says. *I keep giving birth to him. Over and over.*

Oh, wow, I say. I grab her hand, but not really her hand, mostly just a finger, her longest finger, and I squeeze gently on the tip. *Does it hurt? Is it bad? Why did you . . . ?* but I can't finish my question.

She looks up at me, but really she looks through me, and after a few seconds, I see her focus return to me again.

She says, *Maybe I don't believe in God and in spirits, but at night it feels like I can talk to my octopus baby and I can hear him calling me Mommy.*

I want to say, *What does your baby tell you?* I want to say, *Maybe our next book can be about babies and moms.* I want to say, *Is my boy becoming your octopus baby?* I want to say, *I love you.*

What I say is, *Wow.*

And then the wings arrive. And we stop talking. We grab them. And we eat. These wings demand full attention. They are like a codependent relationship. They don't let you take on other interests. They don't let you have outside friendships. They don't let you work late or sleep in. They need you. You need them. They consume you. You consume them. Your hands are filthy with them. Your mouth is full of them. It is too messy to take on anything else until you've eaten them to the bone and there is nothing left but scraps.

Better than a fuck, Kitty says when we're done.

We both need to wash our hands and faces after the whole experience. Since they only have one bathroom, we go in there together and lock the door. She washes her hands and face first and I stand behind her waiting. I know I'm in trouble because the way she washes her face with her hands and breathes air and spits water is sexy to me.

When she's done with the sink, I get in there. Instead of leaving, she sits down to pee right next to me. I almost choke on the water from nervousness. It's a weird feeling because I've only done this kind of thing with Julia. And I don't know what to do with a pissing Kitty next to me like this. What I do is I take longer to wash my face so I don't have to think about where to look while she's peeing.

I want to watch her. Does that make me creepy?

While washing my face and actively not looking at her, and while she pees what seems like a zillion gallons of liquid, I say to the running faucet, *I think things are different than before. Would you want to try to start to begin to approach dating again?*

She doesn't answer. She just keeps peeing and I'm wondering if the water plus her pee drowned out my question.

I stop the sink and instead of looking towards her, I go for the paper towels and wipe my face and hands.

When I open my eyes, Kitty is standing up and pulling up her cute purple underwear and her jeans and she wiggles her hips in a way that is almost too much to bear.

I don't say anything. I don't move. I just watch her wash and dry. And I stand out of the way so she can walk out of the bathroom and just ignore the frozen idiot statue in the corner. But instead, she walks up to me. She grabs my cheeks and pulls my face close to her and kisses me on the lips, and she says, *We started dating when we ate those wings.*

#

```
{ error : "expected an error but no error found,
          so maybe you're safe,
          happily ever after or whatever . . ." }
```

#

In those last years, my mom would ask me about my writing, but it didn't give me a terrible feeling like when others asked. She didn't care about publications or publishers. She didn't care if the book was a critical success. She asked about how it all felt, or she asked what I had discovered. The last time I remember her asking me anything, we were on the phone and she was drunk and I was so frustrated by the drinking that I failed to appreciate her question: *Have you learned anything new and icky about yourself?*

"trouble at #work? well just keep it all in
perspective by remembering how your mom was
eaten by the enormous french fry machine
she dedicated ten years to building . . .
#frenchfrylivesmatter" —@ya_mama_so_thin

Chapter Eighteen: The Immortal Gefilte Fish

This company doesn't have an HR department, so I meet directly with Freddy Callahan, the CEO of Quirkitunity Inc., maker of that crazy, buggy dating app that once told me that I was unsuitable for a mate. I spent way too many hours this week analyzing the company and now I have to deliver the information to Freddy, information which I don't think will help CollaborationHub's three-million-dollar contract one bit.

Freddy is a big, bald man who looks great in a grey silk suit and red tie. He looks powerful. He looks charming. He also looks like he can be a real asshole when he wants to be.

So lay it on me, Freddy says when I walk into his office. *What are we doing wrong with your software?*

I sit down on his couch. The man has a couch in his office. And a full bar.

He asks me if I want something to drink and I shake my head. But he serves two shots of bourbon anyway and puts them both on the coffee table. I feel like I'm speaking with an arrogant exec from a 1960s advertising agency.

He sits in a chair across from me, and takes a gulp of bourbon.

I say to him, *It's a tricky situation.*

But aren't you supposed to be some big shot? Like The Wolf or something like that? Maybe not quite The Wolf. He looks at me for a few seconds and laughs. *So you're no Harvey Keitel, but maybe you're like a fierce squirrel.*

I don't know about a squirrel, I say, not exactly sure if he is insulting me or just joking around. Maybe there's no difference. *Think of me as an immortal gefilte fish.*

What does a gefilte even look like? He twists his head at me and I can tell he has no idea what this thing is, which isn't such a surprise, because even Jews who tolerate eating it a few times a year probably don't know what the hell it is.

Long, ferocious tentacles, I say, while I use two fingers to pretend like I have fangs. My Jewy metaphor's a mess.

He nods like I said something perfectly coherent. *OK,* he says. *So let's have it.*

Well, I say. *You've got a weird situation. Your employees aren't bad at using collaboration software. They just suck at collaboration. They don't seem to have any respect for each other. It's mostly a bunch of brilliant, belligerent cowboys who want to do their own thing. Everybody is ranting in their own posts, but nobody is reading other people's posts. Impact metrics are embarrassing. And when people try to work together, they talk all crooked.*

You say that like it's a bad thing, he says.

Freddy, 80 percent of your online groups have less than three members.

Look, he says, losing a little faith in me. *That's what makes the product quirky. I'm not going to sacrifice our secret sauce.*

Yeah, I say. *I don't want to mess up the charm of your dysfunctional software. But there are still things that make this environment unhealthy.* His office smells like cigars.

He is looking at me like he still doesn't get it.

Look, I say. *I'm talking about respect. I'm talking about boundaries. I'm talking about direct communication.*

Yuck, he says. *You sound like my ex-wife.* And he winks at me.

There is something weird and familiar about this man, and I can't put my finger on it. I know I haven't met him, but I feel like I know him.

You know, he says to me. *I named the company after her.* He laughs a little and then says, *Boy, she hated when I called her quirky.*

I get dizzy from the shock of putting it together. His big obnoxious presence, his poor sense of boundaries, his annoying charm, his insistence on calling his ex quirky.

Wait a second, I say. *You're Kitty's ex-husband.*

He has this knowing look that convinces me he read all the private stuff I wrote into his stupid app. He opens up his arms. *In the fat flesh*, he says.

I want to walk right out of here. I want to yell at him. I want to hit him. There are so many things. But instead, I take a deep breath.

Listen, I say. *You've got to stop being a dishonest asshole. Learn to be straight and honest and real, with your people.*

That sounds like a pain in the ass.

It is, I say. *But the other kind of pain is worse. You should know this by now.* And I say this with more confidence than anything I've ever said.

He nods, and then drinks the shot of bourbon that he poured for me.

How's my Kitty cat doing? he asks.

Freddy, I say. *I'm here to talk business.*

He nods, as if he understands, but then he says, *That woman was something else. I sure miss her. You should have seen the parties we had.* He sucks on his empty shot glass and he stares right through me for a few seconds and then he suddenly looks directly at me. *Oh*, he says. *I almost forgot. You had a drunk mom. That's too bad.*

This is where the scene almost falls apart. This guy who knows everything about me. I want to destroy everything about Freddy and this company and get his app permanently banned from the App Store. Not just because of what he knows about me and how much I hate him for talking about my mom, but also because partying with Kitty is something I'll never be doing and I'm sad to not have this thing to share with her.

I think about how Kitty used to talk about wanting to cut this man's cock off. That sounds about right. But then I think about how calm she looks when she talks about that meditation retreat thing and I try to pretend that I've also been to that place.

I breathe in and out and then back in and then back out.

I say, *Can you afford to fly your whole team to one location for one week every quarter?*

He goes back to the bourbon and grabs himself another shot and drinks it down and says in the midst of the bourbon, *I can do anything I want.*

Well, then do that. First day is for team building. Hire a psychologist to teach better communication skills. I can give you some recommendations. Do some of those bullshit ice breaker games that force team collaboration. Then one day for a retrospective. One day of planning. And the rest of the time is just play time, you know, like a few days at Timberline Lodge, you can even reenact scenes from The Shining *up there.* I can totally picture Freddy slamming an axe at a door and sticking his head through and yelling out, *Heeeeeeeeeeerrrrreeee's Freddy!*

He makes some kind of sound that sounds like a horse's neigh. *Sounds like a big fat waste of time,* he says.

Listen, I say. *Your team needs actual time together. Real-life time together. They need to learn how to work with each other. I think you can make the software less buggy, while keeping it, you know, quirky.*

So wait a minute, he says to me, drinking another shot that he conjured up from who knows where. *What am I supposed to do with your software?*

Oh, I say. *You don't need our software for a damn thing. It's a cesspool in there.*

He looks down at the ground and he nods and he makes a grunt or a burp or some small sound that is more on the inside than the outside.

Look after Kitty, he says to me. *You seem like a decent guy and probably know that she's a catch. I was too much of a dick to keep her.* He looks down at the empty shot glasses and this big intimidating man turns into a sad-looking boy.

I know, I say to him.

On the way out the door, I turn back around and say, *Listen, it might also help things around here if you work on your drinking. I know about a meditation retreat that might do you some good.*

He smiles, not too big but not too small, and says, *I'll take it under consideration.* I don't know how to interpret his response except maybe as a way to thank me for being concerned but also that he doesn't plan to do a thing about it.

Kitty once told me that if you squint your eyes and hold your nose and cover your ears that this man had some charm, and I can see that now. He has so many bad qualities, but it's still hard not to like the guy.

#

Anne tells me that she wants to talk to me right away. She knows that I no longer respond to @ mentions, so she texts me. She has us booked at Death Glider on the third floor. Which is a room that is too small, has no display, and poor Wi-Fi reception.

I walk in there and Anne is already waiting, staring at me. It feels like I've come into this office for that first interview however many years ago. She says, *I got a call from Freddy just now. What did you do?*

I say, *I told him the truth.*

So why did he order three times as many licenses as last year?

Oh, I say. *He did?*

That's three times more licenses than he can possibly use.

What can I say? I give good evangelism. But you should have told me that he was Kitty's ex.

She looks down at the ground and scrapes some invisible dirt with her foot. *I'm sorry,* she says. *I wasn't sure if it would help or hurt.*

It's alright, I say. *But I don't want to meet with him again.*

OK, she says, and for some reason it feels like we're just regular adults talking about adult things. I kind of like it. *By the way,* she says, *thanks for the help with the Rick thing. I sort of panicked. You are a surprisingly calming person to be around, you know.*

How are things on that front?

Oh, just fine. Your schedule worked brilliantly. He loved it. We made some small tweaks and we're going to run with it starting on Saturday.

Great, I say. I want to hear more about Rick and Anne. I want to tell her how much I like getting to know Rick and that I practically think he has some decent ideas. But I can tell Anne is working through an invisible agenda.

Enough about my traumas, she says. *Let's get back to your traumas. Thanks for handling so many companies for us. I know it's probably not what you expected to be doing around here.*

It's fine, I say. *I can take care of myself.*

Really? she says. *That sounds suspiciously confident.*

Yeah, I say, a little bit proud. *I am doing some useful backbone exercises.*

Ha, she says. *How did you hurt your back anyway?*

Long story, I say. I quietly do a few abdominal exercises while sitting there.

Well, you look good.

I say, *I'm so healthy that I now have a back that is only twenty years older than the rest of me.*

So, she says, with a weird smile on her face that makes me uncomfortable, *it's good that you have a good back because I think you're ready to take your collaboration skills to the next level.*

Uh oh, I say. *You aren't going to try and set me up with someone else, are you? Because I'm practically not miserable right now.*

No way that I'm messing around with your personal life anymore, she says, totally joking around I know, but still it somehow makes me sad. *This is about CollaborationHub. This is about your J-O-B job. This is about a once-in-a-lifetime opportunity.*

Uh oh, I say. *That sounds even worse.*

Listen, Saul. Anne puts both her palms on the table, and then pushes herself up. She walks behind me and puts her hands on my shoulders. Like a massage, but without enough pressure. I try to look back at her, but I can't see her face from this angle. *Do you like your job?*

I kind of do, I say. And I only say "kind of" because it's hard to admit that I like it way more than I ever imagined, even if I'm working too many hours.

That doesn't surprise me. You're good at your job. I knew you would be. But you're better than good. You're great at it. And I want you to lead our evangelism team. Our real evangelism team. Double the salary. Our top clients around the world. You'll rack up so many frequent flyer miles that you can take the boy to Japan without even thinking twice about it.

There is a tingle in me when she calls me great. But when she gets to the talk of my boy, the tingle disappears.

I say, *Who will look after Auggie if I'm traveling the world for my S-O-B job?*

Oh, she says. She lets go of my shoulders and walks back to her chair and swats her hand in the air as she sits down. *You can pay your nanny to look after him when you're busy.*

I don't have a nanny. I say it with no affect, no irony, no humor.

You don't?

Anne understands so many things and has helped me in so many ways. But there's also a part of my life that she does not understand at all.

Well, she continues, *didn't your ex want him more of the time anyhow?*

I start to get impatient with her. *Anne, I don't want to spend less time with my child.*

Just think about it, she says. *I don't need an answer today.*

Good, I say. *Because today I'm focused on other things. Like the final touches to my book.*

Right, she says. *How is that little book thing of yours?*

#

Here's the weird thing about the book: I'm proud of it. Kitty's drawings are just fabulous. We've gone back and forth a few times to clean up the words and the pictures, but we have the same vision for what we want out of this book. And it turns the book into something new. I love the Papa in this story even more looking at these pictures, even when I know he is going to make a mess of things. He'll be a disappointment to his wife and his son—both his fictional son and his real son. But everything is a disappointment if you look at it a certain way. Papa is also the hero of the story. I can see that now with every word and every stroke.

The other weird thing is that I've started writing about my mom. Some of it is real, some of it is made up. But it feels connected to the story of Papa. When I write it, it is like I'm writing a sequel to the Papa book, even though the plot is completely unrelated, and the kid in this new book is me.

Instead of sending Papa off to any publishers or literary agents, I send him to Anne to see what she thinks after spending so much time criticizing me for writing all these years.

Her reply is short and (not so) sweet: *You know bookstores are dying, right?*

Her second reply says: *What would I need to say for you to take that evangelism job?*

Her third reply doesn't even have caps or punctuation: *sent to lit agent friend*

I message Kitty about the whole meeting-her-ex-by-mistake thing. I'm not sure how casual to be about it. I feel some guilt even though I don't think there should be any guilt, but she gives me such a nice and clean response: *Ha! It was inevitable. At least you got away without any scars.*

Then I get an email from my dad. The subject is: *Mom Emails*

#

It's a mystery how my father learned to zip a bunch of emails and send them to me, but the bigger mystery is what's inside these emails. He doesn't say anything in his email to me, so I just unzip the file and start with the first one from my mom.

```
I am going to try and tell you everything,
starting from the beginning. I have kept many
secrets and this is me trying to stop with the
secrets. It is complicated to be who I am. I don't
know if you love me anymore, after everything
I've done, I wouldn't blame you, but I love you,
and you deserve to know these things. If you
don't care to know, just click Delete. I'm sure
there's a delete button somewhere on your side.
There always is.
```

I stop reading the note. It feels weird reading this. It's for my dad. Does that matter? I still want to read it. I'll probably read them all eventually.

I turn off my device, walk over to my couch, lie down, and close my eyes.

#

This memory is different than the other memories. When I remember it, I remember it cloudy. Not cloudy like it's vague, but cloudy like there is actual fog in the air. And in our house. As usual, I was five or eight or seven or ten or whenever. I was playing in the backyard, alone, one summer day, pretending that I was saving a caterpillar from an army of roly-polies, but I decided to come inside early. I had to pee. But there, in the bathroom, was my mom.

There were at least fifty bottles of medicine all around the bathroom sink—those orange bottles with the important-looking labels. Some were open, some were closed, some were on their sides, and there were pills of all colors all over the counter.

My first thought was: *These pills will be awesome for my roly-poly battle!* And then I saw my mom. Not directly, but through the mirror. The red lightning bolts in her eyes. The wet cheeks. The way she stared at herself like she didn't recognize who she was. It tickled in my chest in a horrible way to see her.

Mom? I said.

What? she said to the me in the mirror, like she was angry with the me in the mirror.

The real me started crying. Loud or quiet, I don't know, but the crying hurt my head and throat and chest.

She didn't respond right away, who knows how long she stood there, not very long, or way too long.

And then it was like she woke up. She turned around to look at me.

She said, *Oh. Don't worry, baby. Mama's just organizing her life. It's all OK.*

It didn't feel any better for her to talk to me like this even though her words were warm words, I guess. She wouldn't even touch me or hug me.

She said, *Just leave Mama alone for a minute in here and it will all be better.*

I left the room. I imagined her jumping out the bathroom window and never coming back. It hurt so bad I couldn't even cry. I went back outside and tried to get back to my caterpillar game, but the game was over.

Even from outside, I heard my mom coughing in the bathroom. And then flushing. And then coughing. And then flushing. I'd later understand that the coughing was more like vomiting up the medicine, but even back then I understood it on some level. And then she came outside to see me. My mom had come back from running away. She straightened her pants, even though her pants were already straight, and she said to me, *Let's go get a banana split.*

I ran over to hug my mom and when she squeezed me, her body was soft and warm and she held me tight and I didn't want to let go of her, not even to get a banana split.

#

We're lying on my old couch side by side, with me behind Kitty, and we watch *The Godfather* and *The Godfather: Part 2*, all in one sitting, or in one lying, except for a few bathroom breaks. That's more than six hours of mafia bliss. I get a little distracted because it's nice to sniff the back of her neck while we watch. I don't know what she smells like, it's not a smell in the way I think of smells, more subtle than big obnoxious things like flowers or farts, she just smells like her, and I'm a little high from the sweetness of it. It's fun to be in this early phase of dating, even though I know the intensity will wear off, and then we'll have to deal with more complicated relationship stuff. I don't realize that my neck and back are aching from the terrible position until the credits roll and we stand up to stretch.

That was nice, she says. *For a dude movie.*

What do you mean a dude movie? It's a human movie. It's a movie about family. It's about connection and disconnection. Who doesn't love that? I can feel myself wanting to manologue, to defend the movie, and to defend my gender.

OK. OK, she says, a little amused by my excitement. *It was good. I admit. But next time I get to pick.*

Which movie? I say, oddly nervous about what she might choose.

She comes up to me like she's going to whisper the answer. Instead, she whispers, *It's a surprise.*

Kitty starts putting on her shoes, so I say, *Where are you going?*
I've got to run.

Run where? I don't want her to run. I say, *If you stick around, I'll make*
you a Sicilian omelet.

She smiles, *It's tempting, but I'm off to meet a girlfriend.*

It hurts my feelings. Because this right here right now is nice. Why
does she have to stop the niceness because of some girlfriend? It's a Saturday afternoon and I don't pick up Auggie until tomorrow evening and I
just want to linger with this woman for longer. I want to watch more movies, eat more meals, do more fucking, tell more stories, drink more nonalcoholic beverages, play more games, take more naps, read more books, tell
more jokes—with her. I'm totally nervous about where this is all going,
and I'm cautious about how it affects Auggie, but something has opened
up in me. I'm letting myself enjoy it more. Not totally. But a little more:
Now with 13.5 Percent More Enjoyment!™

As she is getting her shoes on, she stops partway. *Can I ask you something?* she says.

Maybe, I tell her.

Are we really ready to do this? I mean, are you sure you like me? And are
you over that . . . marriage of yours?

Are you? I say, kind of stalling for time. It's not that I don't have a proper
answer, but I'm just aware of the number of landmines in this area.

She puts on her second shoe and then says, *You first.*

So I take in a big breath and get ready for an answer. *Look*, I say. *I don't*
know for sure. But I do know that I'm finally OK about being divorced. And
I'm less mad at her too. I feel like I'm untangled from something. And I know
this because of how much I love, and then I correct myself and say, *like . . .*
who you are in an entirely different way. Remember the first time we met
and you said you wanted to cut off your ex's cock?

She covers her eyes and says, *Oh no, that.*

I gently pull her hands off her eyes. *Oh yes*, I say, *that. Well I love that. I*
love how you say exactly how you feel and you don't coat it with any bullshit.
You're more real than anyone else I've ever dated. I can totally appreciate
that now.

Oh, she says. I can see in her blushy smile that she took this in as the real thing that I meant it to be.

I reach out to hold her hand. Handholding in a new relationship is so tingly and sparkly and electric.

What about you? I say.

She pulls her electric hand away from me. *Yeah*, she says, *well I still have some messy feelings for him, but the cock-cutting gets less pronounced each day. And I just like how you're so sensitive and funny and thoughtful and neurotic and goofy. And sexy.*

Wow, I say and my face gets warm. *Can I tack on other compliments than just my cock-cutting one? I feel bad that you had like six things and I just talked about cock chops.*

She put her finger to my mouth. *Not today*, she says.

We both stand up from the couch.

I don't know who initiates it, but we kiss. A real kiss. A mouth kiss. A tongue kiss. A TMI kiss, as Auggie calls it when it happens on TV.

She looks at me. She takes a good, long breath, like she's breathing me the way I breathed her, and I feel self-conscious about me and my smell. She says, *I like this.* She rubs her fingers on my three-day-old scruff. And then across my lips. She whispers, *I like you.*

And then she leaves.

Chapter Nineteen: The Next Level

I was kind of hoping that everything was OK again with the gamification plug-in after it sent me that "no error found" message and no other messages for the week. But then I get this text on a Sunday morning:

```
{ title       : "assessment complete",
  next_step   : "publish internal posts
                to external locations",
  timer       : "20,000,000 milliseconds" }
```

My first thought is: Cool. It's finished. So I won't be hearing from this thing again.

My next thought is: What does "publish internal posts to external locations" mean exactly?

My instinct is to worry about it on Monday.

But then I calculate that twenty million milliseconds is less than six hours away. If this thing is going to do anything horrible, Monday is too late.

I have that chest tightness I used to get when I was a kid and knew that my mom wasn't feeling right even if she wasn't telling me about it.

I send a message to Jessie the developer, but he doesn't answer.

Then I think about how I swiped some of the gamification code from that public GitHub project. So I get online and track it down to see if it's as bad as the threatening message makes it sound.

It's a lot worse.

I text the emergency alert to our company's on-call team: *Emoticon Level 1.*

I don't make it all the way to the bathroom when I vomit the Laughing Planet burrito I had last night.

#

Within two hours, I'm in the Millennium Falcon conference room with Anne, the VP of engineering, Don the deployment director, Jessie, and another developer named Susan. We're here on an actually-sunny Sunday afternoon. The developers and Anne seem only slightly annoyed, but the director and the VP both seem totally pissed to be here. Don the Director keeps pushing on his temples like he's got a migraine. I don't know much about him other than his individual contributors call him Don the Director and he doesn't talk much and he always looks angry.

The VP says to me, *You said it was an emergency. So dish it out.* He's wearing a tuxedo and duckie slippers. Auggie would love those things.

I stand up, walk to the whiteboard, and grab a red dry-erase marker even though it doesn't take any whiteboarding to turn around and say, *The gamification plug-in is going to post all of our private posts and our customers' private posts to public social media sites in less than three hours.*

What? Anne says. And she stands up so fast that her chair falls over, into the corner with all the half-broken chairs, like it was ready to die with the rest of them.

The two devs, Susan and Jessie, both look up from their phones, hoping they misheard the outside world. Susan is actually holding two phones in her hand—an iPhone and an Android phone—one on top of the other.

Jessie says, *Harvey balls of fire.*

I never quite understand that guy.

So, the VP says, *what's this mean exactly?* He points at me with one of the duckie bills from one of his slippers.

I say something that will make his stomach cramp up and his chest feel tight the way I feel. I say, *Remember the time you got so fucked up at the company holiday party that you made Jessie take that video of you dancing in your boxers while yelling about how our biggest client could go ahead and suck all of your dirty toes?*

Oh. The VP smacks his duckie foot on the ground and says, *Is that still on CollabHub?*

Jessie and Susan both immediately say, *Yes.*

And that's not even the worst of it, I say. *Not only are we all fucked, but our customers are fucked too. Think of the shit our customers are saying privately using our software. Quirkitunity. Tea Tootlers. Gun Freaks. Beer Barons. Flower People. TeleDildonics, LLC. All that crazy shit is going to be on Facebook, Twitter, Instagram, TikTok within a few hours.*

Anne puts her hand on her stomach. *Oh, God. How did this happen?*

I look at the dead chairs, and at the people and the devices in the room, and at my dear friend, Anne.

I really fucked up, I say to Anne in a way that makes me feel so small and so childish like I'm fessing up to my mom for going through her purse and taking those dollar bills—not like someone who is ready to become a great evangelist. I shake away my mom and then repeat it to the room with more authority. *I fucked up. I swiped some half-baked open-source code from a very baked coder and stuck it into our gamification plug-in code.*

The VP says, *How do you know the code is messed up? I made sure that you don't have access to our codebase anymore.*

I say, *I've been getting messages from the plug-in. The last message was the most alarming. So I reviewed the code that I swiped online and it's bad.*

Jessie says, *I don't remember anything getting code reviewed.*

Susan says, *Did you even get this code tested?* She is young enough to be my child, even makes Jessie seem like an old veteran, but I can tell she knows her shit. She's wearing a smartwatch and a Fitbit on the same wrist.

I shake the red marker in my hand like I'm revving up for a speech. I feel like a dumb old fool for what I have to say. But I say it anyway: *No tests. No reviews. I snuck it in there. I'm an idiot. Give me access to the codebase and I'll fix it.*

The VP says, *I don't know if I want to do that.* He's tapping his left duck slipper on the ground. The plastic eye is half peeling off the slipper.

Anne says, *Can't we just take it all down?*

Don the Director is still pressing on his temples and looking at the ground when he says, *Every server, every cache, every instance, every customer. It would be messy. And you could kiss our high-availability metrics goodbye.*

I hand the red marker over to Jessie. He suspiciously and reluctantly takes the marker. Then I look over at the VP and say, *We can have Don look into the feasibility of shutting all the servers down. Meanwhile, let me pair program with Jessie. Susan can review and test it. We'll fix the code and then do an emergency patch on every one of our customers that has the gamification plug-in installed.*

Anne asks, *Is this even possible in three hours?*

The deployment director says to the dead chairs, *We've never done it this fast before. Since we're only updating the plug-in, it's possible we can pull it off. Assuming you guys can fix the code ASAP and there are no hiccups.*

I say, *This is why we need to move to a multi-tenant service-oriented architecture.*

The VP points at me and says, *You have officially lost the right to armchair quarterback our fucking software.* The man is actually scarier in those duckie slippers. He says, *Just fix the damn code. And then . . .* and he pauses thinking of what comes after that. The duck eye is now totally gone from his left slipper.

I know what comes after that. It is clear to me. I say, *And then I will leave the company.*

Nobody argues with me. Not even Anne, though she doesn't look me in the eyes.

I say, *We'll set up Millennium as the War Room. Developers only for now. We fix this thing. We test this thing. And then we deploy it.*

#

We get the fix into the codebase, me and Jessie working together at his laptop.

Susan then runs through some unit tests and integration tests. I have no idea how she learned how to do all this stuff at the company so fast.

When I ask her, she says, *Hush up, No-Test Charlie. I don't like to talk when I'm testing.* She somehow says this with charm, not annoyed like everyone else.

I can tell I would've liked working with this woman, but it's too late for me in this CollabHub saga.

As we wait for Susan to review and accept our changes, Jessie says, *You're not as shitty a coder as I expected.*

Who said I was shitty? I ask.

Well, I noticed that pyramid of doom in your code last month, so I figured you didn't know how to code worth a damn. And you also act like you don't know what you're doing all the time.

Really? I say, surprised to hear it. *I had no idea.*

Yeah, like how you're acting right now. And he points at me as proof. *I figured you were one of those schmucks who got promoted because of your seniority more than your chops.* He smacks me on the back hard enough that it hurts. *But you actually know how to code.*

And to fuck up the code.

He smiles at me. I've never seen him amused before. He says, *It takes a coding bad ass to fuck up code as bad as you did.*

Susan merges our code into the codebase. And then it's up to Don to get all our not-fucked-up code onto every single customer instance.

While all this is happening, Anne sends me a text: *step into my office when you're done unfucking things*

I take a few deep breaths to see if I can unknot the knots in my chest. It only half works.

I send Auggie a message that is just a heart emoji. He replies with a thumbs-up reaction, which is more noncommittal than I was hoping for, but I'll take what I can get right now.

#

Anne's office has a beautiful view of our horrendously ugly parking lot, which is even more ugly without the Korean-Mexican fusion food cart that is only there on weekdays. Anne is sad. The frown on her face is as unsubtle as my fuck-up.

She says, *You don't have to leave, you know. I've already spoken with some of the execs, and they still want you to lead the evangelism team.*

I do have to leave.

The overhead light in her office is off and the sun is setting behind us and it's dark and ominous in here. She looks at her watch, and the bright display of her watch glows against her face. She says, *But if you pulled us through this thing unscathed, then . . .*

Too late, I say. *I'm scathed.*

She has a confused look, which I guess I like better than a sad look.

But things are changing around here, she says. *We're becoming a better company than we were before. Don't you want to be a part of that?*

Look, I tell her. *I need to get out of here. I appreciate what you've done for me. And I love the job you tricked me into, but I'll always be stuck if I stay here.*

What do you think you're going to do? You'll never make enough money off your book, even if it is good.

If.

I know, I say to her. I'm almost flattered that she thinks I have such high hopes for my book. The truth is that I'd love to quit everything and write. But I'd never do that. I have a kid to take care of. And anyway, my creative brain shuts down when it's tethered to the bottom line. I know myself well enough to know that.

I say, *I've run some numbers, and with my connections, I can make a decent living consulting.*

Consult? she says, and she even chuckles. *Consult what?*

You know, I say. *Help companies with their collaboration skills.*

Right, she keeps on giggling. And then sees that I'm serious. She says, *But that's what you already do here.*

I know, I say. *But what if what they need isn't software?*

She doesn't like this question at all. Now she plays hardball. She says, *What about our non-compete agreement?*

I get a message from Auggie, who asks me if I can measure the iPad he sewed for me because he wants to sew an iPad cover for it, to keep it safe. I tell him that I'll send him the measurements when I get back home.

I try my version of hardball on Anne. I say, *I looked into it. Collaboration-Hub can't stop me from doing the work I'm trained to do. And you can trust me. I won't be sharing any of our valuable IP. You already know that I don't find our intellectual property all that valuable.*

You looked into it, Anne says, repeating my words.

I close my eyes and while my eyes are closed I say the thing that I feel inside of me, even when I know it might sound ridiculous to say it out loud: *The way that I'm going to take collaboration to the next level isn't related to CollabHub, it's going to be by spending more time in the real world with people I care about, talking about real things.*

When I open my eyes, it surprises me that I'm still sitting here inside this building, like I expected to be floating above it all. But I'm not floating. I'm sitting here in this darkening room right next to Anne.

Anne stares at me like my words were asymmetrically encrypted.

The VP of Duckie Slippers gets on the intercom and yells out, *We're in the fucking clear! Long live CollaborationHub! We love you, Saul. But also, fuck you for almost destroying the company and for totally destroying our weekend.*

We sit for a moment and bask in the relief. Anne is gazing right through me and I am gazing right through her. It is completely dark outside now and the only light inside is just one dim table lamp on her desk that is pointing at the desert rose cactus, the plant that I thought was replaced by a Wi-Fi extender a long time ago. Funny how I didn't notice the plant until it got dark enough in here for the thing to stand out. The cactus is even blooming a bright pink bloom.

My watch taps me with a message from Kitty that says, *I miss your lips.* For a moment, my lips savor the compliment.

Anne finally says, *I think I understand.* She gets a stern look on her face, one that I don't like until she says, *As long as you include me as one of your real world friends.* She uses finger quotes when she says the word "friends." I'm pretty sure she meant to use it for "real world."

Definitely, I say to her, also using finger quotes. I'm pretty sure she knows I'm serious about considering her a real world friend.

She takes a long breath and looks around her fancy room. *But I'll miss you around the office. And I'll miss your inappropriate messages from the restroom.*

I'll miss you too, I say. *I'm sorry I don't get to see you tell those damn good ol' boys that girls are better at this job.* I get up to hug her. As we hug, I say, *I guess it's time for me to go out as my own Corinthian merchant.*

What? she says. She steps back from my hug as she tries to process what I've said.

Oh, I say, a little embarrassed for voluntarily bringing religion into the equation. *You know, the story of the Corinthian merchant from the Bible?*

Anne laughs, and I'm afraid that I might've said something blasphemous.

What's so funny? I say.

She's tearing up a little. She says to me, *I totally made up that story to get you on the right track.*

You mean, I say, *you made up that terrible story about a murdered merchant to get me motivated?*

Yeah, she says as if it's so obvious, *I figured you'd find more charm in a story with a messy plot and a messy hero.*

As highly as I've always regarded Anne, I still underestimated her.

#

Auggie gets in the car and we wave goodbye to his mom. I like the ritual of waving goodbye with the idea that we don't have to do it again for a whole week. A more clear boundary. Except I can sense the sadness in Auggie as we drive off.

We're quiet for a few blocks and then he says, *I think I'm done with* The Octonauts.

Really? I say, while trying to figure out why this line hits me harder than it should. *Nobody made fun of you about it or anything?*

No, Dad, he says. *I just think I'm old enough for something new.*

I'm sad about this. They have been such a part of our world for so long, and I'm not prepared to let go. How am I going to handle the teenage years when I can barely handle saying goodbye to an annoying set of land animals in an undersea space station?

What's wrong? he asks me.

I don't know, I say. *I'll miss those guys.*

Some of them are girls, he says.

So what do you want to get into now?

I don't know, he says to me. *Maybe* Pokémon *or* My Little Pony *or* The Hunger Games *or just a regular superhero.*

You're a bit young for The Hunger Games, I say.

Yeah, he says. *Jeremy told me it isn't just fun games with people who are hungry.*

It's dark and cloudy outside, and it's starting to drizzle, even though my weather apps all assured me that it would clear up by now.

I say, The Octonauts *are still cool to me.*

It's just too simple, Dad. They never get in serious trouble.

Maybe so, I say. *But they're cute.*

Dad, cute isn't everything.

I can hear him scratching against something on the car seat beside him, but I can't see what he's doing in the rearview. I say, *What are you doing back there?*

He says, *Was this really your mom's car?* He never calls her anything like Grandma or Bubbie or Granny or anything else. Which, I guess, makes sense since he never needed to call her anything.

Yeah, I say. *She didn't drive all that much. She was dealing with other things.* It's amazing the car hasn't given me more trouble. It's needed a few things over the years. A transmission, a couple gaskets, some new tires, a few doohickeys that I don't know what they're for. I obediently give it gas and oil and the car just putters along without any complaints. Even does well on these wet and slippery roads.

He says, *Why did she drink?*

I take a few deep breaths. I sit there and I think. Long enough for Auggie to say, *The light turned green.*

I don't know, I say. *She was looking for something she could never find.*
Did she love you?
Yes, I say, without a second thought.
But, he says, *she was still never happy?*
It's fascinating to try and follow his stream of consciousness. The puddles between his words. Even this little seven-year-old is hopping around in this amazing way from one stone to another and I can never be sure how the stones are connected, and what we're stepping over to get there.

I say, *I know you don't like me saying it's complicated, but people can be complicated. Sometimes you just don't know why people are the way they are and why they do the things they do.*

He looks out the window and I can tell he's squinting real hard at whatever he's looking at. Maybe I need to get him an appointment with an optometrist.

He says, *I wish I had a regular family with just you and Mom.*

I keep missing all the green lights on this drive home and I'm getting impatient with all the stops and starts and the stupid weather. I want to be at home right now while having this conversation with him. I don't like having to multitask between the road and him.

With a regular family, I say, *you would have never met Kitty or Daniel.*
Maybe they could have just been our friends.

I know this is all pretty messy, I say. *It's not easy to have a relationship with another human being. Sometimes things don't work out between two people.*

But you'd never break up with me. Right?

I say, *That's different.*

But isn't that also a relationship with another human bean?

My boy is out-thinking me and it takes some time to come up with an answer. I say, *Being a parent is different than a romantic relationship. I will NEVER break up with you.*

He says, *But you might break up with Kitty?*

I wish I could bring in a team of therapists right now to help me with this. *I'm not going to lie to you,* I tell him. *Kitty and I are trying to find our way. I really hope it works out.*

He says, *Can we have a party sometime and invite Kitty and Mama and Daniel?*

I want to say, *It's complicated*, but I don't say that. I say, *Sure.* Maybe things aren't as complicated as adults make them out to be.

Dad? he says.

What is it? He probably hears the tiredness in my voice. I'm not sure how many more heavy questions I can handle today.

Do you know why I cry when I leave Mama's house?

Why? I say. I'm about to cry without even hearing the answer.

It makes me sad when I think how you and Mama never say goodnight to me on the same night.

Oh, I say.

Auggie starts laughing all of a sudden. And it scares me. I'm afraid I just cracked him.

What is it, Auggie? I say.

The traffic out there is messy and it takes a few seconds before it's safe to look in the rearview mirror at him. There's this joy on his face. Not like a little kid sort of joy. Older. I picture him much older, like maybe a teenager, or a young adult, or even an old man thinking back fondly on years that are long gone. We make eye contact in the mirror and we both smile simultaneously, even though I don't know why he's smiling and I don't know why I'm smiling, but it doesn't feel like there's any layer between us, it doesn't feel like we are only looking at reflections of each other. It's as real as anything.

My son says to me, *I guess sometimes complicated is better than just Octonauts.*

He's scratching his fingernails on the car seat again and the sound is both comforting and annoying.

Maybe it is, I tell him.

It's not a punchline to a joke. It's just this small moment. A moment that we might remember for many years to come, even if nobody tweets or posts or snaps or emails or emojis it. It might even be a moment that my son will recall when I'm old and fragile and weeping into a gelato at the mall (if malls still exist): the memory of the two of us riding along on a rainy afternoon in this old car that once was my mother's, talking about *The Octonauts* and families and break-ups. And how complicated it is to be who we are.

Acknowledgments

Writing a novel is a crazy stupid thing to do. And trying to boil down the acknowledgments in under five hundred words is even crazier and stupider. To all the amazing people who have helped me during the craziest and stupidest hours I spent writing this book, thank you.

• My dear family—Sheri, Savi, Dashiell. ♥ Especially to Sheri, who read the hell out of this book and learned how to kick my writerly ass when that was necessary . . .

• Dreamies—Jackie Shannon Hollis, Joanna Rose, Kate Gray, Mark Lawton, Cecily Patterson, Bruce Barrow. For the wisdom and love and support that comes from this writing group. For the patience to read ∞ drafts of this book.

• Fab 4—Liz Prato, Jackie (again!), Scott Sparling. I treasure all our IRL and virtual time together.

• My agent, Rayhané Sanders—Your passion and insights are astounding to me.

• Red Hen Press—An amazing press doing amazing things. I'm so appreciative of what y'all do and how damn well y'all do it.

- The Pinewood Table—Stevan Allred and Joanna Rose, and all the people who've had the privilege of sitting at this real, and sometimes metaphorical, table.

- To the larger community of writers in PDX, I can't thank all of y'all properly, but you make a lonely guy who hides in the attic 12.5% less lonely.

- Cheryl Strayed, who made me feel a little less awkward about sharing my awkward characters with the awkward world.

- Margaret Malone and Monica Drake, for your support and brilliance and your general fabulosity.

- Anne Mendel, who sparked this damn book into existence, and may or may not resemble the character named Anne in this book.

- Joey Helpish—You helped me *way* more than just -ish.

- Even though I wrote this book after the days I was at Antioch in LA, that time was precious to me. And I still treasure that community of writers. To Kate Maruyama, Stephanie Westphal, Jae Gordon, Telaina Eriksen, Kristen Forbes, Stephanie Glazier, and all the other fabulous folks who love telling stories.

- I've missed so many people with this incomplete list. I'm sorry.

I'd also like to acknowledge my chronic migraines. If not for this constant struggle, I'd never appreciate the value of the moments that are happy, productive, and pain-free. My heart goes out to anyone with chronic pain and to all the lovely supporters of those people.

Biographical Note

Yuvi Zalkow is the author of the novel *A Brilliant Novel in the Works* (MP Publishing 2012). His short stories have been published in *Glimmer Train*, *Narrative Magazine*, *Carve Magazine*, *Rosebud*, the *Los Angeles Review*, and others. He received an MFA from Antioch University. Yuvi also uses his poor drawing skills to make YouTube videos and mobile apps that ooze with his worries and anxiety. You can find out too much information about him at yuvizalkow.com. Yuvi lives with his wife, kid, and grumpy cats in Portland, Oregon.